PENGUIN BOOKS

DIGGING UP
THE MOUNTAINS

Neil Bissoondath was born in Trinidad in 1955. He emigrated to Canada in 1973 and studied French at York University, Toronto. He later taught French and English as a second language while beginning his writing career. He is now working on a full-length novel and new short stories.

NEIL BISSOONDATH

DIGGING UP THE MOUNTAINS

SELECTED STORIES

PENGUIN BOOKS

Penguin Books Ltd, 27 Wrights Lane, London W8 5TZ (Publishing and Editorial)
and Harmondsworth, Middlesex, England (Distribution and Warehouse)
Viking Penguin Inc., 40 West 23rd Street, New York, New York 10010, USA
Penguin Books Australia Ltd, Ringwood, Victoria, Australia
Penguin Books Canada Ltd, 2801 John Street, Markham, Ontario, Canada L3R 1B4
Penguin Books (NZ) Ltd, 182–190 Wairau Road, Auckland 10, New Zealand

First published in Great Britain by André Deutsch 1986
First published in the USA by Viking 1986
Published in Penguin Books 1987

Copyright © Neil Bissoondath, 1986
All rights reserved

Filmset in Bembo
Printed and bound in Great Britain by
Cox & Wyman Ltd, Reading

TO THE MEMORY OF MY MOTHER
and
FOR MY FATHER

CONTENTS

DIGGING UP THE MOUNTAINS

1.

Hari Beharry lived a comfortable life, until, citing the usual reasons of national security, the government declared a State of Emergency.

"National security, my ass," Hari mumbled. "Protecting their own backsides, is all."

His wife, anguished, said, "Things really bad, hon."

"*Things really bad, hon,*" Hari mimicked her. He sucked his teeth. "Looking after their own backsides."

"The milk gone sour and the honey turn sugary." She gave a wry little smile.

Hari sucked his teeth once more. "Don't give me none of that stupid nonsense. 'Land a milk and honey', my ass."

"You used to call it that."

"That was a long time ago."

"Rangee used to blame it on independence. He used to blame the British for—"

"I know what Rangee used to say. It ain't get him very far, eh? Shut up about Rangee, anyway. I don't want to talk about him."

"Again? Still? Like Faizal? They tried to help you."

"Why you like to talk about dead people so much?" he demanded irritably.

"Because you don't. You ain't mentioned their names once in the last two weeks."

"Why should I?"

"Because you might be next."

"Don't talk nonsense."

"Because *we* might be next, me and the children."

"Shut up, woman!"

Hari stalked angrily out to the back porch. The evening air, cooled by the higher ground which made the area so desirable to those who could afford it, tempered the heat of the day. The bulk of the mountains, cutting jagged against the inky sky, allowed only the faintest glow of the last of the sunset.

In those mountains, Hari had once found comfort. His childhood had been spent in the shadow of their bulk and it was through them, through their brooding permanence, that he developed an attachment to this island, an attachment his father had admitted only in later life when, as strength ebbed and distances grew larger, inherited images of mythic India dipped into darkness.

The island, however, was no longer that in which his father had lived. Its simplicity, its unsophistication, had vanished over the years and had been replaced by the cynical politics of corruption that plagued all the urchin nations scrambling in the larger world. Independence—written ever since with a capital I, small i being considered a spelling mistake at best, treason at worst—had promised the world. It had failed to deliver, and the island, in its isolation, blamed the world.

Hari's father had died on Independence night and Hari had sought consolation in the mountains. He'd received it that night and continued to receive it many nights after. Now things had changed: the mountains spoke only of threat. He didn't know if he could trust them any more.

The emergency legislation had shut his stores. Hari was idle, and the sudden idleness made him irritable. If only he had someone with whom he could discuss the situation, someone who would make him privy to state secrets, as his old friends used to do. But the government had changed, his friends were no longer ministers, and the new ministers were not his friends. He could no longer say, "Eh, eh, you know what the Minister of National Security tell me yesterday?" The former Minister of National Security was in prison, put there by the new Minister for State Security. No one was left to show Hari the scheme of things; he was left to grapple alone, his wife useless, whining, demanding escape.

The darkness of the evening deepened. Hari felt a constriction in his throat. In the sky the first stars appeared. Hari reached into his back pocket and took out a large grey revolver. Its squared bulk fit nicely into his hand, its weight intimated power. He raised his arm with deliberation, keeping the elbow locked, and fired a shot at the sky. His arm, still locked, moved rapidly down and left; he fired another shot, at the mountains. The reports mingled and echoed away into the depths of the hidden gully.

"Come, you bastards, just try and come."

Only the barking of the German Shepherds answered him.

2.

It had started—when? Five, six, seven months before? He couldn't be sure. So much had happened, and in so short a time, event superseding grasp, comprehension exhausted. And it had all begun, quietly, with rumor: a whisper that had rapidly bred of itself, engendering others, each wilder, more speculative, and, so, more frightening than the last; rumor of trouble in the Ferdinand Pale, the shanty area to the east of the town.

Hari had dismissed the rumors: "Trouble, my ass. Shoot two or three of them and bam!—no more trouble."

But it hadn't worked out that way. The police had shot several people and had arrested dozens more, yet the rumors and the troubles persisted.

Hari had obtained a pistol from his friend, the Minister of National Security.

Hari said to the minister, "To protect the shops, you know, boy."

And to his wife, Hari said, "Let them come here. This is my land and my house. Let them come. It's bullet in their backside."

But no backsides presented themselves. Occasionally Hari would go out to the back porch and brandish his pistol: "Let them see what they walking into," he would say to his children who stood in the doorway staring wide-eyed at him. And to the darkness he would say, "Come, come and try."

Unexpectedly, the rumors dried up. Tension abated and fears were packed away. Life resumed. Hari called in the contractor, and gardeners—dark, sullen men of the Pale—started putting the yard in order, tugging out rocks and stones and laying out the drainage, preparing the ground for the topsoil.

Hari spent much of his free time overseeing this activity. Constantly followed by the children, he stalked around the yard nodding and murmuring and giving the occasional order, his tall rubber boots sinking deep into the convulsed earth. Slowly, at intervals less frequent than promised by the contractor, trucks arrived with loads of topsoil. Hari railed at the contractor: "But at this rate, man, it going to take five years to cover the whole yard!" The contractor, a fat man with red, wet eyes and a shirt that strained at the buttons, replied with exasperation: "But what I going to do, boss? The boys don't want to work, half of them ain't even show their face around the office since the little trouble in the Pale." The soil that did arrive was dumped into one corner of the yard under Hari's direction. He had it furrowed and combed, and had holes dug for the small grove of shade trees he would plant.

He started thinking about giving the place a name, like a ranch: Middlemarch, Rancho Rico, Golden Bough. He tossed the names about in his mind, playing with them, trying to picture how each would look on the personal stationery he was having printed up. He asked his wife's opinion. She suggested Bombay Alley. He stomped away, angry.

Twice he beat his son for playing with the gardeners' tools. "Look here, boy," he said, "I have enough troubles without you giving me more."

Still, the progress of the lawn pleased Hari. The contractor managed to hire additional men; trucks dumped their loads of topsoil at regular intervals. In less than a month, there swept from the base of the house to the base of the wrought-iron fence neatly raked stretches of an opulent brown. Hari, pleased, decided to order the grass.

He was on the phone arguing with the contractor about the price of the grass—it would mean sending three men and a truck to the country to dig up clumps of shoots; the contractor wanted more money than Hari was offering—when the music on the radio was interrupted by the announcement of a sudden call to elections. Hari understood immediately: the government, taking advantage of the apathy that followed the troubles, hoped to catch the opposition, such as it was, off-balance. Hari told the contractor he would call him back.

He poured himself a large whisky and listened to the Prime Minister's deep, bored voice as he spoke of a renewed mandate, of the confidence of the people. Hari thought the use of the island accent a little overdone. Did this election switch from Oxford drawl to island lilt really fool those at whom it was aimed? Did they really believe him to be one of them?

He dialled the number of his friend, the Minister of National Security: "Since when all-you care about mandate, boy? Is a new word you pick up in New York, or what?" Hari laughed. "Or maybe the Americans want a little reassurance before they hand over the loan cheque?" Hari laughed again, and his friend laughed with him.

But things went wrong. It was not a matter of political miscalculation; it was simply the plight of the small country: nothing went as planned, the foreseen never came into sight, and possibilities were quickly exhausted. The government lost. The opposition, on the verge of illegality only weeks before, took power.

Hari was untroubled. Life continued. He had, through it all, remained a financial contributor to both parties; and he liked the new Prime Minister, the scion of an old, respected island family that, adapting itself to the times, often publicly decried its slave-owning roots. The new Prime Minister considered himself a man truly of the people, for in him flowed the blood of master and slave alike.

The Americans handed over the cheque. The Prime Minister, serious and handsome, with a sallow island whiteness, went on television: ". . . the land of milk and honey . . . new loans from the World Bank . . . stimulation of industry and agriculture . . . a socialist economy . . ." This became known as the Milk and Honey speech. It was printed in pamphlet form and distributed to all the schools in the island. It was reported on the BBC World Service news.

The rumors started once more about a month later: trouble in the Ferdinand Pale. There were reports of shootings. Death threats were made against the new Prime Minister. Hari, without knowing why, sensed the hand of his friend, the former Minister of National Security. Pamphlets began appearing in the streets, accusing several businessmen of collusion with "imperialists". Hari's name cropped up time and time again. Letters—typed askew on good-quality paper, words often misspelt—began arriving at the house. Occasionally the phone would ring in the middle of the night, giving Hari the fearful vision of sudden death in the family. But always the same voice with the lazy island drawl would say in a conversational tone: "Damned exploitationist . . . Yankee slave . . ."

Hari complained to the police. The sergeant was apologetic: there was nothing they could do, their hands were full with the Ferdinand Pale.

The letters, less accusatory, more threatening, continued; the phone calls increased to three and four a night. Hari bought a whistle and blasted it into the phone. The next night the caller returned the favor. Hari's wife said, "You ask for that, you damn fool."

Hari complained directly to the Ministry for State Security. He was called in; the minister wanted to see him.

Hari had never met the minister, and the new title, more sinister, less British, worried him. Before he entered the cream-colored colonial building on Parliament Square, Hari noticed that his shirt was sticking to his back with perspiration. He wished he could dash back home to change it.

The minister was cordial. A big black man with a puffy face and clipped beard, he explained that his men were investigating the threats—a man of Mr. Beharry's standing deserved "the full attention of the security forces"—but that it was a slow process, it would take time. "Processes," the minister said, and Hari noticed he seemed to smack his lips when he pronounced the word, as if relishing it, "processes take a long time, they are established by law, there's paperwork. You understand?"

Hari nodded. He thought: How can I trust this man? The minister used to be what was called a "fighter for social justice". He had studied in the United States and Canada, until he was expelled from Canada for his part in the destruction of the computer centre at Sir George Williams College in Montreal. He had returned to the island as a hero. The papers had said he'd struck a blow for freedom and racial equality. In Hari's circle he'd been considered a common criminal; the former Minister of National Security had said at a party, "We have a cell reserved for that one." Now here he was, Minister for State Security, growing pudgy, wearing a suit.

The minister offered a drink.

Hari asked for Scotch. "Straight."

"Imported or local?"

"Imported." Then he changed his mind. "Local."

The minister buzzed his secretary. "Pour us some whisky, Charlene. Local for Mr. Beharry, imported for me." The minister smiled. He said to Hari, "I never drink the local stuff, disagrees with my stomach."

Hari said, "Too bad. It's good." And he knew instantly that he was grovelling.

The minister swung his chair around and stood up. A big man, he towered over Hari. "Mr. Beharry, you are a well-known man here in our happy little island. You are an *important* man. You own a chain of stores, the Good Look Boutiques, not so? You are a rich man, you have a nice family. In short, Mr. Beharry, you have a stake in this island." He paused as the secretary came in with the drinks. As Hari took his glass, he noticed a tremble in his hand, and he was aware that the minister too had noticed it. The minister smiled, raised his glass briefly at Hari, and sipped at the whisky. Then he continued: "It is because of all this, Mr. Beharry, that I want you to trust me. I am responsible for the security of this island. Trust between people like us is vital. And that is why, right now, I am going to reveal to you a state secret: in a few days we are going to ask everybody to turn in their guns, you included. It's the best way we know how to clean up the island. This violence must stop."

Hari's palm became sweaty on the glass. He said, "But is my gun, there's no law—"

"The law will be pushed through Parliament tomorrow. No one can stop us, you know that."

Hari, suddenly emboldened by the minister's smugness, said, "You know better than me. I never went to university."

The minister, unchastened, said, "That's right, Mr. Beharry."

Then they drank their Scotch and talked soccer. Hari knew nothing about soccer. The minister talked. Hari listened.

A few days later, Hari turned in his gun. Before handing it over at the police station, he jammed a piece of wood down the barrel.

The letters and phone calls were still coming. Hari threw the letters out unopened and put the telephone into a drawer. His wife, constantly worried, asked him, "How we going to defend ourselves now, hon?"

Hari said, "Don't worry."

That night, he went to his parents' old house, locked up and deserted. He hadn't been there in months. The place hadn't changed: the furniture was where it had always been, his parents' clothes still hung in the closets. Dust lay everywhere. Thieves, assuming the house contained nothing, had never bothered to break in. The air was musty, the familiar smells of childhood gone forever. Those smells, of food frying, of milk boiling, of his mother's perfumes and powders, had lingered several months after his mother's death and given

Hari a haunted feeling. It was because of them that he'd stayed away so long, leaving the house and its ghosts to their own devices.

He went into his parents' bedroom. The bed had never been stripped and the sheets, now discolored by dust, lay as they had been thrown by the undertakers who'd taken his mother's body away. He wondered if the impression left by the body in its attitude of death could still be seen. He rejected the thought as morbid but couldn't help taking a look: he saw only dusty, rumpled sheets.

Ignoring the dust, he lowered himself to the floor and felt around under the bed with his hand. He found what he was looking for: a rectangular wooden box the size of a cookie can. He opened it and took out a large grey revolver, the kind worn by American officers during the war. His father had bought it off an American soldier stationed on the island in 1945. After so many years of lying around, of being considered a toy, it would finally find a use.

Hari slipped the revolver into his pocket—it was bigger and heavier than the one he'd turned in and didn't fit as snugly into his pocket—and left the house. He didn't bother to lock the door.

Later that same night, Rangee, Hari's closest friend, telephoned. Hari was in bed, the revolver on the headboard just above him; and the ring of the telephone, startling in the semi-darkness, caused him to reach first for the revolver.

Rangee said, "Listen, Hari, things really bad in the Pale, but watch out. Is not the Ferdinand Pale you have to fear, is the other pale."

Before Hari could ask what he was talking about, the phone went dead. Hari assumed it was another of the frequent malfunctions of the telephone system.

Rangee was found the next day, shot twice in the head, the

receiver still clutched in his hand. The police said it had been a robber: Rangee's watch and wallet were missing. Nothing else in his house had been touched.

Hari returned from the morgue. So many had already left, gone to lands unfamiliar beyond the seas, that he took Rangee's death as just another departure. He froze Rangee in his mind, as he'd done with the others. He was determined never to mention them again: they were like a challenge to him. He sat at the kitchen table, his son and daughter, large-eyed, across from him, and cleaned and oiled the American's revolver. It needed little work: the mechanism clicked sharply, precisely, the magazine full. Hari marvelled at American ingenuity.

About a week after Rangee's death—later, Hari would have difficulty separating events: which came first? which second?—Faizal, another friend and business partner, came to see Hari. Faizal had connections in the army and liked to show off his knowledge of things military. Once, after a dinner party, Hari had told his wife, "Faizal went on and on. I feel as if I just finish planning the whole D-Day invasion."

Seated in the darkened back porch, glass poised between restless fingers, Faizal appeared nervous. He talked about the weather, about business, about the Ferdinand Pale. His eyes, agitated, traced the bulky silhouette of the mountains against the star-strewn sky. He related the story of the Battle of Britain and explained the usefulness of the Dieppe raid.

Hari felt that Faizal was trying to say something important but that he had to work up the courage. He didn't push him.

Faizal left without saying anything. Despite all the alcohol he had consumed, he left as nervous as he'd arrived. Hari assumed he was just upset over Rangee's death, and he was thankful that Faizal had said nothing about it.

Faizal was shot three days later. He'd received two bullets in the head; his watch and wallet were missing. The police concluded it was another case of robbery.

Hari, steeled, said, "Damn strange robbers. All they take is watches and wallets when they could empty the house."

The night after Faizal's death, one of Hari's stores was destroyed by fire. The fire department, an hour late in responding to the call, said it was arson. Then the fire marshal changed his mind: the final report spoke of old wiring and electrical shorts.

It was after this that Hari obtained two German Shepherds and started firing his warning shots into the evening sky.

The troubles in the Ferdinand Pale erupted into riots. Two policemen were killed. The government declared a State of Emergency and sent the army into the streets. Hari said, "Faizal would have been thrilled." It was the last time he mentioned Faizal's name. Members of the former government, including Hari's friend the former Minister of National Security, were arrested, for agitation, for treason. Stores and schools were closed, the airport and ports cordoned off.

It was only after watching the Prime Minister announce the Emergency on television that the meaning of Rangee's strange last words clicked in Hari's mind. The announcement had included news of an offer, at once accepted, of fraternal aid from Cuba. The Prime Minister, exhausted, had looked very, very pale.

3.

The day after the Emergency proclamation, the laborers didn't turn up, as was to be expected. Hari, restless, walked around the yard pretending to inspect the progress of the lawn. There had been problems obtaining the grass. The contractor had, once more, complained of the workmen, their laziness, drunkenness. But Hari guessed at the real problem:

whatever was seething in the Pale had seized them. Only one load of grass had been delivered, and the soil was beginning to harden in spots, to bind to itself.

Hari, feeling the heaviness of the revolver in his back pocket, let his eyes roam over the few rows of grass that had been planted, scraggly little shoots not quite in straight lines. Looking at them he found it difficult to picture the thick, carpet-like lawn he'd envisaged. His eyes moved on, past the ugliness of incomplete lawn, past several piles of wood left over from the construction of the house and not yet carted away, to the deep gully where his wife, if she got the chance, would start her plant nursery, to the wall of forest, dank and steamy, to the mountains beyond, a great distance away yet ever present, like a dead loved one.

Just let them try to take it away. Let them try!

"Hari," his wife called from the kitchen window, "we need milk, you better go to the plaza."

"For sour milk?"

"We need milk, Hari." She sounded tired. Her anxiety had distilled to fatigue. She had given up dreams of a nursery; she wanted only flight—to Toronto, Vancouver, Miami.

He looked at her and said, "This is my island. My father born here, I born here, you born here, our children born here. Nobody can make me leave, nobody can take it away."

"All right, Hari. But we still need milk."

His son came to the door. He was so small that Hari, when drunk, doubted his parentage. His son said, "I want chocolate milk."

His daughter, plump, more like Hari, echoed, "I want chocolate milk too."

Hari sucked his teeth and brushed roughly past them into the house. He snatched up the car keys from the kitchen counter and started to remove the revolver from his pocket. Then he paused and let it fall back, an ungainly lump in his trousers. It was a calculated risk: what if the police stopped him? They could shoot him and announce that Mr. Hari Beharry, well-known businessman, had died of a heart attack during a road-block search; an illegal revolver had been the source of his anxiety. Bullet holes? If the government said he'd died of a heart attack, he'd died of a heart attack. Hari had lived here too long, been too close to the former government, to delude himself. He knew the way of the island: nowhere was truth more relative.

It occurred to him only afterwards that they might have simply shot him, then claimed he had shot first. But this was too simple, the island didn't seek simplicity. With the obvious evidence, it would have been smarter to claim a heart attack: it was more brazen, it would be admired.

He braked at the driveway and glanced into the rearview mirror: the house, white, brilliant in the sun, the windows and doors of mahogany lending a touch of simple elegance, filled the glass. His wife had surprised him with her suggestion of mahogany: he hadn't thought her capable of such taste. With all the trimmings, he'd ended up sinking over a hundred thousand dollars into the house. It was the investment of a lifetime and one that would have caused his father both pride and anguish: pride that the family could spend so vast a sum on a house, anguish that they would. It was in this house that Hari planned to entertain his grandchildren and their children, to this house that he would welcome future Beharry hordes, from this house that he would be buried. The house spoke of generations.

But now, as he drove along the serpentine road, verges broken and nibbled by wild grass, his dreams all managed to elude him. Those scenes of future familial joy that he had for so long caressed had, almost frighteningly, become like a second, parallel, life. And now they had gone out of reach: he could no longer conjure up a future and what did come to him, in little snippets, like wayward pieces of film negative, caused him to shudder.

It wasn't yet ten o'clock but the sun was already high, radiating a merciless heat. Hari could feel the mounting degrees pressing down on him from the car roof. He could see waves rising like insubstantial cobras from the asphalt paving; he dripped with perspiration. The wind rushing in through the window did little to relieve his discomfort. He wiped away a drop of perspiration that had settled in the deep cleft between his nose and upper lip and shifted in his seat, trying to get used to the feel of the revolver under him.

The plaza was only a short distance away but already Hari could sense the change of atmosphere. At the house the heat was manageable. It suggested comfort, security; it was like the heat of the womb. Outside, away from the house, under the blue of a sky so expansive, so untrammelled that it seemed to expose him, to strip him, the heat became tangible, held menace, was suggestive of physical threat. It conjured not a desire for beach and sea but an awareness of the lack of cover, a sense of nothing to hide behind. The familiar of the outside world had undergone an irrevocable transformation.

The revolver, he realized with a twinge of disappointment, gave no comfort. He used to be able to picture himself blazing away at blurry figures, but this image had been the result of too many paperback westerns. The blurry figures had unexpectedly taken on more substance. What had once seemed epic now seemed absurd.

He drove past several empty lots, wild grass punctuated occasionally by the rusting hulks of abandoned cars. In the distance, on both sides, beyond the land that had been cleared for an aborted agricultural scheme (money had disappeared, as had the minister responsible), he could see the indistinct line of forest, recalling a smudged, green watercolor: government land, guerrilla land. And far away to the left, beyond and above forest, the mountains, sturdy, mottled green, irregularly irrigated by vertical streams of white smoke: signs, some said, of guerrilla camps; signs, others said, of the immemorial bush fires.

At last the plaza came into sight, low stucco buildings with teak panelling and light fixtures imported from Switzerland. The fixtures were broken and in several places were marked only by the forlorn ends of electrical wire. The teak had been scratched and gouged, some pieces ripped from the wall for a bonfire that had been lit at the entrance to the bookstore. The stucco, unrecognizable, had been defaced by slogans, both sexual and political, and crude paintings and election posters and askew copies of the Emergency proclamation, unglued corners hanging limply in the hot air.

In front of the barricaded shops, in the shadow of the overhang, lounged a line of black youths, wool caps pulled down tightly over their heads, impenetrable sunglasses masking their eyes.

Hari couldn't separate his fear from his quick anger.

"We need milk, must have milk, chocolate milk," he muttered, vexed, as he pulled into the parking lot. He could hear their voices, his wife, his son, his daughter, and they were like mockery, demanding and insistent, ignorant of his problems and worries.

He pulled carefully into a parking space, stopping neatly in the middle, equidistant from the white lines on either side of the car. An unnecessary vanity, the lot was deserted. He sucked his teeth in irritation and tugged the keys out of the ignition. With the engine dead, an anticlimactic silence fell over the plaza. None of the youths moved and Hari couldn't tell whether they were looking at him. He wished he knew.

He opened the door—it squeaked a little, disturbing the quiet like a fingernail scraping a blackboard—and put one leg out onto the scorching asphalt. Heat waves tickled up his pant leg, sending a spasm through him. Faintly, from the shadow of the overhang, came the sound of a radio, disturbingly gay, the music local, proud, threatening.

Hari let his foot rest on the asphalt and sat still, trying to discern where the music was coming from. As he looked around, it occurred to him that the milk store would be closed, everything was closed by the Emergency; it was a wasted trip. He noted, as if from a distance, a curious lack of emotion within him: it was as if all feeling had dried up.

"Wha' you doin' here, boss?"

The voice startled Hari. Four black faces were at his door, sunglasses scrutinizing him. He could see his reflection in the black lenses, his strained face eight times, each a caricature of himself.

He heard his voice reply, "I come to get milk, *bredda*. For the children. You know. They need milk. They just small." He wondered if the men were hot under those wool caps, but they were part of the uniform.

"Look like you out of luck, boss. The milk store close." He was the leader, the others deferred to him.

"Yeah, I just remember that myself."

Another of the men said, "You better get out of the car, boss."

Hari didn't move.

The leader said, "My friend like your car, boss."

Hari didn't hear him. He was wondering if the leader had bought his pink dashiki at his store.

Hari said, "You buy that dashiki at the Good Look Boutique?"

One of the men said, "What business that is of yours?"

Hari said, "I own the Good Look."

Fingering the dashiki, the leader said, "I know that, boss. And no. My wife make the dashiki for me. You like it? How much you'd sell that for, boss?"

Hari's heart sank.

"Get out of the car."

"Look, all-you know who I am?"

"Yes, Boss Beharry, we know you. Get out of the car."

"What you want, *bredda*?"

"Get out. I not going to ask you again."

Hari stumbled out. The men crowded him. Hari reached for the revolver, levelled it at the leader, and pulled the trigger. The hammer clicked emptily. Hari's vision fogged; the world went into a tilt: he had drained the clip at the sky and mountains.

The leader said, "Well, well, boss. So the Americans supplying you with guns now, eh?" He knocked the revolver from Hari's hand with an easy, fluid blow.

"What you want, *bredda*?"

"The keys."

Hari gave the car keys to the leader. Hari noticed he was wearing a large silver ring marked U.S. Air Force Academy, the kind advertised in comic books.

"The money."

"Money?" A sudden presence of mind gripped Hari. The heat scorched his skin, the asphalt solidified beneath his feet, the world righted itself.

Hari said, "Give me room, *bredda*, I'll give you the money." He reached into his pocket and pulled out a thick wad of bills. With a quick movement of the wrist, he flung it high and away. The bills scattered like confetti.

The leader looked perplexed. No one moved. Then suddenly everyone was running, the youths from the shadow of the overhang to the money, the robbers from the car to the money. Only the leader remained; Hari pushed him, hard. The man stumbled and fell. Hari started to run.

At the corner of the farthest building, he looked quickly

back. No one was following him. The leader, standing casually by the car, was dusting himself off and smoothing the creases in his pink dashiki. It was a strangely domestic sight.

Hari had just finished watering the little patch of lawn when the police came to return his car. All the windows had been smashed into tiny crystal diamonds. Glittering in the sunlight, they littered the seats and floor like so many water droplets. The body had been badly dented in several places and the paint maliciously gouged with an icepick. Someone had tried to scratch a slogan into the driver's door. Hari could make out the letters CA but only deep gouges followed, as if the vandal had gotten into a sudden rage. This, more than anything, frightened Hari: it was an elegant, hieroglyphic statement.

"We find it on a back road," the policeman said, cocking his military-style helmet to one side. In the old days Hari might have pulled him up for sloppiness; now he said nothing. "We didn't find no money. The keys was in the ignition."

Hari said, "You didn't find the—" He stopped short, remembering he had had the revolver illegally.

The policeman said, "What?"

Hari said, "Nothing. The men. You know."

The policeman said, "No, nothing. We'll call if we find anything."

Hari took the keys and thanked him. The policeman turned and walked away, up the driveway to a waiting jeep. Four men were sitting in the back of the jeep; they all wore police uniforms and sported impenetrable sunglasses.

As the jeep pulled away, one of the men waved at Hari.

Hari waved back.

A second man raised his arm; in his hand fluttered a pink dashiki. The man shouted, "Thanks, boss."

Hari pulled the children inside and bolted the door.

That evening the Minister for State Security telephoned. He said, "Mr. Beharry, I hear you are leaving our happy little island. That's too bad."

Hari said, "Well, I—"

The minister said, "Are you going to visit your American friends?"

Hari said nothing.

The minister said, "You know if you are out of the island for more than six months, your property reverts to the people, who are its rightful owners."

Hari put the phone down.

Flight had become necessary, and it would be a penniless flight. The government controlled the flow of money. Friends had been caught smuggling; some had had their life savings confiscated. He could leave with nothing. It was the price for years of opulent celebrity in a little place going wrong.

His wife, stabbing at her eyes with a tissue, said, "At least we not dead."

Hari said, "We're not?"

He went out into the back yard. The sun was beginning to set behind the mountains and random dark clouds diffused the light into a harsh yellowness. It would probably rain tomorrow.

Hari went to the tool shed and got a fork. The earth around the patch of lawn was loose and damp. The grass shoots had not yet begun to root; they popped out easily under the probing of the prongs. In a few minutes, the work was done. Hari looked up. The sun had already sunk behind the mountains: Hari wished he could dig them up too.

THE
REVOLUTIONARY

·I had not yet been at the university a week when I noticed him, a mass of woolly hair shooting from his head like so much virgin forest, replete with bramble and twisting vines. Below this bobbing congestion, well-developed shoulders and arms stuck out in bony angularity from his sleeveless army jacket. The muscular arms swung loosely and rapidly, like run-away windshield wipers, but it was the feet that drew most of the attention. Much too large for his minute stature, they were turned outward in Charlie Chaplin manner and, when he walked, they produced a sound not unlike that of swimming flippers on concrete.

When I first saw him walking down the corridor towards me, my defensive instincts went wild. I pictured my head being severed by his arms or, lucky enough to escape that fate, my toes being demolished by his oversized army boots, unpolished to a cadaverous grey.

As we passed one another, I glanced at his face: it reminded me of a piece of plastic softened over heat and shaped until taut by a malicious hand. Droopy eyes, overdone nose, chin brashly off centre, it was less a face than a caricature of one. The gloomy eyes blinked at me and the thick lips parted in a smile, revealing a gap between his front teeth large enough to hold a cigarette.

21

I nodded back, feeling, as I did so, that I was making a dreadful mistake. I quickened my step to the elevators.

Later that day, depressed at not having received any letters from home, I plopped myself down in the over-populated cafeteria to brood over a cup of coffee. My neighbors collected their books and prepared to rush off to a class. In the confusion, I missed the flapping which would have alerted me.

"Hi, you from Trinidad?" The voice was deep and confident.

My irritated glance was met by a wide, vaudevillian grin, cleaved by a dark space.

I nodded silently, my learned response to a question I'd heard several times too often. He deposited his army surplus satchel on the table in front of me.

"I from Trinidad too," he said. "My name is Eugéne Williamson. You want some coffee?"

My instinct was to run. Declining his offer I reached for my books.

"Eh eh! But what happen, man? I's one of you, a Trinidadian just like you. C'mon, nah man, have some coffee with me, eh? Wha'cha say?"

Eugene's enthusiasm conveyed itself to the farthest reaches of the large, crowded cafeteria. I could practically feel the vocal waves washing over me. Irritated glances were shot at us; I was sympathetic. People walking past the cafeteria looked in to see what was happening.

I nodded weakly and let my books fall to the table as a gesture of defeat.

As Eugene placed the steaming Styrofoam cup in front of me, he asked the inevitable second question: "So what part of Trinidad you from?" His voice had, thankfully, fallen to a low shout.

"Ellesmere Park," I said, knowing it was the wrong answer.

"But I was born in the country, in Sangre Caliente."

The middle-class name, followed by the country name, had a remarkable effect on Eugene: his face darkened and then brightened, as quickly as a brief dimming of the moon by a sailing cloud.

"Ahh, Caliente," he sighed, "a good, grass-roots place. That's where you does find the real people, you know, the proleteriet."

"The what?"

"The pro-le-ter-iet, you know, the hard-working people, the exploited masses who not afraid to get down on their hands and knees and get some dirt under the fingernails."

"Oh, I see," I said. "Yes, you could find some hard-working people in Caliente."

His eyes took on a dreamy look, accentuating his crow's-feet. I decided he must be well into his thirties. "Yeah, man," he said, "is a good place to live, in the country, surrounded by nature and heroic people. All that fresh air, birds whistlin' in the trees, flowers growin' all over the place." He nodded strenuously. "Good place, good place."

His trees, birds, and heroic people didn't figure in my re-collection of Sangre Caliente. Rather, I remembered that the people had a certain penchant for plastic flowers—they were easier; they didn't need watering and they didn't fade if you kept them out of the sunlight—and the birds were too busy being shot or captured to sing very much. I was trying to think of a gentle way of breaking the news to him when he interrupted his reverie.

"So what you studying up here? Spanish? English?"

It was with a kind of pride that I replied, "Neither. French."

Immediate surprise registered on his face. "Really? You know, is a nice language. I did study it once in high school but I couldn't prononks them words, man. For me, t-a-b-l-e is

table and it don't make sense to prononks it another way. I
suppose it wasn't my thing, you know what I mean?"

I laughed. "What you doing?"

"English Lichecher. You know, Shakespeare, Dickens, and
all them cats."

"Having a hard time?"

He wrinkled his generous nose. "It hard, man. I ain't know
why, but I did never have all this trouble back home. I think is
because all the damn profs think they know how to talk better
than us."

He paused and sipped suspiciously at the murky coffee.

Then he asked, "When you finish you going back to teach
or what?"

My reply was cautious. "I don't know yet. It have so many
things I don't like in Trinidad, I don't know if I could live
there. . . ."

Eugene nodded. "Yeah, I know what you mean. But I make
up my mind already. I going back to help change things, I
want to make life easier for the masses, for our heroic people." He sighed, wearily, like a man resigned to a difficult but
necessary task, and ran his fingers through his bramble.

"You going into politics?" I asked. I could picture him on a
platform haranguing a sleepy crowd, his arms circular blurs,
his bramble bouncing like Scarlett O'Hara's hoop skirt.

"Politics? You joking or what?" He chuckled. "No way,
brother. Besides, I did never like that expression, 'going into
politics'. The way I look at it is, a big lawyer or a big doctor
does go into politics just like he went into law or medicine.
They not interested in helping the people, just in making a
career. I don't trust anybody who want to make a career out
of politics, they always out for themselves and only themselves. If you really want to help people, you does just do it,
you doesn't go into politics."

I said, "So no politics?"

"Brother, the suffering masses need more than lies from politicians. Not that I would lie if I went into politics, of course, is just that it have a better way to do things."

"What way?"

"A gun. Is the only way the socio-economic situation in Trinidad going to change. A gun!" He literally spat out the last word: tiny circles described themselves on the surface of my coffee and I gingerly set the cup aside.

"What you mean, a gun?" I asked. "Revolution?"

"Yes," he whispered, his eyes glazing over. "The glorious, liberating path of socialist-proleterien revolution."

"You think revolution possible in Trinidad?"

His eyes and brows rose dramatically. "Remember 1970?" he said, recalling the island's brief fling with notoriety and headlines. "That was just the trialrun, man, just the trialrun. Since then the country been getting riper and riper, just like a mango, and you know what does happen to a mango when it get too ripe."

"Yeah," I said, "it does stink and you have to throw it away."

He said, "Exactly."

I said, "You going to throw Trinidad away?"

He looked momentarily puzzled. Then he said, "Listen, man, the place almost ready for revolution. Don't fool yourself. History on the march and nothing can stop it. The masses just waiting for the word to seize the day. They know the day coming when we going to free ourself from the white imperialist-colonialist oppression machine and nothing going to stop us." Eugene leaned back in his chair, rocking it onto its back legs. He took a deep breath.

Obviously, Eugene's mind had been set afire by the reading of much Progressive Literature. I did have an objection though. "Eugene," I said, "I think you have a problem. I don't know if you thought about it but, you know, to make revolution you have to sweat. All the government have to do is give out free rum, some fancy clothes, and declare a carnival and fffffftz! End of revolution."

Eugene was startled. He reached out and firmly grasped my right forearm. His unblinking eyes stared fanatically into mine and he half-whispered in an earnest voice, "No, man. It have a lot of guerrilla bands in the island just waiting for the word from the leader. And they well-armed too. The police ain't know nothing about them."

"That's why nobody else ever hear about them either?" I sucked my teeth in irritation. "Come on, eh man? Stop acting."

"Lo-lo-look," he stammered, imploring belief, "you ever hear about the Popular Insurrection Service Squad? Or the Caribbean Region Association of Patriots? No? Well, them's just two of the guerrilla groups. Don't think I joking, man, I dead serious now."

I nodded and allowed myself a small smile. "So what's your plan?"

He stretched his arms overhead and bellowed a bloated yawn. "Well," he paused to rub at his eyes with his knuckles, "when I graduate, I'll take my wife and my son back to Trinidad and contact one of the groups."

"Wife and son?" I interrupted. "You're married?"

"Oh yes." He seemed surprised by the question. He took his wallet from his satchel and a photograph from the wallet. He held it out to me. "My wife, my son, Tara and Tarot."

"Tara and Tarot?"

The photograph, black and white and grainy, showed mother holding baby. Tara was thin and tired and her eyes, small, dark, and grave, were disturbing. Tarot, a tiny lump of fat with undefined features, was crying. His nose was running. The photographer had attempted to be artistic, to manipulate shadow and sunlight. Neither had co-operated. The result was not a photograph for a wallet. It seemed to capture nothing but distress. I returned it to him with a strange sense of relief.

"Anyway," he continued, slipping the photograph back into his wallet, "we'll contact one of the groups and go live in the Northern Range with them, to carry on the glorious struggle."

I said, "In the Northern Range, like—"

"Like Che and Fidel in the Serra Mistra," he completed the sentence for me. "Then, when the iron is hot, we will strike and free the heroic, oppressed masses from the killing yoke of capeetalist exploitation. We going to throw the imperialist aggressors into the sea, just like that." He gestured dramatically with his arms, pretending to throw something heavy. "We going to kill all the local agents of the criminal colonialists and all reactionaries." He clenched his right fist. Horrified, I thought he was going to thrust it into the air. However, he simply put it under his chin for support.

"And what going to happen afterwards? When you overthrow the government, what then?" A casual smoker, I suddenly needed a cigarette. I looked around for a familiar face with a cigarette pack. No luck, but just as suddenly I didn't need one.

"That have nothing to do with me," Eugene declared emphatically. "My job is to go in like a hurricane and destroy the blood-sucking superstructure of the whole fascist-capeetalist regime in the place. All I have to do is destroy everything— free the masses—and then I'll leave, after doing my socialist duty."

"Your socialist duty? But you not going to build anything? Who do you think you helping?"

Eugene blinked twice, reached wordlessly into his satchel and extracted two books. "The future of Trinidad in these two books," he intoned reverentially.

The first was a thick, grey volume published in Moscow: *Articles on the State* by V. I. Lenin. The second was a copy of Mao Zedong's sayings—"Revised and Abridged"—bound in expensive red leather.

A new sales slip peering out of Mao aroused my suspicion: "You read these books as yet, Eugene?"

"No, but some of my friends have. They say that only Vladamir Ill . . . Ill . . . ahh Lenin and May-o have the rightest ideas to free the proleteriet. They say the little red book even tell you how to do farming, everything." His enthusiasm, I noted, was muted.

He took the books from me and held them against his ribs, the way I had seen priests carrying Bibles. His eyes fixed on me: "You want to join the movement? This is your chance to get on the future train."

"The future train? You mean you have an organization here too?"

"Yes, an arm of the revolution flourishing here at the university. These books are for the Future Train Movement's library."

"And a library!"

"Yeah, with librarians. I'm one of the assistant librarians. We have five, you know."

"Five assistant librarians. The book collection must be pretty big."

His eyes shifted away from mine. "Well, it ain't so big yet but it growing fast."

"You have a president or a leader or something like that?"

His eyes still averted, Eugene replied, "We have a Central Committee, and above that we have a Politburo and we have a chairman of the Politburo. A chairman, we have a chairman."

"Sounds very democratic," I said.

"It is." Then, for no apparent reason, his face grew solemn.

His dark eyes gazed emptily at the coffee cup twirling between his thick fingers. In a voice streaked with awe, he whispered, "Imagine! I have to go back to Trinidad to lead men to their deaths!"

And in the best tradition of freedom fighters, this guerrilla leader crushed the Styrofoam coffee cup in his powerful right fist. Coffee splattered over the table and splashed onto his lap.

I said, "How does Tara feel about the whole thing? Living in the Northern Range and killing and the rest of it?"

He said, "What Tara feels is of no business to me. I have my mission and I must fulfil it or die." His eyes curled up to meet mine. "You want to join the Future Train?"

"Let me think about it," I said.

Eugene left me sitting at the table. He said he had to attend a tutorial on William Woodsworth. As he flapped his way to the door, the assistant librarian of the Future Train Movement—his head held high from pride or from the necessity of preventing his hair from crushing him—tripped over himself. Vladamir Ill Lenin, May-o, and the future of Trinidad went sprawling to the ground.

I pretended not to notice.

A SHORT VISIT TO A FAILED ARTIST

His brother Willie says he is an intellectual.

His sister-in-law Shushilla says, "He had great ambitions, artistic ones." She seems to stress the tense of the verb.

They both say he and his wife and baby have just moved from Montreal to Toronto. They have not found an apartment, they cannot afford one. They are staying with Willie and Shushilla in their Ontario Housing Corporation apartment.

Willie and Shushilla invite me to meet Adrian. And his wife Charming, too, they add as an afterthought.

The baby is not further mentioned.

He is reading *Deep Throat*, which he throws aside as we enter the apartment. He snuffs out his cigarette with studious attention to the act, shakes my hand, and lights another cigarette.

His face fits my conception of Bellow's Humboldt—square, handsome, beaten, with finely formed lips and nose, but his eyes are matt black and squinting, slices of shadow hemmed in by converging wrinkles. His hair is shock white and his teeth are tobacco-stained. He is barefoot and his shirt hangs open all the way down: I see a thin, tight, light-brown body with just hints of softness around the middle. He is not yet fifty.

He turns and shouts down the darkened corridor to the bedroom: "Charming! Charming! Come here!"

Charming shouts back in an unfriendly voice: "Shut up, you'll wake the baby."

"Come here, girl."

The bedroom door opens and a much younger woman than I anticipate—her voice old, as beaten as her husband's face—emerges from the darkness. Her eyes are red and tired, and tufts of hair, like black, curly cotton wool, stick out from her tight afro. She shakes my hand wearily, her palm moist and lifeless.

Adrian says, "Go back in the bedroom."

"Yes, darling," Charming replies. "Anything you say, darling."

Adrian says, "Watch your mouth, girl."

Charming, unmoved, disappears into the corridor.

Adrian says, "Women."

"What about them?" Shushilla challenges.

"Women are shit."

"You're shit, Adrian."

"Don't talk damn nonsense, girl. Shit. Women are shit."

"Don't talk nonsense, Adrian. You're shit."

Willie, compact in navy-blue turtleneck and jeans, beckons me to the kitchen. I go with relief, leaving behind in the living room the emotional clutter.

Willie hands me a beer. "They're just joking, you know."

"Sure," I say. "I know. Just joking."

He says, "Adrian is a fool." He grasps his beer bottle in both hands, rubs the bottle, contemplates it like a man struggling not to turn the object he holds into a missile.

Adrian comes into the kitchen. "Where's our guest. Give him a beer, Willie."

I hold out my bottle. "I've got one."

He throws himself into a chair at the small Formica dining

table and lights another cigarette. "Where's Rachel," he asks.

Willie says, "At a class."

"When is she coming back."

"I don't know."

"What do you mean you don't know."

"I don't know when she's coming back. She's got a class."

"Maybe she's screwing in some downtown hotel."

"You care if she is?"

Adrian looks at me: slices of shadow that give me the uncomfortable sense of being stared at by a blind man. "You don't know Rachel."

Then he turns away. No answer is necessary. He says, "Women are shit. Who gives a damn. Especially about Rachel. Slut."

Willie, leaning against the fridge, says nothing.

Again Adrian turns to me. "Have a seat." He pulls heavily on the cigarette. Smoke pours from his mouth, his nostrils. "Rachel's a slut. Mother Nature's a slut. Rachel will screw anyone anywhere anytime. Give her two glances and she's as hot as a bitch in heat."

Willie says, "Don't pay any attention to him. Rachel's a cousin of Shushilla's. He's just vexed with her because she hit him in the balls when he tried to get her into bed." He chuckles.

Adrian turns his shadowed gaze on him. "That's not true. That's what Rachel claims. Rachel's a slut and sluts always lie. Give me a beer."

Willie says, "Get it yourself, Adrian."

"Why? You're standing in front of the fridge."

Willie, wearily, gets him a beer.

As Adrian takes a long swig, Adam's apple bobbing like a pump, the front door opens and a thin, tall girl with long black hair comes in. She is wearing tight shorts and a T-shirt marked THE CIA SUCKS.

She says loudly, "Hi, everybody."

Adrian ignores her, making a great play of it. He swigs his beer again, puts his back to the wall, and stretches out his legs, blocking the entrance to the kitchen.

Willie introduces me to Rachel and we say hello over Adrian's legs. Her fingernails are two inches long and carefully painted a deep purple. Her manner—flip, cultivated sexy—slots her as an off-duty, high-class whore, a courtesan at rest. An unjust impression: Adrian has already provided the angle of vision.

She says, "Move your feet, Adrian."

"Why?"

"I want to get something from the fridge."

"Step over them."

"Why don't you sit properly? The chair has a back for leaning on. Shift your backside."

"No."

"Why not?"

Adrian grins. The stains on his teeth remind me of the shadowing on a charcoal sketch. "This is a good defensive position in case I'm attacked."

"Shit." She flings the book she's been holding past Adrian's face onto the table and runs into the living room.

Adrian, staring at the wall before him, says, "Look at her swinging that backside. Slut." And then, more quietly, to himself, "Shit."

Charming, wearing a faded blue nightgown, appears in the doorway. "Why you don't move, Adrian?"

"I don't want to. I like having my back to the wall. I don't have to worry about being stabbed in the back."

She sighs, and all her fatigue seems to concentrate in the sound. "Who going to stab you in the back? You think you worth it?" She nods sadly at him and walks away.

Adrian shouts, "Charming, you have any more cigarettes?"

There is no reply.

"Charming, you have any more cigarettes?"

"No!"

"Well, go get some. Becker's still open."

"You want cigarette, go get it for yourself."

"And what you going to do?"

"Sleep."

"Lazy bitch."

Willie says, "I'll go get them." He is unenthusiastic. I am about to offer to accompany him, for relief, when Adrian produces a new pack as if by magic.

He says, "No, no, I have some."

I say, to cut the tension, "You smoke a lot."

He says, "Three, four packs a day," and there is a kind of pride in his voice. He peels the cellophane off the pack and lights a cigarette.

Suddenly he springs to his feet. "I have something to show you," he says and rushes out of the kitchen.

Willie, ill at ease, shifting his weight from one foot to the other, offers another beer.

I decline, not having yet finished the first. I want to ask why he has brought me here, why this exhibition of Adrian, but his discomfort is complete. I do not wish to add to it. Instead, I busy myself by glancing at Rachel's book: Pierre Vallière's *White Niggers of America*.

He says, "Failed artists always have trouble with women."

"He's a failed artist?"

"In the worst way. He's tried everything. Writing, painting, sculpting, acting. Even tried to dance once. Somebody told him he had the body for it. Didn't have the talent, though."

"What's he doing now?"

"Trying to earn some money. He works at a computer place or something like that. He scrubs the floors."

Adrian comes into the kitchen clutching several sheets of paper and a fat envelope. His eyes, I notice, are even more squinted, mere slits now, the wrinkles at the corners knotted into tight bunches. He says, "Look at these," and passes the sheets to us.

They are photocopies of a hand—Adrian's hand—held at different angles. Every groove, every line of his flesh stands out in etched ugliness. In one he is holding his middle finger up with the others folded back into his palm. In another, two fingers form a V.

Adrian says, "Isn't that fantastic."

Willie mumbles, "Interesting."

I say, "You can get cancer from exposing your hands too much to those rays." No other comment seems quite adequate.

Adrian says, "The possibilities are enormous. A whole new art form." And for the first time that evening, I detect a note of uncalculated excitement in his voice. It is embarrassing.

Willie says, "What's this one?" He holds up a sheet with jumbled angles and faded lines, as if a washcloth had been held to the machine.

Adrian says, "I tried to photocopy my face," and he looks with interest at the enigmatic smudge.

Rachel bustles into the kitchen and snatches the sheet from Willie. She laughs. "Best picture you've ever taken, Adrian."

Adrian, angered, shouts, "Get out, slut. Doesn't know a damn thing about art."

"You know more than me?"

"I said, get out."

"All right, all right. Going." She retrieves her book from the table, says it is nice to have met me but she's tired, she's going to bed.

Adrian says quietly, "What you expect when you spend the whole afternoon screwing." Then, forgetting her, he opens the envelope, reaches into it with thumb and forefinger, pinches something and spreads it in Willie's palm: cream paper dots.

Willie says, "What's this?"

"Leftovers from the computers," Adrian says. "From where they punch the holes in the cards."

Rachel looks in and says, "Computer shit."

Adrian ignores her. "They throw out boxes of the stuff every day. Imagine the possibilities."

I nod.

Willie says, "I'm imagining."

Adrian says, "I think I'll get some boxes and see what I come up with."

Willie's eyes glaze over. He says, "Good idea."

Adrian puts the computer dots and the photocopies into the garbage can, sits once more at the table, and lights a cigarette. I sense the abandonment of yet another artistic endeavor.

Suddenly he stares at me. "What's your name?"

Willie, embarrassed, says, "He told you earlier."

"Let him tell me again." Adrian thinks for a minute, then adds: "A name is a label. I don't like labels."

I tell him my name anyway.

"I hear you're studying French."

"Yes."

"How do they teach it?"

I explain that, in one exercise, the professor gave two or three of us a situation to which we were required to react and interact in French. It was like acting, except that we wrote the script as we went along.

"I'll give you a situation," Adrian says. "React in French for me."

Guarded, I ask, "Like what?"

"Let's say you're parked somewhere with your wife. A

man comes up with a gun, ties you to a tree, throws your wife on the ground in front of you, and rapes her." He pulls on his cigarette, crosses his legs. "Now, react."

"That situation is somewhat different from—"

"Can you do it?"

"I'm too tired." I find myself contemplating violence: a kick to a sensitive part of his anatomy.

Willie says, "He's tired of you, Adrian."

Adrian looks at me and says, "Is that true."

Willie, hurried, says to me, "Come, I'll drive you home if you're ready."

"I'm ready."

"I'll just go tell Shushilla."

As Willie steps over his legs, Adrian says to himself, "Well, I might as well go to bed too." Without acknowledging me, he gets up and leaves the kitchen, a burning cigarette between his fingers. Behind him he leaves a silence that is like rock; and for the minute that I stand alone, feeling lost, waiting for Willie, its weight presses in on me with hard edges.

Then, suddenly, Rachel's voice rasps, "Oh shit, Adrian, you kicked me."

Adrian, with equanimity, says, "I didn't see you. It's dark in here."

Charming, muffled, says, "Come to bed, Adrian."

Adrian, impatient now, says, "Coming, I'm coming."

There is silence in the apartment.

After a minute, Willie comes to the door of the kitchen, motions to me. The car keys tinkle in his hand. "Shushilla's asleep. Let's go."

I put the beer, now warm and odorous, on the table and follow him to the front door. The living room is dark and only a pale, refracted light comes in through the curtainless window. Asleep on the floor, wrapped tightly in a white sheet like a broken limb in a cast, is Rachel. On one side of the bed, a pillow over her head, lies Charming. Adrian, stripped to his underpants, sits on the other side, his back against the wall. He is smoking. He does not notice us leave. He is staring at Rachel.

THE CAGE

My father is an architect. Architects are good at designing things: stores, houses, apartments, prisons. For my mother, my father, not an unkind man, designed a house. For me, my father, not a kind man, designed a cage.

My father is a proud man. He traces his ancestry back nine generations. Our family name is well known in Yokohama, not only because of my father's architectural firm but also because of those nine generations: his name is my father's greatest treasure.

It is not mine.

At the Shinto shrine in the backyard my father mumbles the names of his ancestors, calling on them, invoking their presence. With those names he swears, expresses pleasure, offers compliments. He knows those names better than he knows mine.

When I was small, I used to stand at the window of the living room watching my father as he mumbled before the shrine. He almost always wore a grey turtleneck sweater; he suffered from asthma and said that the air that blew in off the sea, over the American warships and docks, came heavy with moisture and oil. On especially damp mornings he would return to the house with the skin under his eyes greyed and his cheeks scarlet. He coughed a great deal, and I could see his chest laboring rhythmically beneath his sweater.

I often wondered why, even on the worst of mornings, with drizzle and a grey mist, he went out to the shrine: couldn't the ancestors wait a day? A few hours? Were they so demanding? One day I asked him why and he just stared back at me in silence. He never answered. Maybe he couldn't. Maybe it was just something he knew deep within him, an urge he bowed to without understanding. Maybe it was to him, as to me, a mystery.

I shall never forget the day he called me Michi, the name of his father's mother. She was the person he loved best in the world, and for many years after her death he would visit her grave, to cry. He called me Michi because he had simply forgotten my name. He became angry when my mother reminded him.

When I was a child he took only occasional notice of me. I was my mother's charge. He was not a bad father. He was just as much of one as he was capable of being. His concerns were less immediate.

His attention grew during the teenage years, for he feared them most. When I was fifteen, I told my parents I no longer wanted to take piano lessons. I saw distress on my mother's face: she had, in her youth, before marriage, wanted to be a concert pianist. When I practised, she would often sit quietly behind me, listening, saying nothing. I could feel her ears reaching out to every key my fingers hit, every sound my touch produced. At times I felt I was playing not for me but for her, giving her through the pain and fatigue in my fingers a skein of memory. But music cannot be a duty. It must come naturally. I am not a musician. I grew bored. My fingers on the piano keys produced a lifeless sound. My father, admitting this, agreed to let me stop. My father, after quietly invoking his ancestors, said it was a bad sign. But he would agree if I accepted the *ko-to* in place of the piano. I agreed. It gave me my way and allowed him to assert his authority.

However, his distrust of my age continued. One day he searched among my clothes and found a packet of letters. It was a modest collection, three from girlfriends in foreign places, one from a boy I had known briefly in school. His family had moved to Osaka and he had written me this one letter, a friendly letter, a letter to say hello. My father ignored the letters from my girlfriends and handed me the letter from the boy. He demanded that I read it to him: a friendly letter, a silly letter; finally, a humiliating letter. When I finished, he took the letter with him. I never saw it again. At dinner that evening he searched my eyes for signs of crying. He saw none. He exchanged worried glances with my mother.

I hadn't cried. Instead, I had thought; and the lesson I learned was far greater than mere distrust of my father. I learnt, more than anything else, how little of my life was my own, in my father's eyes. It was the horror of this that prevented tears; his claim to my privacy that, finally, caused me to regard him with eyes of ice.

I had few friends. My peers and I had little in common. They liked to talk of husbands, babies, houses; boredom was my response. No simple explanation offered itself, nor did I seek one. Maybe it was my age, maybe it was my temperament, but I accepted this situation. Often, in the middle of a gathering of schoolmates, I would slip away home, to my room.

For there, among my school texts, was my favorite companion, a child's book that had been a gift many years before from my father. It was a large book, with hard covers and pages of a thick, velvety paper. It related the story of the first foreigners to come to Japan. Every other page contained an illustration, of the sea, of the ships, of the mountains of Japan, in colors so bright they appeared edible.

The picture that most attracted me presented the first meeting between foreigners and Samurai. They stood, clusters of men, facing one another: foreigners to the right, grotesquely bearded, drab in seafaring leathers; Samurai to the left, resplendent in outfits of patterned and folded color. Behind them, with a purity borne only in the imagination, lay a calm, blue sea tinged here and there by whitecaps of intricate lace. On the horizon, like a dark brown stain on the swept cleanliness of the sky, sat the foreigners' ship.

My father, in giving me the book, had stressed the obvious: the ugliness of the foreigners, the beauty of the Samurai. But my mind was gripped by the roughness, the apparent unpredictability, of the foreigners. The Samurai were of a cold beauty; you knew what to expect of them, and in this my father saw virtue. For me, the foreigners were creatures who could have exploded with a suddenness that was like charm. Looking at them, I wondered about their houses, their food, their families. I wanted to know what they thought and how they felt. This to me was the intrigue of the book, and I would spend many hours struggling with the blank my mind offered when I tried to go beyond the page before me.

I remember one day asking my father to tell me about the foreigners. He was immediately troubled. He said, "They came from Europe." But what did the word "Europe" mean, I asked. Europe: to me, a word without flesh. "This is an unnecessary question," he replied, his eyes regarding the book and me with suspicion. I took the book from his hands and returned to my room.

Not long after this I showed the book to a school friend. We were both about twelve years old at the time and I hoped to find in her companionship of spirit. She looked through the book and handed it back to me, saying nothing. I asked her opinion of it. She said, "It is a very pretty book." And those words, so simple, so empty, created distance between us.

The book has remained in my room ever since, safe, undisplayed.

At eighteen, when I graduated from high school, my parents tried to marry me off. He was an older man from my father's firm, an architect like my father. They made me wear a kimono to meet him. At first his glances were modest, but as the evening wore on he became bolder. Angered, I returned his searching gazes. He faltered. He became modest once again. Finally, he left.

My behavior had not gone unnoticed. Afterwards my mother scolded me.

I said, "I do not want to marry."

My mother said, "The choice is not yours, it is not any woman's."

My father said nothing. He left the room.

My mother said, "You have made your father very angry."

I said, "I do not want to marry. I want to live with a man."

My mother looked at me as if I had gone mad. "We are sending you to university. You will not waste your education in such a way."

"I want to have a career."

"We are not giving you an education so you can work. Men want educated wives."

"I do not want to be a man's wife."

"Where are you getting such ideas? You associate with the wrong people. Such ideas are foreign to us." Then she too left the room.

The "wrong people" has always been one of my mother's obsessions. I remember inviting a schoolmate to my house. She met my mother. They talked. When my friend left, my mother said, "I do not think you should associate with such people." I was still obedient at the time; I never spoke to the girl again. I understood why my mother took this attitude.

The girl's home was in one of the poorer sections of Yokohama, her mother worked as a clerk in a department store. This was the first time my mother was too busy to drive one of my friends home. And for me, guilt came only years later, too late, as with everything in retrospect.

My mother. She once played the piano. She has a degree in opera from Tokyo University. She could have had a career. Instead, she got married. She talks of her life now only to say she is happy. But what is this happiness—who can say? Not I, for I could never be happy in her situation. I maybe know too much. Yet I cannot contradict my mother. I can only say I doubt her. This self-sacrifice—she has given her all to her husband, to her son, to me; she has rejected all possibility of leading her own life, of developing her talent—this self-sacrifice is not for me. She has the ability to put up with things even when she is at odds with them. I suppose this shows strength. Sometimes, though, I wonder if this is not so much strength as a simple lack of choice. My mother does not have the ability to create choice where there is none.

I am, in the end, tangible proof of my mother's failure as a woman.

Once during this same summer that ushered me from high school to university my mother expressed a desire to spend the vacation in Kyoto. My father said he wished to visit Kobe; he was adamant. Later, I heard my father, unaware of my presence, telling my brother to observe his handling of the situation. All along, he said, he had wanted to visit Kyoto but he would let my mother beg a little, cajole him, fawn over him; only then would he agree to visit Kyoto. My mother would think she had won a great victory. And that was the way it worked out. My mother never realized the deception, and my sadness prevented me from revealing it to her. It was too, I knew, part of the game she had long ago accepted.

My mother and women like her, my father and men like

him, will tell you that the man's world is in his office, the woman's in her house. But in my parents' house, designed by my father, built by him, his word is law. My mother, if she really believes in the division of domain, lives in a world of illusion.

This facility for seeing the wrong thing, asking the wrong question, already a barrier between acquaintanceship and friendship, made my relations with my brother difficult. I resented having chores to do—washing dishes, making beds, both his and mine, cleaning the house—while his only duty was to protect the family name by staying out of trouble. I resented having my telephone callers interrogated, my letters scanned, my visitors judged, while he was free to socialize with people of his own choosing. I resented the late hours he was permitted to keep while I was forced to spend my evenings practising the *ko-to*, producing music that bored me to tears and put my father in mind of his ancestors, never far out of reach. I resented my brother's freedom to choose from among the girls he knew while I could meet only those men selected by my father, always architects, always older, always pained by courtship conducted before the boss.

My brother and I have never spoken. He is as much a stranger to me as I am to him. What I know of him I do not like. He is too much like my father. They occasionally pray together at the shrine in the backyard.

I had been accepted at Tokyo University, in dietetics. This field was not my choice, but my father's. From a magazine article he had got the idea that dietetics would be a fine, harmless profession, and one easily dropped for marriage. I would have preferred literature but I had no choice. It was my father's money that afforded me an education, and his connections that brought me entry to prestigious Tokyo University.

I left for Tokyo at the end of the summer, with my mother as temporary chaperone. She settled me in and, after three days, left with the lightest of kisses. She had grown into her role, my mother, and had spent much of her time with me worrying about my father and brother. The moment she left, uncertainty became my sole companion. I was as tentative as a spider's web in wind. I avoided people, grew close to no one. My life was my books, and I emerged from chemistry and anatomy only to attend the occasional gathering organized by the dietetics department. Attendance at these "social evenings" was informally obligatory: even in the wider world, you belonged to a family and owed certain obligations. Nothing exciting ever happened at these parties. You went, you drank a little, ate a little, chatted politely, you left. Little was achieved, save homage to the concept of the group. Maybe occasionally a student would get a low grade raised a little.

It was at one of these gatherings halfway through my first year at university that I met Keisuke, a well-known Japanese poet. I had never heard of him, for my father, probably remembering the childhood incident with my story book, had proscribed literature. So at first I treated Keisuke in an offhand manner. I distrusted his name, Keisuke, a fine old traditional name; it seemed to reflect all the values my father held dear. Nor was he particularly attractive in any way. His physique was undistinguished, tending, if anything, to softness around the middle; and the whites of his eyes were scrawled by a complicated system of red veins, from lack of sleep. At one point in the evening, I heard him say that it was his habit to drop in when he could on the gatherings of the different departments. This declaration, made not to me but to a group that had politely formed around him, scared me a little. It was not something that was done and, although there was a general assent that this was a good idea, I could see the hesitation that preceded the required politeness, the easy discomfort quickly submerged in nods and smiles. And I could see, too, that Keisuke had not missed it. He looked at me and smiled: we shared a secret.

After, when he had left, there were a few whispered comments about how odd he was. One of the professors, a small, balding man, said slyly, "But he's a poet. You know what *they're* like. . . ."

The next day at lunch in the cafeteria, Keisuke appeared at my table and sat down, without asking permission. "So," he said. "Did they find me very odd?"

Flustered at hearing the same word in his mouth as had been used to describe him the previous evening, I instinctively said, "Yes."

For a second there was silence, and then we both began laughing. Our secret, understood by a smile the evening before, was made explicit by the laughter. I became comfortable with him. He asked me to call him "Kay", and he mocked his own name, describing it with the English word "stuffy", which he had to explain to me since my English was not very good at the time.

We talked a great deal. He told me he had lived and studied in America for seven years. His father, an executive with the Panasonic Corporation, had been transferred to New Jersey when Kay was sixteen. Kay knew New York City well, and as he described it—the lights, the noise, the excitement—I wondered why he had returned, after all that time, to Japan.

He smiled at my question. "I am Japanese," he said.

I nodded, but the answer discomforted me. It was my father's explanation of too many things.

Kay and I became friends. He invited me to his apartment not far from the university. It was a small place, and cluttered. On the walls he had hung framed American film posters, all at different heights so that any thought of uniformity was banished. Everywhere—on his desk, on the coffee table, on the kitchen counters—he had stacked books and magazines and papers. We would sit together in a corner on a *tatami*, reading or talking under the yellow light of a wall-lamp.

I told him about my father, my mother, my brother. He showed me some of his poetry. I read it. I understood little. He asked what literature I had read. I told him about my father's prohibition on books and of his final admonition on the night before I left for Tokyo. Stay away, he had said, from books full of fine words. Kawabata, Tanizaki, Mishima would not help my chemistry marks and, besides, writers always had strange ideas anyway, ideas unfit for young female minds.

Kay listened to my story in silence. Then he said, "Your father is a man full of fears." This was like revelation to me.

I confessed that I had read Mishima, for my brother had on the bookshelves in his room the complete works, a gift from our father. I had read them surreptitiously and, at the time, untrained, unaware, I had seized only upon the eroticism. Kay, unsurprised, explained to me what I had missed: the mingling of the sex with blood, and the brooding sense of violence. "Mishima was mad in many respects," he said. "A twentieth-century Samurai. His end was fitting." And now, now that I understand Mishima, I worry about my brother, and I fear him.

One evening, after a light dinner of *sashimi* and warm sake, Kay seduced me. As I write this, I realize what an un-Japanese admission it is. It scares me a little.

After, lying on the *tatami*, smoking my first cigarette and enjoying the warmth and soreness that clasped my body, I felt as if I had been given a precious key, but a key to what I wasn't sure. This too Kay, lying wet next to me, understood. He suggested I read Ibsen and, in the following months as my first year of university drew to a close, he supplied translations to help my shaky English through the Ibsen texts he'd studied in America. We discussed his works, among others, and the

more intense our discussions became, the more I found myself
articulating thoughts and ideas that would have made my
father blue with rage.

Kay, one of those writers with strange ideas whom my
father so feared, gave me the ability to put into words what
had been for me, until then, ungrasped feelings. With his
help, I arrived at last at a kind of self-comprehension, although
a confusion—guilt, Kay called it—remained. He said this
was so because, although my ideas were coming into focus,
their source remained hidden.

However, I do not want to give the impression that I
always sailed smoothly. At times, especially after another of
the tedious meetings with one of my father's architects—for
which I was periodically called home—I felt that the seduction was less a key than a betrayal. As I sat there in my
father's spare living room, serving the men, smiling at them, I
felt that Kay had heightened my confusion rather than diminished it. But these periods of doubt were shortlived.

The rest of my university career was uneventful. Kay and I
continued to see one another from time to time but the intimacy of that first year was never repeated. He had too much
work, I had too much work. At least, it was the excuse we
used.

I graduated as a dietitian and had no trouble finding a job in a
hospital in Yokohama. I worked there for a year, in a profession not of my choosing, counting day after day the calorie
intake of patients. Counting calories becomes tedious after a
while and the patients soon became little more than mathematical sums in my mind, defining themselves by what they
could eat.

At the end of one particularly trying day, I called on a
patient, an old woman, chronically ill and querulous, to discuss
her rejection of prescribed food. She explained to me in a

cross voice that she wanted, of all things, mayonnaise on her food. I told her this was impossible. She became abusive. I became abusive. I hit her with my clipboard. She started to cry, silently, like a child, the tears filling the wrinkles and creases of her crumpled face. It was then, looking at her through my own tears, that I realized I could not continue.

The tedium of the job, living once more in my father's house, smiling at his architects, practising the *ko-to*, these were all taking their toll on me.

I confronted my parents with my decision. They offered an alternative. They had never been happy about my working; a working wife is in short demand. It would be better, they said, if I were to concentrate on what really mattered. I was getting old, already twenty-three. In five or six years I would be considered an old maid, an also-ran in the race to the conjugal bed. I had better get cracking.

But, as usual, I had my own idea. I had managed to save a tidy sum during my year of work, money my father considered part of a future marriage contract. In Japan, women marry not for love but for security. The man acquires a kind of maid-for-life. For a person with my ideas, marriage means compromise, an affair not of the heart but of the bank account. Therefore, my savings compensated a bit for my advanced age and my father never failed to mention the money when one of the suitors called.

I, however, wanted to travel. My father said it was out of the question; neither he nor my mother could leave Yokohama at the time. I said I wanted to travel alone. My father said this was preposterous, and he called on his ancestors, all nine generations of them, to witness the madness of his daughter.

Kay had once said to me, "Learn from the past but never let it control you." I think it was a line from one of his poems. At that moment the line ran through my mind. If my past would not control me, I decided, then neither would my father's. I told them I was leaving. My father threatened to restrain me physically. He called my brother to help. He came. I did not protest; it would have served no purpose. My father and brother were as one. Even their eyes, black circles trapped behind the same thick lenses, framed by the same black plastic, were indistinguishable. It was these eyes that I saw come at me. As they led me off between them, my mother started crying. But she said nothing. They locked me in my room and told the hospital I was sick.

For a week I lay or sat alone in my room. My mother, silent always, brought me my meals, of which I ate little. I slept a lot, tried to read, spent long hours looking at my picture book: the splendid Samurai, the bearded foreigners. At one point—I no longer remember whether it was day or night; time, after a while, was of no importance—I felt myself slipping into the painting, becoming part of it. I could feel the weight of heavy sea air on my face, the soft tingle of sand beneath my feet; I could hear the broken whisper of softly tumbling surf. I was prepared to surrender myself but something—a voice, a rattle of dishes—tugged me back. For the first time in my captivity, I cried. My tears fell onto the pages of my book and there the stains remain.

They let me out after a week and I returned to work. My father had spoken to the administrator of the hospital, an old friend. Since other members of the staff had complained about the old woman's behavior, no action was taken against me, save a kindly lecture on the virtues of patience.

The next two months were, however, not easy. I was never allowed a moment to myself; my every movement was monitored, every minute accounted for. Even at work, I found out, the administrator asked discreet questions about me. My father had spoken to him about more than my problems with the old woman.

My life became like that of the four song-birds my brother

kept in bamboo cages suspended from the ceiling of his room. They would whistle and chirp every morning, each making its own distinct cry, sometimes sounding as if in competition against one another. The birds would sing at precisely the same time every morning, demanding food. I thought they saw this ability to wake him as power, but my brother knew who controlled the food.

One day, with the sense of reserved delight he shared with our father, my brother brought home a new song-bird. It was the smallest of them all, a tiny creature of a blue and a red that sparkled when brushed by the sun. But there was a problem: while the others sang, this new bird remained silent. My brother tried coaxing music out of him, in vain. He tried attacking with a stick, but the bird was unmoved. My brother first tried withholding food, but later when the incentive was offered the bird ignored it, and twice he knocked over his dish, scattering the seed.

The bird uttered only one sound in his week in my brother's bedroom, a pure, shrill whistle. The cry brought my brother, my mother, and me to the room. The bird was lying on the floor of the cage. My brother opened the door and poked the little body with a finger, at first gently, then more roughly. Satisfied it was dead, he picked it up by a wing, took it to the kitchen, and dropped it into the garbage can. He dusted his hands casually and returned to his breakfast. He showed no regret.

I watched my brother with horror. At that moment I hated him. I went to my room and I cried, for the bird, for myself.

He replaced it that evening with a more pliant bird. This one sang easily, and it was fed.

The next day I began playing the traditional daughter. I quit my job, I never complained, I welcomed the architects, smiled at them, hinted to my father of grandchildren: a game, a game for which my real personality had to be hidden away like the pregnant, unwed daughter of a rich family. It was not very difficult, for I discovered in myself a strange determination.

After two months of this, my father, watchful always, put his suspicions aside. He said to my mother, "I have exercised the power of my ancestors. They cannot be resisted." Then he went to visit the grave of Michi, his father's mother.

During this period I grew closer to my mother, for she was most often my guard. One night—it turned out to be my last in my father's house—we sat talking in my room. We had turned off the lights and opened the window. Above the silhouetted trees and roof tops, we could see the sky turning dark, as if expiring. As yet, no stars were visible. The night air was cool and we could hear insects chirping and cluttering in the shrubbery outside. My mother put on a sweater over her kimono, an oddly touching sight, and folded her arms, not sternly as I had once thought, but wearily, like a woman undone. We sat on the bed, I on one side, she on the other, with a great expanse between us.

I asked her, "Have you ever thought of the possibility of leading your own life?"

She sighed. "I used to think of it when I was small but I always knew it would be impossible."

"Why?"

"You are playing games now." She smiled sadly. Without looking at me, she said, "Whatever happens, I am always your mother. Wherever you are, whatever you are doing, you can call me. I will help."

"Who can you call?"

"Your father."

"You once had friends."

"Yes, but your father comes first. Friends just . . ." She waved her hands, searching for words. ". . . just get in the way."

"But you haven't got any friends."

"I am content. I have all I want, all I need. Now say no more about it."

I couldn't see her face. She was all in shadow. But her voice was tender.

The next day, for the first time in many months, she left me alone, unguarded. I packed my bags and called a taxi. The night before, although I hadn't known it, she had been telling me goodbye.

I had always believed I could trust none of my relatives: my father, made in the image of his ancestors; my mother, made in the image of my father; my brother, a stranger. It took me a long time to realize that my mother was my friend. I do not think she really understood me but I was one of those things she put up with even though we were at odds. I hope she can one day understand my attitude but I do not expect this. I can only hope.

I spent two months in Tokyo, in an apartment lent to me by one of Kay's friends. Kay visited me from time to time. We couldn't talk. He seemed uncomfortable with me and, through this, I became uncomfortable with him. We were like polite strangers. This distance, and the silences it brought with it, depressed me; and I, in turn, depressed him.

One evening, after a particularly silent dinner, I asked him to tell me exactly what was wrong.

He said, "Nothing." Then he closed his eyes and said, "I have not been able to write. Your mood affects me. It is not good."

I couldn't reply. There was nothing to say.

He opened his eyes, the whites red-veined, the skin around them reddened, and looked slowly around the apartment. It was very much like his, the film posters, the stacks of books and magazines. He had started a style among his friends.

"There is something else, too," he finally said. "I have been wondering . . . well, do you think you did the correct thing in leaving your father's house?"

·I looked at him: it was all I could do. The one person of whom I had been sure. I said, "Keisuke. Keisuke."

He left a few minutes later, after putting the dishes into the kitchen sink.

His visits grew less frequent and finally stopped altogether. Without him, I found myself enmeshed in the freedom I had sought, friendless, guideless, at liberty to choose my own way. "Without him": the irony does not escape me.

I found a job, again ironically, playing the piano in a bar. I eventually moved into my own little apartment and developed a small circle of friends, all connected in one way or the other with the bar. One night the owner, an overweight man who dressed in flashy American clothes, tried to pressure me into sleeping with him. I never went back to the bar and so had yet another place to avoid, another place to run from.

In Tokyo, anonymity was easy to obtain: it is not difficult to be alone in a crowd of thousands. Privacy came more easily in large, overpopulated Tokyo than in the smaller, relatively slow-paced Yokohama. Tokyo, the least traditional, most western, of our cities is, for me, the safest.

But it was still Japan. I was invited to parties. Japanese parties, like marriages, are business occasions in disguise. Men go to a party to get a promotion or to clinch a deal. The women smile and serve. The men drink and talk. When they have drunk enough, they talk sex and arrange package tours to Korea, where they enjoy the prostitutes of a people they detest.

I felt I had to get away. My first thought was: Europe. But I quickly realized there were yet other places I had to avoid, the usual Japanese destinations: much of Europe, much of

America, especially Boston or Philadelphia or New York. So I changed my money to travellers' cheques and bought a plane ticket to Toronto. It was new space. I expected nothing.

Many Japanese think of snow and bears and wonderful nature like Niagara Falls when they think of Canada. But Toronto, a big city, bigger than Tokyo, less crowded, with more trees and flowers, did not surprise me. I do not know if it was Toronto or me. Probably me.

I rented a room in a big house across from a park. My landlady, Mrs. Harris, lived on the first floor with her sister, Mrs. Duncan, and her cat, Ginger. She was a small woman of about fifty, with hair too blonde for her age. "We are all widows," she said with a smile the first time I went to the house. "Ginger's Tom died last week. A car, poor dear." I thought her a strange woman but she smiled often, the skin on her face stretching into congruent wrinkles.

The second floor was rented to people I never saw. But they liked rock music. Their stereo worked every day, from early morning to late at night. I rarely heard the music but I was always aware of it because of the thump of the bass beneath my feet, like a heart beating through the worn green carpet.

The third floor was divided into two small rooms. It was one of these that I took. The ceiling followed the contours of the roof, and the walls were painted a white that reflected the little sunlight that came in through the small window. The furniture was sparse: a bed, an easy chair, a table with a lamp. My window overlooked the tops of trees and, to the left, fenced-in tennis courts. Sometimes, on a clear day, I could see Lake Ontario on the horizon, a thin ribbon of blue barely distinguishable from the sky.

I did little in my first weeks in Toronto. I walked. I visited the tourist sights. I learned my way around the city. The last heat of the summer exploded down from the sky every day. It exhausted me, and I spent much time sleeping. My memories of the time are dull, everything seems to have rounded corners, everything seems somehow soft.

On weekends, many people came to the park across the street, to walk, to eat, to talk. I would sit at my window observing them, many forms in blue denim or shades of brown, the occasional red or yellow or purple: glimpses of lives I would never touch, for I stayed at my window.

Looking. Looking. Looking.

One hot afternoon, returning groggy from my walk, I came across my third-floor neighbor sitting in the small front porch. She was a tall lady with red hair and very white skin. Perspiration slicked her forehead. She wore a thin white T-shirt and shorts. In her right hand she held an open beer bottle.

"Hello," she said as I walked up the stairs. "Hot, isn't it."

I said, "Yes," reaching for the doorknob. It was no cooler in the porch than it had been in the sun, only the heat was different. Out there, the sunlight burned like an open flame; here, it was like steam. I was exhausted. I did not want to deplete the last of my energy by talking. English was still a strain.

"It's like a goddam oven up there," she said, pushing a chair towards me. "Hell, it's like a goddam oven down here. But at least it's open."

I sat down. We had seen each other twice before but each time she had been in a hurry. I had been shy. We had just said hello.

"You from Hong Kong?" she asked.

"No, I am from Tokyo. I am Japanese." Across the street, the browned grass of the park cowered in the shadow of the trees.

"Oh." She sipped from her beer. "What are you doing here?"

"I plan to take English lessons." My words surprised me. It had been something to say, an excuse for being there, but as I heard myself I thought it a good idea.

"Oh." Then there was silence. On the road a car sped by in a spasm of loud music.

"What do you do?" I finally asked; it took courage.

"I dance. I'm a dancer. My name is Sherry."

"Ballet? Jazz?"

"Table."

"Table?"

"I work in a strip joint."

"What is 'strip joint', please?"

She laughed. "It's a place where ladies like me take off their clothes. For men."

"*Hai*. Yes. I see." The heavy air wrapped itself around my skin like a steamed napkin, and for a second I smelled the oily brine of the Yokohama harbor. "Excuse me, please," I said getting up. The smell, as brief and as powerful as vision, had frightened me.

She watched me open the door. "Like a goddam oven," she said.

The next day I checked the Yellow Pages for a school and went down to their office. It was on the edge of the Yorkville area, a place of expensive stores and restaurants. The sidewalks were crowded: many young people with perfect hair and clothes; many old people trying to look like the young people. On one corner a young man with a clown's face juggled colored balls for a small crowd. On another, a young couple in tuxedos played violins while people hurried by.

I was uncomfortable among these people: their numbers didn't offer anonymity. It was just the opposite, in fact. The people, by their dress, by their extravagance of behavior, demanded to be noticed; they were on display. I walked quickly to the office building where the school was located, into the lobby of marble that created echo in the fall of my footsteps, into the elevator that at last brought relief.

Behind the green door that carried only a number, a man with grey hair and glasses was sitting at a desk. In front of him were a telephone, an ashtray so full that the ashes formed a little mountain, and a messy pile of papers. He was playing Scrabble when I walked in, a rack with tiles at either side of the board. No one else was in the office; he was playing against himself, right hand against left hand.

"Good morning," he said, standing up. "Can I help you?" His suit, of a dark blue, showed chalk smudges at the pockets and on the right shoulder.

"Yes, please, I wish to improve my English language."

He offered me a seat and went to another room to get coffee. The walls of the office were bare; in the far corner a large climbing plant, green leaves dulled by dust, clung weakly to its wooden staff.

He returned with two Styrofoam cups of coffee. He placed one on the desk in front of me, the other on the Scrabble board. As he sat down he asked me if I was from Hong Kong. Then he told me about himself. He spoke some French, some Spanish, some German. He had lived and worked in many places. He didn't like Greek food, cats, and American cigarettes. Finally, after an hour, he told me about the school and we managed to arrange private English lessons for me.

I began the following week. My teacher, a tall, nervous young man with a moustache, was a student at the University of Toronto. He dressed poorly, and was so thin and white that at times, under the fluorescent light of the classroom—desk, chairs, walls bare but for the black rectangle of the chalk board—I thought I could see through him. He said he was a vegetarian.

He wanted to talk about Japan and *hara-kiri*, although he knew nothing about Japan or *hara-kiri*. We discussed food. He insisted that I, being a Japanese person, never ate bread, only rice and vegetables and raw fish and nothing else. He would not believe that I had tasted my first Big Mac in Tokyo.

At one point he said, "Ahh, yes, I understand. American imperialism."

"No," I replied. "Good taste."

He did not appreciate my attempt at humor. He became angry and drilled me severely on grammar and vocabulary, refusing to discuss anything.

I settled in to a routine: Classes every morning at the school; a light lunch, then a walk in the afternoon; back to my hot room for a nap; dinner at a restaurant and then my room again, for homework and reading. It was an easy, uncomplicated life. For the first time I knew what it was to anticipate the next day without tension.

Sometimes I saw Sherry, my third-floor neighbor. We would exchange a few words of politeness. Once she asked my opinion of a perfume she had bought. Another time she held up to herself a new blouse. Through these brief encounters, I grew comfortable with her, even to like her a little.

My one shadow was a nightmare. Gentle and vivid, it came again and again, at first sporadically, later with greater frequency: my father and Keisuke, both in the dress of Samurai, standing on a beach, swords unsheathed, while behind them the sea wept with the voice of my mother. I would awake with the sound of sobbing in my ears and I would have to speak to myself: *I am in Toronto. I am in Toronto.*

Toronto: a place where my personality could be free, it was not a city of traditions in a country of traditions. It was America, in the best implication that word held for us Japanese: bright, clean, safe, new. Life experienced without the constraints of an overwhelming past. I shall never forget my joy when, awaking one night in a sweat from the nightmare, I realized that here I was a young person and not almost an old maid, that by a simple plane flight I had found rejuvenation.

For two months I lived with a joy I had never imagined possible, the joy of an escape that did not demand constant confrontation with the past.

At the school, the director's hands continued to challenge one another to Scrabble. My teacher grew thinner, shaved his moustache, grew it back, added a beard. I practised grammar, vocabulary, sentence structure.

I was so comfortable I even wrote a short note to my mother, to let her know I was all right.

Summer began signalling its end. The trees across the street lost some of their green; the heat of the day was less severe and at night my room cooled enough that I needed to cover myself with a sheet. At school, I got a new teacher. The first had come in one morning with the shaved head and salmon robes of a religious cult, and had spent much of one class trying to convince me to drop English in favor of Hindi. He was fired.

One evening I saw Sherry in the restaurant where I had dinner. I was surprised, for she usually worked in the evenings.

"How's your English?" she said loudly, motioning me to her table.

"Fine, thank you. I have learnt much. How are you?" I sat down. She had already eaten. The plate before her was empty but for smeared ketchup.

"Not so great. Can't work."

"I am sorry. Are you sick?"

"Not quite. I had an operation."

"It is not serious, I hope."

She laughed. "No. I had a tit job."

"Pardon me, I do not understand."

"They cut my breasts open. Cleaned 'em out. Put in bags of water. Size makes money."

"*Hai*. Yes. I see." Suddenly I was no longer hungry. My

eyes swept involuntarily from her face to the table.

She pushed her chair back and picked up her cigarettes. "It hurts," she said softly, a look of pain on her face. "I better go." She stood up. Her face turned into the light. I saw bags under her eyes, wrinkles I had not noticed before, and I realized I had never before seen her without makeup. The light shone through her curled hair, thinning it like an old person's. "See you," she said.

"Yes, sleep well." I watched her go, feeling her take some of my joy with her.

Two weeks later, as I was doing my homework late at night, I was disturbed by noises from Sherry's room. I put my book down and listened. At first there was nothing. Then I heard a quiet groan. I became worried. I went to my door and listened again. Another groan. I opened my door, put my head into the corridor, and said, "Sherry, what is it, please?" I listened. There was no answer, no sound. Uncertain, I closed my door and went back to my books. A few minutes later, Sherry's door slammed and heavy footsteps hurried down the stairs. The front door slammed.

My door flew open. Sherry walked in slowly. She was wearing a bathrobe. "Well, little Miss Jap, you pleased with your work?" She was calm, but it was the calm of anger, the same restraint my father and my brother displayed in times of emotion.

"I am sorry?" I put down my book.

"You just cost me two hundred dollars."

"I do not understand."

" *What is it please, Sherry?* " she mimicked me. "The john went soft on me. You think I got paid? Eh? That's two hundred dollars I'm out of, lady."

"Who is John, please?"

"Jesus Christ! What are they teaching you at that school, anyways?"

I was very confused. I said, "I am sorry. Please explain."

"What are you? Some kinda moron?" Then she turned and walked back to her room. Her door slammed.

I got up and closed my door. It was getting cold in the room. I shut the window and got into bed, pulling the sheet tightly up to my neck. That night my nightmare came again: my father, Keisuke, and my mother weeping like the sea.

When I came in from school the next day, Mrs. Harris the landlady called me into the kitchen. She was sitting at the dining table with Mrs. Duncan, Ginger the cat on her lap. The little television next to the fridge was on but the sound was turned down.

Mrs. Harris said, "About last night, my dear, I just wanted to let you know it won't happen again. Sherry's gone. I asked her to leave this morning."

"What happened last night, please? I do not understand." I had tried to seek an explanation from my teacher at the school but, upon hearing the story, she had grown uneasy and talked about the English subjunctive.

"Oh dear," said Mrs. Harris. She glanced at Mrs. Duncan. "Well, you see, dear, she was a stripper. Do you know what that means?"

"I know. She told me." Mrs. Duncan held out a plate of cookies to me. I took one.

"And sometimes, quite often in fact I found out this morning, she brought men back to her room with her. They paid her, you see. To . . . well, you know."

"*Hai*. Yes. I see." I understood now, with horror, the two hundred dollars.

"But she's gone now, thank God."

I went up to my room, the cookie growing moist where the tips of my fingers pressed into it. The door to Sherry's room was open, the bed stripped, the dresser and table cleared of the cosmetics and perfumes Sherry collected. Beneath my feet, the neighbors' stereo beat in its steady palpitation. I felt very alone.

The weather in Toronto grew cold. The trees outside my window turned gold and brown, and in one night of wind lost all sign of life. The lake in the distance became a sliver of silver beneath a heavy sky. Now, no one came to the park. The view from my window was of desolation, of bared trees and deadened grass. I rarely looked out. My afternoon walks came to an end. Instead I went directly home from school, to my room.

I talked from time to time with Mrs. Harris and Mrs. Duncan. They spent almost every afternoon in the kitchen. They would drink coffee and eat cookies and talk about the boyfriends they had when they were young. How different from my mother, who could never acknowledge past boyfriends and could not even have a friend to talk to.

At four o'clock every afternoon Mrs. Harris would put on the little television and they would smoke and look at a soap opera. Sometimes they cried a little. I often felt, watching them blow their noses into tissues, that they were crying not for the people in the show but for themselves, for the people they might have been and the people they were. Their own lives were not so interesting as those they saw on television at four o'clock every afternoon.

I found it strange that they never told me their first names. It was as if they had lost them. One cold, rainy afternoon, an afternoon on which shadows became airborne and floated about in the air, I asked Mrs. Harris why she called herself by her husband's name.

Stroking the cat, she thought for a minute. "It's tradition, dear. Christian tradition."

"Yes, dear," Mrs. Duncan said, "it's as simple as that. It's what women have always done."

"And what do you do with your own names? Are they no longer of importance?"

"A name is a name is a name," Mrs. Harris said. She lit a cigarette and the cat leapt from her lap with a growl.

I saw that Mrs. Harris did not like my questions.

Mrs. Duncan said, "Poor Ginger. She doesn't purr any more."

Mrs. Harris said, "She's gone off her food too." There was worry in her voice.

I went to my room. Through the window, the park hunched gloomily against the rain and cold. I thought of Ginger, and of my mother and Mrs. Harris and Mrs. Duncan, and I remembered the bird that would not sing.

That night my nightmare came again, but now I sensed my own presence, and I no longer knew from whom—my mother or myself—came the sound of the weeping sea.

Two days later I received an envelope from my mother. I left it unopened for several hours: I feared it, feared what it might say and, more, what it might not. Finally, I ripped it open.

It was a short letter. In it, my mother told me that my father, on discovering my disappearance, had said nothing, had done nothing. He hadn't even called on his ancestors. She said that my father never mentions me. She then explained, briefly, the mystery of myself to me. She spoke of Michi, the idol of my father. Michi had been, my mother said, a strong and independent woman, a woman with her own ideas. She had been beaten into submission by my great-grandfather and was left, in the end, with little but her grandson, my father, as outlet for her sense of life. It was all my mother knew but she hoped the knowledge would help me.

The letter brought me once more directly before the life I had managed to ignore during these months in Toronto. It reminded me that I faced nothing here, that this life of free-

dom was one without foundation, that it would all inevitably
end with a twenty-hour plane flight. That night I did not
have my nightmare, for I did not sleep. I spent the night
crying, and I could not understand why it was the memory of
my father coughing before the Shinto shrine that caused me
the greatest sadness.

Depression: the English word is inadequate to describe that
which seized me, which took hold of my heart, my lungs, my
intestines. This was more like a sickness, a sickness of the
soul.

Two nights later it snowed. My coats were too thin for the
climate. Instead of buying a new coat, I took out my return
plane ticket.

When I arrived in Tokyo, it was raining.

I now work as a language teacher, instructing foreigners,
mostly Americans, in Japanese. In return, one of them prac-
tises my English with me.

It has been over a year since I left my father's house. Since
my return to Japan, I have telephoned my mother once, just
to hear her voice. We both cried on the phone, but I did not
tell her where I live. Not yet.

The sea no longer weeps in my dreams. Instead, some
mornings I wake up with wet cheeks and a damp pillow. I do
not know why.

Or maybe I do.

There is an English expression, "No man is an island." Or
woman. Expressions always contain a grain of truth and this
is an expression I wish I had never learned, for it brings into
too bright a light what I have come to understand: I am a
woman, I am a Japanese woman—I still look to the east when
I take medicine—and the ties of tradition still bind me the
way they bound Michi. To understand oneself is insufficient.
Keisuke has yet to realize that his precept of refusing to let

the past impede the future applies, in my country, but to one sex. This is, perhaps, why I failed to understand his poetry when I first read it; it was too alien in too many ways. Keisuke to one side, my father and brother to the other, but it is always the men. For them all, the common sentence: I am Japanese.

There is, as one of my businessmen students puts it, no leadership potential in me. I do not lead, I never have. I have only practised avoidance.

Accepting my father's values would make life easier for me. But I cannot do this automatically. I am not a clock. As a first step, therefore, I am taking a course in flower arranging, a small step, but important in its own way.

For I shall, I fear, return one day soon to my father's house, to the *ko-to*, to the architects; for I have learned that the corollary of tradition's pride is tradition's guilt. Keisuke was right: I feel guilty for having betrayed my father's name and his nine generations of ancestors. Keisuke helped me recognize my guilt but he did not equip me to deal with it. In this, and not in the seduction, lay the real betrayal.

Tradition designed my cage. My father built it. Keisuke locked it. In returning to my father's house, I betray my mother's faith but the load is lighter on my shoulders than that of the nine generations.

I shall pack away my picture book: it is a child's book. I shall save it for my children, my daughters and my sons. It is to them that I bequeath my dreams.

And in the meantime, I continue to arrange my flowers. Even a cage needs decoration.

INSECURITY

"We're very insecure in this place, you know." Alistair Ramgoolam crossed his fat legs and smiled beatifically, his plump cheeks, gouged by bad childhood acne, quivering at the effect his words had had. "You fly down here, you look around, you see a beautiful island, sun, coconut trees, beaches. But I live here and I see a different reality, I see the university students parading Marx and Castro on the campus, I see more policemen with guns, I see people rioting downtown, I see my friends running away to Vancouver and Miami. So you can see, we are very insecure down here. That is why I want you to put the money your company owes me into my Toronto bank account. It is my own private insurance. The bank will notify me the money has been deposited and the government here won't notice a thing."

Their business concluded, the visitor pocketed Mr. Ramgoolam's account number and stood ready to leave. He asked to use the phone. "I'd like to call a taxi. My flight leaves early in the morning."

"No, no." Mr. Ramgoolam gestured impatiently with his plump arm. "Vijay will drive you into town. You're staying at the Hilton, not so?"

The visitor nodded.

"Vijay! Vijay!" Mr. Ramgoolam's silver hair—stirred, the

visitor noticed, by the slightest movement—jumped as if alive.

Vijay's voice rattled like a falling can as it came in irritated response from the bowels of the house. "Coming, Pa, coming."

The tick-tock of Vijay's table-tennis game continued and Mr. Ramgoolam, chest heaving, bellowed, "Vijay!"

Still smiling beatifically, Mr. Ramgoolam turned to his visitor and said, "So when you'll be coming back to the islands again?"

The visitor shrugged and smiled. "That depends on the company. Not for a long time probably."

"You like Yonge Street too much to leave it again soon, eh?" Mr. Ramgoolam chuckled. The visitor smiled politely.

Vijay, rake thin and wild-eyed, shuffled into the living room.

Mr. Ramgoolam saw the visitor to Vijay's sports car, the latest model on the road. "You won't forget to get the letter to my son, eh? Remember, it's Markham Street, the house number and phone number on the envelope. You won't forget, eh?"

"I won't forget," the visitor said. They shook hands.

Mr. Ramgoolam was back in his house before the gravel spat up by the tires of the car had settled. He followed the tail-lights through a heavily burglar-proofed window—Vijay was speeding again, probably showing off; he'd need another talking to. Nodding ponderously, he muttered, "We're very insecure in this place, yes, very insecure."

Alistair Ramgoolam was a self-made man who thought back with pride to his poor childhood. He credited this poverty with preventing in him the aloofness he often detected in his friends: a detachment from the island, a sneering view of its history. He had, he felt, a fine grasp on the island, on its history and its politics, its people and its culture. He had developed a set of "views" and anecdotes which he used to liven up parties. It distressed him that his views and anecdotes rarely had the desired effect, arousing instead only a deadpan sarcasm. He had written them down and had them privately published in a thin volume. Except for those he'd given away as gifts, all five hundred copies were collecting dust in cardboard boxes under the table-tennis board.

Mr. Ramgoolam had seen the British when they were the colonial masters and he had attended the farewell ball for the last British governor. He had seen the Americans arrive with the Second World War, setting up their bases on large tracts of the best agricultural land; and he had seen the last of them leave, the Stars and Stripes tucked securely under the commander's arm, more than twenty years after the end of the war. He had seen the British, no longer masters and barely respected, leave the island in a state of independence. And he had seen that euphoric state quickly degenerate into a carnival of radicals and madmen.

His life at the fringe of events, he felt, had given him a certain authority over and comprehension of the past. But the present, with its confusion and corruption, eluded him. The sense of drift nurtured unease in Mr. Ramgoolam.

He would always remember one particular day in late August, 1969. He had popped out of his air-conditioned downtown office to visit the chief customs officer at the docks. As an importer of foreign foods and wines, Mr. Ramgoolam made it his business to keep the various officials who controlled the various entry stamps happy and content. On that day, he was walking hurriedly past the downtown square when a black youth, hair twisted into worm-like pigtails, thrust a pink leaflet into his unwilling hands. It was a socialist tract, full of new words and bombast. Mr. Ramgoolam had glanced irritatedly at it, noticed several spelling mistakes, crumpled it up, and thrown it on the sidewalk. Then he re-

membered he was a member of the Chamber of Commerce
Keep-Our-City-Clean committee and he picked it up. Later
that evening he found it in his pants pocket. He smoothed it
out, read it, and decided it was nothing less than subversion
and treason. At the next party he attended, he expounded his
views on socialism. He was told to stop boring everyone.

Not long after the party, riots and demonstrations—dubbed
"Black Power" by the television and the newspaper — oc-
curred in the streets. Mr. Ramgoolam's store lost a window
pane and the walls were scribbled with "Socialism" and
"Black Communism". The words bedevilled the last of Mr.
Ramgoolam's black hairs into the mass of silver.

As he watched the last black stripe blend in, Mr. Ramgoolam realized that, with an ineffectual government and a
growing military, one night could bring the country a change
so cataclysmic that the only issue would be rapid flight. And
failing that, poverty, at best.

He had no desire to return to the moneyless nobility of his
childhood: pride was one thing, stupidity quite another, and
Alistair Ramgoolam was acutely aware of the difference.

He began looking for ways of smuggling money out of the
island to an illegal foreign bank account. A resourceful man,
he soon found several undetectable methods: buying travellers'
cheques and bank drafts off friends, having money owed him
by foreign companies paid into the illegal account, buying
foreign currency from travellers at generous rates of exchange. His eldest son was attending university in Toronto, so
it was through him that Mr. Ramgoolam established his
account.

The sum grew quickly. Mr. Ramgoolam became an ex-
porter of island foods and crafts, deflating the prices he
reported to the island's government and inflating those he
charged the foreign companies. The difference was put into
the Toronto account. Every cent not spent on his somewhat

lavish lifestyle was poured into his purchases of bank drafts and travellers' cheques.

The official mail service, untrustworthy and growing more expensive by the day, was not entrusted with Mr. Ramgoolam's correspondence with his son. Visitors to or from Toronto, friend or stranger, were asked to perform favors.

Over the years, with a steadily developing business and ever-increasing foreign dealings, Mr. Ramgoolam's account grew larger and larger, to more than forty thousand dollars.

He contemplated his bankbooks with great satisfaction. Should flight be necessary—and the more time passed, the more Mr. Ramgoolam became convinced it would—there would be something to run to beyond bare refuge.

The more insecure he saw his island becoming, the more secure he himself felt. From this secure insecurity a new attitude, one of which he had never before been aware, arose in him. The island of his birth, on which he had grown up and where he had made his fortune, was transformed by a process of mind into a kind of temporary home. Its history ceased to be important, its present turned into a fluid holding pattern which would eventually give way. The confusion had been prepared for, and all that was left was the enjoyment that could be squeezed out of the island between now and then. He could hope for death here but his grandchildren, maybe even his children, would continue the emigration which his grandfather had started in India, and during which the island had proved, in the end, to be nothing more than a stopover.

When the Toronto account reached fifty thousand dollars, Mr. Ramgoolam received a letter from his eldest son. He reminded his father that Vijay would be coming to Toronto to study and that the fifty thousand dollars was lying fallow in the account, collecting interest, yes, but slowly. Wouldn't it be better to invest in a house? This would mean that Vijay— Mr. Ramgoolam noticed his eldest son had discreetly left himself out—would not have to pay rent and, with the rapidly escalating property prices in Toronto, a modest fifty-thousand-dollar house could be resold later at a great profit.

His first reading of the letter brought a chuckle to Mr. Ramgoolam's throat. His independent-minded son, it seemed, was looking for a way of not paying rent. But then he felt a ripple of quiet rage run through him: his son had always made an issue of being independent, of making it on his own. Paying for the privilege, Mr. Ramgoolam thought, was the first requisite of independence. He put the suggestion out of his mind.

Later that night, just before bed, he read the letter aloud to his wife. This had long been their custom. She complained continually of "weakness" in the eyes. As he lay in bed afterwards, the words "great profit" stayed with him.

His wife said, "You going to buy it?"

He said, "Is not such a bad idea. I have to think."

When he awoke at four the next morning for his usual Hindu devotions, Mr. Ramgoolam's mind was made up. He walked around the garden picking the dew-smothered flowers with which he would garland the deities in his private prayer room and, breathing in the cool, fresh air of the young dawn's semi-light, he became convinced that the decision was already blessed by the beauty of the morning.

After a cold shower, Mr. Ramgoolam draped his fine cotton dhoti around his waist and prayed before his gods, calling their blessings onto himself, his wife, his sons, and the new house soon to be bought, cash, in Toronto. It was his contention that blessed business dealings were safer than unblessed ones.

He spent the rest of the morning writing a letter to his son, giving instructions that before any deals were made he was to be consulted. He didn't want any crooked real estate agent fooling his son, Toronto sophisticate or not. He also warned that the place should be close enough to Vijay's school that he wouldn't have to travel too far: a short ride on public transportation was acceptable but his son should always remember that it was below the station of a Ramgoolam to depend on buses and trains.

That was an important point, Mr. Ramgoolam thought. It might force his independent son to raise his sights a little. He probably used public transportation quite regularly in Toronto, whereas here on the island he would not have heard of sitting in a bus next to some sweaty farmer. The letter, Mr. Ramgoolam hoped, would remind his eldest son of the standards expected of a member of his family.

The letter was dispatched that evening with the friend of a friend of a friend who just happened to be leaving for Toronto.

A week passed and Mr. Ramgoolam heard nothing from his son. He began to worry: if *he* were buying a house, you could be sure *he'd* have found a place and signed the deal by now. That son of his just had no business sense: didn't he know that time was money? A week could mean the difference of a thousand dollars! Mr. Ramgoolam said to his wife, "I just wish he'd learn to be independent on somebody else's money."

He was walking in the garden worrying about his money and kicking at the grass when Vijay shouted from the house, "Pa, Pa! Toronto calling."

Mr. Ramgoolam hurried in, his cheeks jiggling. "Hello." It was the real estate agent calling.

The operator said, "Will you accept the charges?"

Accept the charges? Mr. Ramgoolam was momentarily unsettled. "No." He slammed the phone down. He glared at Vijay sitting at the dining table. "What kind of businessman he is anyway? Calling collect. He's getting my money and he expects me to pay for his business call? He crazy or what, eh?" Incensed, he ran out into the garden. Every few minutes, Vijay could hear him muttering about "cheapness".

The telephone rang again half an hour later.

This call was from his son and, luckily, not collect. The first thing Mr. Ramgoolam said was, "Get rid of that cheap agent. I don't trust him. Get somebody else."

The son agreed. Then he asked whether his father would be willing to go above fifty thousand, to, say, sixty or sixty-five. Only such a sum would assure a good house in a proper location. Less would mean a good house, yes, but a long way on public transportation for Vijay.

Mr. Ramgoolam pictured Vijay riding on some rickety bus with a smelly fish vendor for company. He broke out in a cold sweat. "Now wait up a minute . . . awright, awright, sixty or sixty-five. But not a cent more. And close the deal quickly. Time is money, you know."

Time dragged by. Nothing was heard from Toronto for a week. Mr. Ramgoolam began to worry. What was that no-good son of his up to now? Wasting time as usual, probably running off somewhere being independent.

Another week went by and Mr. Ramgoolam began brooding over the house in Toronto. He couldn't get his mind off it. He stopped going to the office. Not even prayer seemed to ease his growing doubts. Wasn't it better to have the cash safely in the bank, slowly but surely collecting its interest? And what about Vijay? The money for his schooling was to have come from that account: now he'd have to take money with him, and Mr. Ramgoolam hadn't counted on that. Above all, the house was going to cost ten to fifteen thousand more than the Toronto account contained; that was a lot of money to smuggle out. Would it mean a mortgage? He hated mortgages and credit. He hated owing. Buy only when you could pay: it was another of his convictions.

After three more days and a sleepless night, Mr. Ramgoolam eased himself out of bed at 3.30 a.m. He might as well pray. It always helped, eased the mind however little.

There was very little light that morning and the flowers he

collected were wilted and soggy. He stubbed his toe on a stone and cursed, softly, in Hindi. The cold shower felt not so much refreshing as merely cold.

He prayed, his dhoti falling in careless folds, his gods sad with their colorless flowers.

When he finished he wrote a quick letter to his son, ordering him to leave all the money in the bank and to forget about buying a house. He couldn't afford it at the present time, he said.

He signed it and sealed it. He wondered briefly whether he should telephone or telegram but decided they were both too expensive. The next problem was to find someone who was going to Toronto. That was easy: the representative of his biggest Toronto client, the one staying at the Hilton, would be coming to the house this evening to finalize a deal and to get the Toronto account number. He could take the letter.

Five days passed and Mr. Ramgoolam heard nothing from his eldest son. Once more he began to worry. Couldn't the fool call to say he'd got the letter and the money was safe? He spent the morning in bed nursing his burning ulcer.

On the morning of the sixth day the call came.

"Hello, Pa?" His son's voice was sharp and clear, as if he were calling from across the street. "You're now the proud owner of a house in Toronto. The deal went through yesterday. It's all finalized."

Mr. Ramgoolam's jaw fell open. His cheeks quivered. "What? You didn't get my letter?"

"You mean the one the company rep brought up? Not yet. He just called me last night. I'm going to collect the letter this evening, before the ballet."

"Be-be-be-fore the ballet?" Mr. Ramgoolam ran his pudgy fingers down the length of his perspiring face. He could feel his heart thumping heavily against the fat in his chest.

"Yes, I'm going to the ballet tonight. Good news about the house, eh? I did exactly as you told me, Pa. I did it as quickly as possible. Time is money, as you always say."

"Yes-yes," said Mr. Ramgoolam. "Time is money, son, time is money. We're very insecure in this place, you know."

His son said, "What?"

"Nothing." Mr. Ramgoolam ran his hand, trembling, through his hair. "Goodbye." He replaced the receiver. The wooden floor seemed to dance beneath him and, for a moment, he had a sense of slippage, of life turned to running liquid. He saw his son sitting in the living room of the Toronto house—sitting, smiling, in a room Mr. Ramgoolam knew to be there, but the hardened outlines of which he could not distinguish—and he suddenly understood how far his son had gone. Just as his father had grown distant from India; just as he himself had grown even further from the life that, in memory, his father had represented and then, later in life, from that which he himself had known on the island, so too had his eldest son gone beyond. Mr. Ramgoolam had been able to picture the money sitting in the bank, piles of bills; but this house, and his son sitting there with ballet tickets in his hand: this was something softer, hazier, less graspable. He now saw himself as being left behind, caught between the shades of his father and, unexpectedly, of his son. And he knew that his insecurity, until then always in the land around him, in the details of life daily lived, was now within him. It was as if his legs had suddenly gone hollow, two shells of utter fragility.

There was only one thing left, one thing to hold on to. He hurried to his room and, brushing his wife aside, dressed quickly. Then he swallowed two hefty gulps of his stomach medicine and called out to Vijay to drive him to the office.

THERE ARE
A LOT OF WAYS
TO DIE

It was still drizzling when Joseph clicked the final padlocks on the door. The name-plate, home-painted with squared gold letters on a black background and glazed all over with transparent varnish to lend a professional tint, was flecked with water and dirt. He took a crumpled handkerchief from his back pocket and carefully wiped the lettering clean: JOSEPH HEAVEN: CARPET AND RUG INSTALLATIONS. The colon had been his idea and he had put it in over his wife's objections. He felt that it provided a natural flow from his name, that it showed a certain reliability. His wife, in the scornful voice she reserved for piercing his pretensions, had said, "That's all very well and good for Toronto, but you think people here care about that kind of thing?" But she was the one people accused of having airs, not him. As far as he was concerned, the colon was merely good business; and as the main beneficiary of the profits, she should learn to keep her mouth shut.

He had forgotten to pick up his umbrella from just inside the door where he had put it that morning. Gingerly, he extended his upturned palm, feeling the droplets, warm and wet, like newly spilled blood. He decided they were too light to justify reopening the shop, always something of an event because of the many locks and chains. This was another thing she didn't like, his obsession, as she called it, with security. She wanted a more open store-front, with windows and show-cases and well-dressed mannequins smiling blankly at the street. She said, "It look just like every other store around here, just a wall and a door. It have nothing to catch the eye." He replied, "You want windows and showcases? What we going to show? My tools? The tacks? The cutter?" Besides, the locks were good for business, not a week went by without a robbery in the area. Displaying the tools would be a blatant invitation, and a recurrent nightmare had developed in which one of his cutters was stolen and used in a murder.

Across the glistening street, so narrow after the generosity of those he had known for six years, the clothes merchants were standing disconsolately in front of their darkened stores, hands in pockets, whistling and occasionally examining the grey skies for the brightening that would signal the end of the rain and the appearance of shoppers. They stared blankly at him. One half-heartedly jabbed his finger at a stalactitic line of umbrellas and dusty raincoats, inviting a purchase. Joseph showed no interest. The merchant shrugged and resumed his tuneless whistling, a plaintive sound from between clenched front teeth.

Joseph had forgotten how sticky the island could be when it rained. The heat, it seemed, never really disappeared during the night. Instead, it retreated just a few inches underground, only to emerge with the morning rain, condensing, filling the atmosphere with steam. It put the lie to so much he had told his Canadian friends about the island. The morning rain wasn't as refreshing as he'd recalled it and the steam had left his memory altogether. How could he have sworn that the island experienced no humidity? Why had he, in all honesty, recalled tender tropical breezes when the truth, as it now enveloped him, was the exact, stifling opposite? Climate was not so drastically altered, only memory.

He walked to the end of the street, his shirt now clinging to his shoulders. The sidewalk, dark and pitted, seemed to glide by under his feet, as if it were itself moving. He squinted, feeling the folds of flesh bunching up at the corner of his eyes, and found he could fuzzily picture himself on Bloor Street, walking past the stores and the bakeries and the delicatessens pungent with Eastern European flavors, the hazy tops of buildings at Bloor and Yonge far away in the distance. He could even conjure up the sounds of a Toronto summer: the cars, the voices, the rumble of the subway under the feet as it swiftly glided towards downtown.

Joseph shook himself and opened his eyes, not without disappointment. He was having this hallucination too often, for too long. He was ashamed of it and couldn't confess it even to his wife. And he mistrusted it, too: might not even this more recent memory also be fooling him, as the other had done? Was it really possible to see the tops of buildings at Yonge from Bathurst? He wanted to ask his wife, pretending it was merely a matter of memory, but she would see through this to his longing and puncture him once more with that voice. She would call him a fool and not be far wrong. Were not two dislocations enough in one man's lifetime? Would not yet a third prove him a fool?

Their return had been jubilant. Friends and relatives treated it as a victory, seeking affirmation of the correctness of their cloistered life on the island, the return a defeat for life abroad. The first weeks were hectic, parties, dinners, get-togethers. Joseph felt like a curiosity, an object not of reverence but of silent ridicule, his the defeat, theirs the victory. The island seemed to close in around him.

They bought a house in the island's capital. The town was not large. Located at the extreme north-western edge of the island, having hardly expanded from the settlement originally established by Spanish adventurers as a depot in their quest for mythic gold, the town looked forever to the sea, preserving its aura of a way-station, a point at which to pause in brief respite from the larger search.

At first, Joseph had tried to deny this aspect of the town, for the town was the island and, if the island were no more than a way-station, a stopover from which nothing important ever emerged, then to accept this life was to accept second place. A man who had tasted of first could accept second only with delusion: his wife had taken on airs, he had painted his black-and-gold sign.

Then the hallucination started, recreating Bloor Street, vividly recalling the minute details of daily life. He caught himself reliving the simple things: buying milk, removing a newspaper from the box, slipping a subway token into the slot, sitting in a park. A chill would run through him when he realized they were remembrances of things past, possibly lost forever. The recollected civility of life in Toronto disturbed him, it seemed so distant. He remembered what a curious feeling of well-being had surged through him whenever he'd given directions to a stranger. Each time was like an affirmation of stability. Here, in an island so small that two leisurely hours in a car would reveal all, no one asked for directions, no one was a stranger. You couldn't claim the island: it claimed you.

The street on which their house stood used to be known all over the island. It was viewed with a twinge of admired notoriety and was thought of with the same fondness with which the islanders regarded the government ministers and civil servants who had fled the island with pilfered cash: an awed admiration, a flawed love. The cause of this attention was a house, a mansion in those days, erected, in the popular lore, by a Venezuelan general who, for reasons unknown, had exiled himself to a life of darkly rumored obscurity on the island. As far as Joseph knew, no one had ever actually seen the general: even his name, Pacheco, had been assumed. Or so it was claimed; no one had ever bothered to check.

Eventually the house became known as Pacheco House, and the street as Pacheco Street. It was said that the house, deserted for as long as anyone could remember and now falling into neglect, had been mentioned passingly in a book by an Englishman who had been looking into famous houses of the region. It was the island's first mention in a book other than a history text, the island's first mention outside the context of slavery.

The house had become the butt of schoolboys' frustration. On their way home after school, Joseph and his friends would detour to throw stones at the windows. In his memory, the spitting clank of shattering glass sounded distant and opaque. They had named each window for a teacher, thus adding thrust and enthusiasm to their aim. The largest window, high on the third floor—the attic, he now knew, in an island which had no attics—they named LeNoir, after the priest who was the terror of all students unblessed by fair skin or athletic ability. They were more disturbed by the fact that the priest himself was black; this seemed a greater sin than his choice of vocation. They had never succeeded in breaking the LeNoir window. Joseph might have put this down to divine protection had he not lost his sense of religion early on. It was a simple event: the priest at his last try at communion had showered him with sour breath the moment the flesh of Christ slipped onto Joseph's tongue. Joseph, from then on, equated the wafer with decaying flesh.

The LeNoir window went unscathed for many years and

was still intact when, after the final exams, Joseph left the island for what he believed to be forever.

The raindrops grew larger, making a plopping sound on the sidewalk. A drop landed on his temple and cascaded down his cheek. He rubbed at it, feeling the prickly stubble he hadn't bothered to shave that morning.

Pacheco House was just up ahead, the lower floors obscured by a jungle of trees and bush, the garden overgrown and thickening to impenetrability. Above the treeline, the walls— a faded pink, pockmarked by the assault of stones and man-goes—had begun disintegrating, the thin plaster falling away in massive chunks to reveal ordinary grey brick underneath. The remaining plaster was criss-crossed by cracks and fissures created by age and humidity.

During his schooldays, the grounds had been maintained by the government. The house had been considered a tourist attraction and was displayed in brochures and on posters. An island-wide essay competition had been held, "The Mystery of Pacheco House", and the winning essay, of breathless prose linked by words like *tropical* and *verdant* and *lush* and *exotic*, was used as the text of a special brochure. But no tourists came. The mystery withered away to embarrassment. The govern-ment quietly gave the house up. The Jaycees, young business-men who bustled about in the heat with the added burden of jackets and ties, offered to provide funds for the upkeep. The offer was refused with a shrug by the Ministry of Tourism, with inexplicable murmurings of "colonial horrors" by the Ministry of Culture. The house was left to its ghosts.

From the street Joseph could see the LeNoir window, still intact and dirt-streaked. He was surprised that it still seemed to mock him.

Joseph had asked his nephew, a precocious boy who enjoyed

exhibiting his scattered knowledge of French and Spanish and who laughed at Joseph's clumsy attempts to resurrect the bits of language he had learnt in the same classes, often from the same teachers, if the boys still threw stones at Pacheco House. No, his nephew had informed him, after school they went to the sex movies or, in the case of the older boys, to the whorehouses. Joseph, stunned, had asked no more questions.

The rain turned perceptibly to a deluge, the thick, warm drops penetrating his clothes and running in rivulets down his back and face. The wild trees and plants of the Pacheco garden nodded and drooped, leaves glistening dully in the half-light. The pink walls darkened as the water socked into them, eating at the plaster. The LeNoir window was black; he remembered some claimed to have seen a white-faced figure in army uniform standing there at night. The story had provided mystery back then, a real haunted house, and on a rainy afternoon schoolboys could feel their spines tingle as they aimed their stones.

On impulse Joseph searched the ground for a stone. He saw only pebbles; the gravel verge had long been paved over. Already the sidewalk had cracked in spots and little shoots of grass had fought their way out, like wedges splitting a boulder.

He continued walking, oblivious of the rain.

Several cars were parked in the driveway of his house. His wife's friends were visiting. They were probably in the living room drinking coffee and eating pastries from Marcel's and looking through *Vogue* pattern books. Joseph made for the garage so he could enter, unnoticed, through the kitchen door. Then he thought, "Why the hell?" He put his hands into his pockets—his money was soaked and the movement of his fingers ripped the edge off a bill—and calmly walked in through the open front door.

His wife was standing in front of the fake fireplace she had insisted on bringing from Toronto. The dancing lights cast multicolored hues on her caftan. She almost dropped her coffee cup when she saw him. Her friends, perturbed, stared at him from their chairs which they had had grouped around the fireplace.

His wife said impatiently, "Joseph, what are you doing here?"

He said, "I live here."

She said, "And work?"

He said, "None of the boys show up this morning."

"So you just drop everything?"

"I postponed today's jobs. I couldn't do all the work by myself."

She put her cup down on the mantelpiece. "Go dry yourself off. You wetting the floor."

Her friend Arlene said, "Better than the bed."

They all laughed. His wife said, "He used to do that when he was a little boy, not so, Joseph?"

She looked at her friends and said, "You know, we having so much trouble finding good workers. Joseph already fire three men. Looks like we're going to have to fire all these now."

Arlene said, "Good help so hard to find these days."

His wife said, "These people like that, you know, girl. Work is the last thing they want to do."

Arlene said, "They 'fraid they going to melt if rain touch their skin."

His wife turned to him. "You mean not one out of twelve turned up this morning?"

"Not one."

Arlene, dark and plump, sucked her teeth and moved her tongue around, pushing at her cheeks and making a plopping sound.

Joseph said, "Stop that. You look like a monkey."

His wife and Arlene stared at him in amazement. The

others sipped their coffee or gazed blankly at the fireplace.

Arlene said witheringly, "I don't suffer fools gladly, Joseph."

He said, "Too bad. You must hate being alone."

His wife said, "Joseph!"

He said, "I better go dry off." Still dripping, he headed for the bedroom. At the door he paused and added, "People should be careful when they talking about other people. You know, glass houses . . . " He was suddenly exhausted: what was the point? They all knew Arlene's story. She had once been a maid whose career was rendered transient by rain and imagined illness; she had been no different from his employees. Her fortune had improved only because her husband—who was referred to behind his back as a "sometimes worker" because sometimes he worked and sometimes he didn't—had been appointed a minister without portfolio in the government. He had lost the nickname because now he never worked, but he had gained a regular cheque, a car and a chauffeur, and the tainted respectability of political appointment.

Joseph slammed the bedroom door and put his ear to the keyhole: there was a lot of throat-clearing; pages of a *Vogue* pattern book rustled. Finally his wife said, "Come look at this pattern." Voices oohed and ahhed and cooed. Arlene said, "Look at this one." He kicked the door and threw his wet shirt on the bed.

The rain had stopped and the sky had cleared a little. His wife and her friends were still in the living room. It was not yet midday. His clothes had left a damp patch on the bed, on his side, and he knew it would still be wet at bedtime. He put on a clean set of clothes and sat on the bed, rubbing the dampness, as if this would make it disappear. He reached up and drew the curtains open: grey, drifting sky, vegetation drooping and wet, like wash on a line; the very top of Pacheco House, galvanized iron rusted through, so thin in parts that a single drop of rain might cause a great chunk to go crashing into the silence of the house. Except maybe for the bats, disintegration was probably the only sound now to be heard in Pacheco House. The house was like a dying man who could hear his heart ticking to a stop.

Joseph sensed that something was missing. The rainflies, delicate ant-like creatures with brown wings but no sting. Defenceless, wings attached to their bodies by the most fragile of links, they fell apart at the merest touch. After a particularly heavy rainfall, detached wings, almost transparent, would litter the ground and cling to moist feet like lint to wool. As a child, he used to pull the wings off and place the crippled insect on a table, where he could observe it crawling desperately around, trying to gain the air. Sometimes he would gingerly tie the insect to one end of a length of thread, release it, and control its flight. In all this he saw no cruelty. His friends enjoyed crushing them, or setting them on fire, or sizzling them with the burning end of a cigarette. Joseph had only toyed with the insects; he could never bring himself to kill one.

There was not a rainfly in sight. The only movement was that of the clouds and dripping water. In the town, the insects had long, and casually, been eradicated. He felt the loss.

He heard his wife call her friends to lunch. He half expected to hear his name but she ignored him: he might have not been there. He waited a few more minutes until he was sure they had all gone into the dining room, then slipped out the front door.

Water was gurgling in the drains, rushing furiously through the iron gratings into the sewers. In the street, belly up, fur wet and clinging, lay a dead dog, a common sight. Drivers no longer even bothered to squeal their tires.

Joseph walked without direction, across streets and through different neighborhoods, passing people and being passed by cars. He took in none of it. His thoughts were thousands of miles away, on Bloor Street, on Yonge Street, among the stalls of Kensington Market.

He was at National Square when the rain once more began to pound down. He found a dry spot under the eaves of a store and stood, arms folded, watching the rain and the umbrellas and the raincoats. A man hurried past him, a handkerchief tied securely to his head the only protection from the rain. It was a useless gesture, and reminded Joseph of his grandmother's warnings to him never to go out at night without a hat to cover his head, "because of the dew".

National Square was the busiest part of town. Cars constantly sped by, horns blaring, water splashing. After a few minutes a donkey cart loaded with fresh coconuts trundled by on its way to the Savannah, a wide, flat park just north of the town where the horse races were held at Christmas. A line of impatient cars crept along behind the donkey cart, the leaders bobbing in and out of line in search of an opportunity to pass.

Joseph glanced at his watch. It was almost twelve-thirty. He decided to have something to eat. Just around the corner was a cheap restaurant frequented by office workers from the government buildings and foreign banks which enclosed the square. Holding his hands over his head, Joseph dashed through the rain to the restaurant.

Inside was shadowed, despite the cobwebby fluorescent lighting. The walls were lined with soft-drink advertisements and travel posters. One of the posters showed an interminable stretch of bleached beach overhung with languid coconut-tree branches. Large, cursive letters read: Welcome To The Sunny Caribbean. The words were like a blow to the nerves. Joseph felt like ripping the poster up.

A row of green metal tables stretched along one wall of the

rectangular room. A few customers sat in loosened ties and shirt-sleeves, sipping beer and smoking and conversing in low tones. At the far end, at a table crowded with empty bottles and an overflowing ashtray, Joseph noticed a familiar face. It was lined and more drawn than when he'd known it, and the eyes had lost their sparkle of intelligence; but he was certain he was not mistaken. He went up to the man. He said, "Frankie?"

Frankie looked up slowly, unwillingly, emerging from a daydream. He said, "Yes?" Then he brightened. "Joseph? Joseph!" He sprang to his feet, knocking his chair back. He grasped Joseph's hand. "How you doing, man? It's been years and years. How you doing?" He pushed Joseph into a chair and loudly ordered two beers. He lit a cigarette. His hand shook.

Joseph said, "You smoking now, Frankie?"

"For years, man. You?"

Joseph shook his head.

Frankie said, "But you didn't go to Canada? I thought somebody tell me . . ."

"Went and came back. One of those things. How about you? How the years treat you?"

"I work in a bank. Loan officer."

"Good job?"

"Not bad."

Joseph sipped his beer. The situation wasn't right. There should have been so much to say, so much to hear. Frankie used to be his best friend. He was the most intelligent person Joseph had ever known. This was the last place he would have expected to find him. Frankie had dreamt of university and professorship, and it had seemed, back then, that university and professorship awaited him.

Frankie took a long pull on his cigarette, causing the tube to crinkle and flatten. He said, "What was Canada like?"

Before Joseph could answer, he added, "You shouldn't have come back. Why did you come back? A big mistake." He considered the cigarette.

The lack of emotion in Frankie's voice distressed Joseph. It was the voice of a depleted man. He said, "It was time."

Frankie leaned back in his chair and slowly blew smoke rings at Joseph. He seemed to be contemplating the answer. He said, "What were you doing up there?"

"I had a business. Installing carpets and rugs. Is a good little business. My partner looking after it now."

Frankie looked away, towards the door. He said nothing.

Joseph said, "You ever see anybody from school?"

Frankie waved his cigarette. "Here and there. You know, Raffique dead. And Jonesy and Dell."

Joseph recalled the faces: boys, in school uniform. Death was not an event he could associate with them. "How?"

"Raffique in a car accident. Jonesy slit his wrists over a woman. Dell . . . who knows? There are a lot of ways to die. They found him dead in the washroom of a cinema. A girl was with him. Naked. She wasn't dead. She's in the madhouse now."

"And the others?" Joseph couldn't contemplate the death roll. It seemed to snuff out a little bit of his own life.

"The others? Some doing something, some doing nothing. It don't matter."

Joseph said, "You didn't go to university."

Frankie laughed. "No, I didn't."

Joseph waited for an explanation. Frankie offered none.

Frankie said, "Why the hell you come back from Canada? And none of this 'It was time' crap."

Joseph rubbed his face, feeling the stubble, tracing the fullness of his chin. "I had some kind of crazy idea about starting a business, creating jobs, helping my people."

Frankie laughed mockingly.

Joseph said, "I should have known better. We had a party

before we left. A friend asked me the same question, why go back. I told him the same thing. He said it was bullshit and that I just wanted to make a lot of money and live life like a holiday. We quarrelled and I threw him out. The next morning he called to apologize. He was crying. He said he was just jealous." Joseph sipped the beer, lukewarm and sweating. "Damn fool."

Frankie laughed again. "I don't believe this. You mean to tell me you had the courage to leave *and* the stupidity to come back?" He slapped the table, rocking it and causing an empty beer bottle to fall over. "You always used to be the idealist, Joseph. I was more realistic. And less courageous. That's why I never left."

"Nobody's called me an idealist for years." The word seemed more mocking than Frankie's laugh.

Frankie said, "And now you're stuck back here for good." He shook his head vigorously, drunkenly. "A big, idealistic mistake, Joseph."

"I'm not stuck here." He was surprised at how much relief the thought brought him. "I can go back any time I want."

"Well, go then." Frankie's voice was slurred, and it held more than a hint of aggressiveness.

Joseph shook his head. He glanced at his watch. He said, "It's almost one. Don't you have to get back to work?"

Frankie called for another beer. "The bank won't fall down if I'm not there."

"We used to think the world would fall down if not for us."

"That was a long time ago. We were stupid." Frankie lit another cigarette. His hand shook badly. "In this place, is nonsense to think the world, the world out there, have room for you."

Joseph said, "You could have been a historian. History was your best subject, not so?"

"Yeah."

"You still interested in history?"

"Off and on. I tried to write a book. Nobody wanted to publish it."

"Why not?"

"Because our history doesn't lead anywhere. It's just a big, black hole. Nobody's interested in a book about a hole."

"You know anything about Pacheco House?"

"Pacheco House? A little."

"What?"

"The man wasn't a Venezuelan general. He was just a crazy old man from Argentina. He was rich. I don't know why he came here. He lived in the house for a short time and then he died there, alone. They found his body about two weeks later, rottening and stinking. They say he covered himself with old cocoa bags, even his head. I think he knew he was going to die and after all that time alone he couldn't stand the thought of anyone seeing him. Crazy, probably. They buried him in the garden and put up a little sign. And his name wasn't really Pacheco either, people just called him that. They got it from a cowboy film. I've forgot what his real name was but it don't matter. Pacheco's as good as any other."

"That's all? What about the house itself?"

"That's all. The house is just a house. Nothing special." Frankie popped the half-finished cigarette into his beer bottle, it sizzled briefly. He added, "R.I.P. Pacheco, his house and every damn thing else." He put another cigarette between his lips, allowing it to droop to his chin, pushing his upper lip up and out, as if his teeth were deformed. His hands shook so badly he couldn't strike the match. His eyes met Joseph's.

Joseph couldn't hold the gaze. He was chilled. He said, "I have to go."

Frankie waved him away.

Joseph pushed back his chair. Frankie looked past him with

bloodshot eyes, already lost in the confusion of his mind.

Joseph, indicating the travel poster, offered the barman five dollars for it. The man, fat, with an unhealthy greasiness, said, "No way."

Joseph offered ten dollars.

The barman refused.

Joseph understood: it was part of the necessary lie.

Grey clouds hung low and heavy in the sky. The hills to the north, their lower half crowded with the multicolored roofs of shacks, poverty plain from even so great a distance, were shrouded in mist, as if an inferno had recently burned out and the smoke not yet cleared away.

Some of his workers lived there, in tiny, crowded one-room shacks, with water sometimes a quarter-mile away at a mossy stand-pipe. There was a time when the sight of these shacks could move Joseph to pity. They were, he believed, his main reason for returning to the island. He really had said, "I want to help my people." Now the sentence, with its pomposity, its naivety, was just an embarrassing memory, like the early life of the minister's wife.

But he knew that wasn't all. He had expected a kind of fame, a continual welcome, the prodigal son having made good, having acquired skills, returning home to share the wealth, to spread the knowledge. He had anticipated a certain uniqueness but this had been thwarted. Everyone knew someone else who had returned from abroad—from England, from Canada, from the States. He grew to hate the stock phrases people dragged out: "No place like home, this island is a true Paradise, life's best here." The little lies of self-doubt and fear.

The gate to Pacheco House was chained but there was no lock: a casual locking-up, an abandonment. The chain, thick and rusted, slipped easily to the ground, leaving a trace of gritty oxide on his fingertips. He couldn't push the gate far; clumps of grass, stems long and tapering to a lancet point, blocked it at the base. He squeezed through the narrow opening, the concrete pillar rough and tight on his back, the iron gate leaving a slash of rust on his shirt. Inside, wild grass, wet and glistening, enveloped his legs up to his knees. The trees were further back, thick and ponderous, unmoving, lending the garden the heavy stillness of jungle.

Walking, pushing through the grass, took a little effort. The vegetation sought not so much to prevent intrusion as to hinder it, to encumber it with a kind of tropical lassitude. Joseph raised his legs high, free of the tangle of vines and roots and thorns, and brought his boots crashing down with each step, crushing leaves into juicy blobs of green and brown, startling underground colonies of ants into frenzied scrambling. Ahead of him, butterflies, looking like edges of an artist's canvas, fluttered away, and crickets, their wings beating like pieces of stiff silk one against the other, buzzed from tall stalk to tall stalk, narrowly avoiding the grasshoppers which also sought escape. A locust, as long as his hand and as fat, sank its claws into his shirt, just grazing the surface of his skin. He flicked a finger powerfully at it, knocking off its head; the rest of the body simply relaxed and fell off.

Once past the trees, Joseph found himself at the house. The stone foundation, he noticed, was covered in green slime and the wall, the monotony of which was broken only by a large cavity which must once have been a window, stripped of all color. He made his way to the cavity and peered through it into the half-darkness of a large room. He carefully put one leg through, feeling for the floor. The boards creaked badly but held.

The room was a disappointment. He didn't know what he had expected—he hadn't really thought about it—but its emptiness engendered an atmosphere of uncommon despair. He felt it was a room that had always been empty, a room that had never been peopled with emotion or sound, like a dried-up old spinster abandoned at the edge of life. He could smell the pungency of recently disturbed vegetation but he didn't know whether it came from him or through the gaping window.

He made his way to another room, the floorboards creaking under the wary tread of his feet; just another empty space, characterless, almost shapeless in its desertion. A flight of stairs led upwards, to the second floor and yet another empty room, massive, dusty, cobwebs tracing crazy geometric patterns on the walls and the ceiling. In the corners the floorboards had begun to warp. He wondered why all the doors had been removed and by whom. Or had the house ever had doors? Might it not have been always a big, open, empty house, with rooms destined to no purpose, with a façade that promised mystery but an interior that took away all hope?

He had hoped to find something of Pacheco's, the merest testament to his having existed, a bed maybe, or a portrait, or even one line of graffiti. But were it not for the structure itself, a vacuous shell falling steadily to ruin, and the smudges of erroneous public fantasy fading like the outer edges of a dream, Pacheco might never have existed. Whatever relics might have been preserved by the government had long been carted away, probably by the last workmen, those who had so cavalierly slipped the chain around the gate, putting a period to a life.

Joseph walked around the room, his footsteps echoing like drumbeats. Each wall had a window of shattered glass and he examined the view from each. Jumbled vegetation, the jungle taking hold in this one plot of earth in the middle of the town: it was the kind of view that would have been described in the travel brochures as *lush* and *tropical*, two words he had grown to hate. Looking through the windows, recalling the manicured grounds of his youth, he felt confined, isolated, a man in an island on an island. He wondered why anyone would pay a lot of money to visit such a place. The answer came to him: for the tourist, a life was not to be constructed here. The tourist sought no more than an approximation of adventure; there was safety in a return ticket and a foreign passport.

There was no way to get to the attic, where the LeNoir window was. Another disappointment: the object of all that youthful energy was nothing more than an aperture to a boxed-in room, airless and musty with age and probably dank with bat mess.

He made his way back down the stairs and out the gaping front door. The air was hot and sticky and the smell of vegetation, acrid in the humidity, was almost overpowering.

Frankie had said that Pacheco was buried in the garden and that a marker had been erected. Joseph knew there was no hope of finding it. Everything was overgrown: the garden, the flowers, the driveway that had once existed, Pacheco's grave, Pacheco himself, the mysterious South American whose last act was to lose his name and his life in sterile isolation.

Joseph began making his way back to the gate. Over to the left he could see the path he had made when going in, the grass flat and twisted, twigs broken and limp, still dripping from the morning rain. He felt clammy, and steamy perspiration broke out on his skin.

At the gate, he stopped and turned around for a last look at the house: he saw it for what it was, a deceptive shell that played on the mind. He looked around for something to throw. The base of the gate-pillars was cracked and broken and moss had begun eating its way to the centre. He broke off a piece of the concrete and flung it at the LeNoir window. The glass shattered, scattering thousands of slivers into the attic and onto the ground below.

His wife wasn't home when he returned. The house was dark and silent. Coffee cups and plates with half-eaten pastries lay on the side-tables. The false fireplace had been switched off. On the mantelpiece, propped against his wife's lipstick-stained cup, was a notepad with a message: "Have gone out for the evening with Arlene. We have the chauffeur and the limo coz Brian's busy in a cabinet meeting. Don't know what time I'll be back." She hadn't bothered to sign it.

He ripped the page from the notepad: he hated the word "coz" and the word "limo" and he felt a special revulsion for "Arlene" and "Brian", fictitious names assumed with the mantle of social status. As a transient domestic, Arlene had been called Thelma, the name scribbled on her birth certificate, and Brian's real name was Balthazar. Joseph avoided the entire issue by simply referring to them as the Minister and the Minister's Wife. The sarcasm was never noticed.

He took the notepad and a pencil and sat down. He wrote *Dear* then crossed it out. He threw the page away and started again. He drew a circle, then a triangle, then a square: the last disappointment, it was the most difficult act. Finally, in big square letters, he wrote, *I am going back*. He put the pad back on the mantelpiece, switched on the fireplace lights, and sat staring into their synchronized dance.

IN THE KINGDOM OF THE GOLDEN DUST

Are they out there, wandering through the crowd? Watching? Pedro, Miguel, and Tomás?

It is the sun I am most aware of, the sun and the silence. Reinforcing each other. Conspirators of heat and stillness. I notice that I notice the sand that hangs in the air with the thickness of disturbed dust. It does not exist in the capital, this gritty, golden fog; but here in my little home town it is how we have come to think of air: as body, as color.

To my right the wooden stage, the small crowd before it motionless: browned faces seized by fatigue and the blankness of a passivity easily assumed. Here and there, the peaked khaki caps and reflective sunglasses of policemen—function, as usual, enigmatic.

Behind them the square, a rutted expanse the grey of ancient bones; in the middle, rising as if in natural formation, our fountain of the Virgin Mary, water gushing from under her feet and down the hidden pedestal to the pool of unfinished concrete black with moisture.

In the distance the western limit of the square: a line of flat-roofed, one-storey buildings a shade or two lighter than the sand of the square, weathered outgrowths with windows shuttered to the heat.

And above, above it all, in a sweep so total it suffocates, thunders a sky of a blue faded as if bleached by the sun.

And all this, all this before me, stilled by the tension that sits passively in my lower stomach, idling, consuming.

A stirring behind me. The other girls—we are ten in all, I the oldest at sixteen—shuffle with a tinge of fear, make way for Lisímaco Gonzalez. As usual he is wearing his police uniform, the khaki shirt, long unwashed, showing consecutive rings of perspiration stains beneath the arms. As he walks past us, short, gaunt, smiling, he says: "Girls . . . "

He drags out the s, and the simple word, offered in greeting, is like a statement of possession: Girls . . .

He mounts the stairs to the stage, pauses at the top, and looks back down at us: His black eyes, round and with a dull shine, never focussing, like a statue with the eyes painted in, squint at us in contemplation; then, quickly, impatience: "Come," he says, "come." His right hand, palm upwards, flicks rapidly at the wrist, urging us to follow him: "You are the stars, not me."

The girls gather around me: I am the eldest, they come to me as to a leader.

"What are you waiting for, Maria Luisa?" says Lisímaco Gonzalez. "Come."

I mount the first step and he reaches down as if to help me up; but his fingers strap themselves firmly around my wrist: not help this, but seizure. I gasp from the jolt of pain that slices along my forearm. He pulls me up to him, takes my left arm in his hand—the grip still that of the policeman—and looks down at the others: "Come."

Slowly they follow me up. Lisímaco Gonzalez has us form a line across the middle of the stage, facing the crowd; then he addresses those faces tense with retreated eyes: "Dear friends . . . "

I look beyond him, sending my gaze to the distance, past the Virgin Mary, to the buildings that, from here, just a few feet above the ground, shimmer in the yellow mist: Surely they are out there somewhere, Pedro, Miguel, and Tomás? I try to picture their faces but cannot, still, not since that morning three months ago. My eyes water, stung by the dust.

"And now our first contestant," says Lisímaco Gonzalez. He half turns and motions Consuelo to him from the end of the line. The golden dust swirls and eddies at the flap of his hand.

And through that movement, for just a few seconds, so few that I know immediately that it is but a trick of the light, I see among the crowd that other face: young and angular, cheeks smooth with boyishness, thin lips compressed beneath pencil strokes of hair, dead eyes shining dully from the shadow cast on the upper half of his face by the lip of his green helmet.

Those tightened lips—twitching at the corners as if with suppressed laughter the morning of the *mistake*, his word, not mine—come back to me. I remember how he turned his face, mask-like, towards me; how that tightness slipped for a brief moment into a smile. And the horror of that moment, a horror that went well beyond that which had already seized me, comes afresh, like slivers of ice scorching through my stomach.

"And now, contestant number two," says Lisímaco Gonzalez.

Consuelo returns to her place in the line.

Rafaela, hesitant, in the plain white dress I associate with funerals and festivals, makes her way over to Lisímaco Gonzalez.

From above, the yellow heat deepens, thickens, caking itself onto my face with the grainy dryness of dead earth.

Lisímaco Gonzalez' right arm encircles Rafaela's waist. It is a gesture I know: friendly from a distance, lightly abusive closer up. I feel for Rafaela, know her confusion, see the tension in her neck between the braids that hang down to each of her shoulders.

Then I notice the little red ribbons with which she has secured the knots of the braids and I feel even more for her. This little protest: the snatch of color that neither screams nor whimpers, but that registers with a subtlety that is like love.

Lisímaco Gonzalez sends Rafaela back to the line and, half-turned, gestures at me. The flapping hand, impatient, like a large, dead leaf flicked at by the wind, tugs at me through the visible air.

Dust swirls.

A hand pushes insistently at my lower back, urging me forward—who? Not Rafaela. Angela, to my left. I slap her hand away and, instantly, I regret my sharpness. Hers is a fear I understand.

The dust thickens before my eyes in a sudden distillation. It is like that other morning: The scene of the *mistake*—the buildings, the faces, the soldiers with guns—remains with me through a milky film, like seeing the world through glasses long uncleaned.

I move forward, towards Lisímaco Gonzalez, but it is not like walking. I do not feel the stage beneath me; I feel myself insubstantial.

"How old are you, Maria Luisa?"

"Seventeen."

The faces of the crowd look up at me: unreadable. Do they feel what I feel? Do they see my shame?

"You write poetry?"

"Yes."

"What do you write about?"

"Anything."

"Flowers? Birds?"

"Yes."

And murder, I want to add.

"And right now you are taking a little holiday from your studies in the capital?"

"Yes."

"What are you studying?"

"Typing."

And then, at the back of the crowd, standing side by side, silent and motionless, obscured by the dust and sun: Pedro, Miguel, and Tomás.

"You are going to become a secretary?"

"Yes."

Pedro, Miguel, and Tomás!

But where are they now?

Gone. Again.

"A secretary, friends! Sec-re-ta-ry! And this, by the grace of God, from our government, Maria Luisa?"

"No. The missionaries. The Canadians."

There is pause, and I feel his confusion. For this brief moment, his control is gone.

"Some applause, friends! Applause for our Maria Luisa!"

Hands move in the crowd. The golden air swirls.

Then, once more, I see them: Pedro, Miguel, and Tomás.

And then I don't.

The sun. The sun.

I move back to the line, still searching the crowd: They must be playing, hiding from me behind the backs of the people.

Angela, moving forward, bumps into me, startles me. I yelp. Lisímaco Gonzalez smiles. And my ears tell me I have made a sound of delight: My shame rises, hot, to my face.

Rafaela puts her arm through mine. "You are sweating, Maria Luisa."

"Pedro, Miguel, and Tomás, they are here, Rafaela."

She pulls her arm away. "No, Maria Luisa, they are dead."

"I saw them. In the crowd."

"Not them, Maria Luisa. Lieutenant Morales, yes, he is out there."

"You too have seen him, then?"

"He was there. In his helmet."

"Then they too are here."

"Morales is not dead, Maria."

"But they go with him. Where he is, they are."

I search the crowd, eyes darting this way and that. They are out there, I am sure, playing with me.

Pedro, Miguel, and Tomás.

In the heat. The terrible heat.

Time suspended in a dense solution of heat and golden dust.

My skin itches, forehead aches; air whistles through my clogged nostrils.

Before me nothing moves. Lisimaco Gonzalez, drooping, khaki shirt blackened with sweat, beside him Estela, the last of his contest. The crowd immobile; the Holy Virgin, always stilled, on her column of crystal.

Only the buildings defy, shimmering like reflections in disturbed water, behind and above them the huge, empty sky exploding in a nothingness of virgin blue.

A movement on the stage in front of me: forms, rounded shapes in a pile.

And there they are: Pedro, Miguel, and Tomás. Lying at my feet.

Pedro, on his back, head tilted away from me, hands resting as if in contentment on his stomach, right ankle thrown casually over left ankle, soccer boots muddied as with chocolate icing.

Miguel, face downwards, arms flung out to either side, a

rug of blood, dark crimson, creeping out from under his chest.

Tomás, head resting on Miguel's legs, staring up glassy-eyed at me, brain hanging from the hole in the left side of his head, mouth echoing voiceless screams.

Slowly Pedro, eyes closed, turns his head towards me and smiles.

Miguel gathers in his arms, turns on his side so that blood and bits of flesh gush from the hole in his chest, smiles and opens his eyes, ovals of coral white, then hops to his feet. His litheness surprises me. Beneath him is their soccer ball, flattened and soaked in blood, an oval in black and red.

Tomás's lips close and widen, tightening into his thin smile. Stiffly, he gets to his feet, the brain jiggling and excreting a green liquid that flows into his blood-matted hair, over his ear and onto his shoulder.

Pedro, lying still, says, "Hi, Maria Luisa. We had you fooled, didn't we. You thought we weren't coming back, didn't you?"

Tomás says: "We were just playing soccer, Maria Luisa, don't be angry."

Miguel says: "We must practise, all the time. Practise, practise, practise!"

Pedro and Miguel chant: "Practise, practise, practise!"

Now they are all around me, ripped, bloodied, talking all at the same time, with one voice yet with different voices, voices I seem to know but am not sure of knowing.

"You look beautiful, Maria Luisa."

"You were born to be a queen, Maria Luisa."

"The police queen!"

"Even just for one day."

"We hope the crown won't be too heavy, Maria Luisa."

"We have a gift for you."

"To congratulate you."

"We *know* you will win, Maria Luisa."

"For the queen!"

"The police queen!"

Tomás says: "Close your eyes."

I close my eyes.

"Put out your hands."

I put out my hands, palms up. The gift, heavy, of warm metal, fills both my hands. I recognize the feel of it, know its shape; and the knowledge of its power suffuses my flesh.

It was before the soldiers came. The boys, dirty and shabby, in the mismatched greens of stolen jungle garb, had spent a week in our town, eating, resting, cleaning their weapons. A young fighter hardly older than I, younger, it seems to me, than the Lieutenant Morales who would come with his men soon after to secure the town for the government, had shown me his weapon. "It is an AK 47," he had said, pointing out the strange markings, "Russian." And we had both marvelled that anyone could read so curious a language; and we had agreed that anyone who could had to be strange and, in a way we could not grasp, wonderful.

I open my eyes. This dust, this dust that puts me in mind of ground gold.

Pedro, Miguel, and Tomas are gone.

In my hands the AK 47: scarred wooden stock, tubes and protrusions of grey metal.

To my sides, my friends, my competitors, brown faces oiled and shining, eyes glazed by the immobilizing heat.

And before me, caught in the thickness of heat and dust, the sky, the buildings, the Virgin Mary, the crowd, and, in drenched khaki, Lisímaco Gonzalez.

He is talking to the crowd. His words do not carry, fall heavily to his feet.

But I do not need his words to know what he is saying, for Lisímaco Gonzalez is doing his job, serving powers in the capital that he will never know, never understand. The killing will get done, and the only true difficulty is to remember who is to be killed when the orders come to kill.

I think this is why I hate him, why I lower the weapon at him, why I squeeze the trigger and watch with emotions inert as a line of holes stitches itself rapidly across his back, from left to right, little roses with centres of black.

He turns, smiling: large teeth whitened by the squinting darkness of the eyes. In his hands, a small silver trophy and a cardboard crown wrapped in tinfoil. He approaches me, growing larger, blocking out the crowd.

The sun pours down, heat heating heat in a golden mist.

He stands in front of me, exuding a salty mustiness.

The crown on my head.

The trophy in my hands.

And an embrace: hot breath, cigarette smoke, and the stench of fresh perspiration.

A kiss: the right cheek, the left cheek. The lips linger, part, the tip of the tongue traces wetly across my skin.

A lizard, I see a lizard.

He pulls away. At last. And from where his tongue has touched, taking with it the taste of my sweat, rises steam, a steam that is my shame made visible.

"Wave," he says, "wave to the people. You are the queen. The police queen."

I raise my right hand.

The crowd, hesitating, urged on by Lisímaco Gonzalez, begins to applaud. Palms meet and separate, slowly, soundlessly, noise absorbed into the thick air.

Suddenly the trophy in my left hand moves. It becomes soft and pliable, melting, as if about to flow away, metal moving with life inexplicably acquired.

I grasp at it, with both hands now, to support it, to contain it. Quickly it lengthens, hardens, acquires weight, a form twice familiar. My eyes run slowly across the angular lettering, more familiar now but wondrous yet, inscribed in the grey metal.

I look up, past the silently applauding crowd, past the Holy Virgin in the square, past the buildings into the sky, into the sun.

And in the moment before I have to turn away, when my eyelids seal themselves and a sparkling darkness fills my head, they come to me, Pedro, Miguel, and Tomás, eyebrows raised in amusement, speaking as one words unintelligible with a sound harsh and fantastic, an eager and magical music that sings of things as yet unimagined from a place that remains well beyond imagination, far, far beyond my kingdom of the golden dust.

AN ARRANGE-
MENT OF
SHADOWS

1.

The clock struck once and it was eight o'clock.

Two pigeons, symmetrical slices of black on the blue sky, swooped and touched down abruptly on the red roof of the clock tower. The hands of the clock—broadswords of a brass long tarnished—were locked as always at four seventeen.

"A.M.," she thought, her mind snatching back to the night years before—ten? twelve?—when they had been jarred into immobility by an early-morning earthquake that she recalled with the precision of a disturbed nightmare: walls swaying as if blown by breeze, glass rattling, dogs barking, shards of dancing light.

The school had never bothered to repair the clock. Its arms stuck; it struck now with its own abbreviated sense of regularity, once every hour, twice every half-hour. It was always one o'clock. So that the earthquake, minor, deserving of notoriety only in a place so small, gained immortality in this static, abandoned way.

She wondered if anyone apart from herself had ever noticed.

And she wondered too why she had spent her life, once so full of possibility, in so remote a place.

Miss Jackson paused at the top of the stairs. Her breathing, more demanding than usual, surprised her.

She had had her fortieth birthday two days before; and three days before, she had received a phone call, thin and crackling, the voice unfamiliar and distant like that of a BBC World Service news reader, telling her that her mother had died. The unfamiliarity of the voice—a neighbor had called, a neighbor she had never known—and its terrifying facelessness had caused a pain greater than the news of the death: there was no one left.

She clutched the books to her ribcage—a defensive attitude, she knew, picked up from the priests of the school who clutched their Bibles in similar posture—and set off down the long corridor, open on the right to the sky and the tops of palm trees, closed on the left by the cream walls and grey doors of shuttered classrooms. The floorboards gave gently beneath her sandals. From beyond the high wall that enclosed the school—this, too, cream, the pyramidal top a pitted grey; such retreating colors, she had always thought, for a tropical island—came the angry vibrations of traffic: horns, tires, voices mingled in a cacophony of protest. Even so early—the morning sun was yet low, casting the shadow of the school building onto the empty parking lot below—exhaust fumes had already heated the air, tinting it with the smell of the singed.

At the end of the long corridor stood Mr. Rahim, tie loosened at the neck, sleeves rolled to the elbow as if for manual labor. His hair, oiled, greying irregularly, was tightly combed. The beginnings of excess weight tightened his shirt at the waist. He brought his right hand to his chin and scratched absently at it, less a man absorbed, she thought, than a man expressing a static contentment. The ring on his hand caught the light and glinted red.

She didn't like Mr. Rahim and Mr. Rahim didn't like her. It was claimed—and he encouraged the claim—that he was a nationalist. At a staff meeting he had once declared her a foreigner in a land, *his* land, that no longer wanted foreigners. But she guessed the reason to be less high-minded, more visceral, reaching back to a night of loneliness and intoxication twenty years earlier when she had found comfort in his body. She knew she had but to admit him and he would be on her side, no longer the nationalist; and she found amusement in this easy new colonialism.

He turned towards her, his eyes darted up, down; then, without acknowledgement, he stepped quickly into the labyrinthine darkness of the staff-room.

The staff-room: it challenged her every morning. The glassed doors, even wide open, admitted none of the searching light which elsewhere seemed to pierce. Within that obscurity, amidst rows of scarred desks—small wooden cubicles covered with books, papers, pens, coffee cups, ashtrays, and stray ashes—the teachers slept and gossiped away their free periods. It disturbed her that there were no books other than texts, there was no discussion beyond gossip and complaint; it struck her as a betrayal, as if the darkness that held the room had penetrated to the very core of the beings who inhabited it. Here for her was purpose, and yet, defeat. She thought with regret of Mr. Bain, tall and portly and assured, who between classes had read the Greek classics in the original and who had, one sunny afternoon, laid his head on an open Euripides and died, without a sound, a white foam like the last of the soapsuds in the kitchen sink bubbling from between his thick, slightly parted lips. Theirs had been a relationship of intellect and mutual interests—her only such support—

and, under stress, she felt his loss with a keenness that was
eviscerating.

This morning she decided to avoid the staff-room, to go
directly to her first class.

She wondered whether Mr. Rahim had yet taken down the
pornographic picture, a small photograph cut roughly from a
magazine of a nude with exaggerated breasts and soliciting
pout, that he'd tacked to his desk the week before. She had
protested quietly and his response had been a smile and a slow
examination of her own rather small breasts. The purple
gleam of his gums had remained with her as a nightmare
vision.

All four doors of the classroom were open. Tall and wide,
they laid bare the room to the outside. She paused at the
doorway, distrustful of the light, the brightness that made of
the doors on the opposite side slabs of almost opaque yellow.
This was not supposed to be; the doors should have been
locked; hers the only key other than the Dean's: he had promised.

And yet, hers was the only room exposed.

The tiled corridor on the other side—those doors too
thrown open with a brazenness she could sense—shone in the
sunlight that was now above the hills to the east, releasing
from shadow the slums that had eaten the western slopes.

Miss Jackson put her books on the table and looked around
the classroom. Unpeopled, its bareness became apparent. The
walls, painted a yellowed cream she associated with the police
stations put up under British administration, were undeco-
rated. Two bare light bulbs, useful only in the darkness before
a storm, hung from grey plastic cords. The desks of old wood,
with channels along their lengths for pens and pencils and
holes, long unused, for inkwells, squatted heavily in rows.

She was more puzzled than angered, and in an uncontrollable reflex assumed for a moment the attitude of the alerted

animal, head lowered, eyes squinting, nostrils minutely flared in olfactory search. But there was nothing beyond the tingle of automobile exhaust.

Her muscles went slack under a sudden melancholy. She turned to the sunlit eastern doors. The balcony railings, of heavy concrete in the shape of urns, painted the grey of storm and battle—as if, it had often occurred to her, to capture in this land of stark primary colors the solemnity of tradition that was of another, older, more northern land—cast fat shadows on the shining tiles. On the hills beyond, the galvanized-iron roofs of the shanty glinted where they had not yet rusted, while the still uneaten vegetation higher up showed a green temporarily enriched by dew. The sky, of a blue as solid and as daunting as open ocean, threatened another day of the sun that had seared her skin into the consistency of soft leather.

The landscape—how foreign a word it now seemed, since she had come to think of it with the local phrase as simply "The Hills"—this landscape, once viewed as a possible watercolor, failed to revive her, depressed her a little more even.

She had lost her sense of the picturesque. Despite herself, she had learnt quickly that the picturesque existed not by itself but in a quiet self-delusion, in that warping of observation which convinced the mind that in poverty was beauty, in atrophy quaintness, the hovel a hut. She had long stopped seeing with the tourist's eye and had come to share the island's distaste for those whose only interest was to use it. She thought of herself now as of the island, and the only unease that rested with her was whether this was strength or weakness, armor or chink.

Armor or chink: the doubts this morning were strong. Her gloom deepened and her thoughts crept back to that other morning six, seven months before when, on a morning very much like this one with the sun and the sky and the hint of exhaust, she had arrived at the school early to search out in the library a passage of literary criticism she had wanted to present to her class. She had noticed with only a passing curiosity that the doors to her classroom were open and she remembered thinking: I didn't hear the wind last night.

She had located the book easily in the large, high-ceilinged room that, years before, had served as assembly hall and that, with the opening of the privileged educational cloister demanded by government aid, had been turned into library and study-hall for non-Catholics during periods of religious instruction. She remembered how the dust had risen from the book into the air yellowed by filtered sun like a sorcerer's cloud, an aqueous dance of fibre and grain, powder and spark. On the shadowed green walls, dusty oil portraits of past principals, stern Irish faces glaring from backgrounds of gloomy mystery, had retreated before the play of movement and light.

She had taken the book with her out to the corridor. Again, the sun, the horns, and the screeching tires, the smell of burning: she recalled a sense of self-possession, a contentment that used to come to her in enveloping spurts, inopportune in their brevity.

The mood had lasted: her handbag balancing easily on her arm; the rough, crumbling quality of the book reassuring between her fingers; each step telling her of her solidity, affirming self. Solidity, a concept novel to her, as if she had never before quite believed in the reality of herself, believed even now only at rare, inexplicable, unexpected moments. Yes, the mood had lasted, right up until she reached the classroom.

There, in the middle of her desk, melting and glistening and turning odorous in a beam of early morning sunlight, had been two thick strips of human excrement.

And there, too, in a rush of fear and physical revulsion, the memory ended.

The clock chimed once. The generic harshness of the light that poured through the doors tightened, sharpened its edges, became geometric, taking on the elongated form of the door where there was bare floor, cracked with a precise angularity where it met the old wooden desks.

Her eyes followed the lines of light, their precision growing steadily sharper as the sun rose. Through the door there now streamed a solid beam of yellow, harsh, lacerating, causing insubstantial diamonds to float before her.

A shadow broke the beam and, squinting, she recognized Father Gries, his long white gown gathered in folds about his withered body, Bible of cracked black leather and dog-eared pages held, shaking, before him in long, bony fingers.

He did not notice her. His absorption in the biblical word, at times so complete, had become legend in the school, and there were times when his presence went barely beyond the physical. Sometimes the boys, with the innate cruelty of their age, would greet him with smiles and obscenities, knowing themselves safe in his deafness; and he would respond, unknowing, with a smile and a blessing. It was at these times that she hated him and wished for his death.

Yet, in his times of lucidity, he inspired fear. He had a reputation; in his teaching days, recalcitrant students would have dividers flung at them, kicks and punches would be delivered with regularity, and at least once he had drawn blood with a well-aimed blackboard eraser. This reputation, probably, she knew, exaggerated by legend, had become real to her. Whenever, by accident, his antipodean gaze happened to settle on her, her stomach would contract and for that second she would feel herself transparent, vulnerable.

He stopped precisely halfway past the door and looked intently down at his Bible. The sun shooting off the whiteness of his gown bathed him in a yellow fuzz, as if he were glowing before disintegration. Then he looked up and turned towards her.

"Miss Jackson."

"Good morning, Father Gries."

His hair, white and fine as a baby's, hung on his forehead like tattered lace. The lips, thin and pinched, moved soundlessly on his desiccated face, giving a glimpse of the teeth that had bent and darkened, already the anthropologist's prize. She pulled back, as she invariably did, from the spectre of mummified age that he presented.

He said, "Father Small is dead."

"Oh, I'm sorry, Father Gries." Father Small was Father Gries's walking companion, another desiccated old priest living out his life on the edge of usefulness. To Miss Jackson he had barely existed, had been little more than animated flesh, and her conviction was muted. The regret she felt was like that she would feel for an animal that had lost its animal companion, a commiseration lightly felt and quickly forgotten.

She said, "My mother died three days ago," and she instantly regretted the words, they were too personal.

Father Gries cupped his palm to his ear. "What? What's that?"

She didn't reply and he let his hand fall, his face a blank, eyes empty.

She thought: At last. They're starting to die out.

She said, "Father Gries, why were my doors open this morning?"

His eyes rose to her face. He hadn't heard her, or hadn't understood her; she didn't know which. Then he turned slowly, step by step, rocking lightly from side to side, and continued along the shining corridor.

Miss Jackson thought: You stupid old fool.

The clock struck once and it was three o'clock. The sun shone now from the west through coagulating rainclouds, a light of a thicker yellow, a light without glow, heavy like egg yolk.

It had been a difficult day. The classes had been restless, inattentive, less furtive with whispered conversation than usual. She had thrown one boy out earlier in the day; another she had tried to humiliate, with a lack of success so blatant that the humiliation had come back onto her. She had tried humor, without response, and anger had found but a void. The boys seemed all to have sunk into a passivity that was not so much solid as porous, elastic, yielding, with a subtle retaliation. It was the mood of torpor, with an added, active dimension. It was a mood she had never before seen, and the effort to tear into it had drained her and created in her a hint of hysteria.

The grating of the school bell cut her off in mid-sentence. She could not, as she usually did, summon the strength to shout above the noise: the bell, louder now it seemed to her than before, marked the end of battle. And yet the faces—black, brown, white—stared at her now with greater attention than before, expectant. Her hysteria grew and she gathered her papers with moistening palms.

She said, "Don't you want to go home?" She had really wanted to say: What's going on? Why are you behaving like this? but the words solidified in her mind, would not transfer into speech. She said, "No football today, Sanders?"

Sanders said, "No, Miss Jackson."

She wanted to scream at them, to hate them. She said, "Go home," and she rose pushing back at her chair.

One by one they stood up, folding papers, closing books, capping pens. Their slowness struck her and once again she saw expectation in their reticence.

She moved quickly, striding away from the low rostrum, aware that they were following her every movement. Like hunters, she thought, like hunters before prey.

Through the door ahead of her the hills, their ugliness bared that morning by brilliance like disease by a scalpel, were caught in a softer light. Angles were dulled, rust could have been shadow, and the shanty took on an aspect of homeliness. It was a view she enjoyed, but rejected at the same time. It was a watercolor she could have done, and would have ripped up upon completion.

Father Gries, Bibleless, was standing in the corridor. He said, "Miss Jackson," and his voice had a precision, conveyed a lucidity, that was like a warning.

"Good afternoon, Father Gries." She hurried past him.

"A moment, Miss Jackson."

She stopped, aware that the class had ceased its shuffling.

Father Gries pushed the white hair from his forehead with a quick, nervous movement of his hand. The hair, fine and wispy, fell back down into place as if lifeless. In the dimming light the age spots on his hands, on his forehead, stood out like shadows that had crept beneath the skin.

He said, "I have a message for you. From the Dean. He would like to see you."

The sky above the hills had darkened. Grey clouds, with a movement that was barely perceptible, were piling up beyond them. The shanty darkened, lost its homeliness. She knew that in the little shacks kerosene lamps that gave a claustrophobic light were being lit. From one spot there suddenly arose a thin, then rapidly thickening, column of black smoke. Illumination turned to conflagration: from here in a few minutes, and with a bit of imagination, it could be a bonfire, destruction transformed.

"Very well, Father. I shall speak with the Dean tomorrow morning before classes."

"No, Miss Jackson, he wishes to see you immediately."

She could now see the flame, a patch of yellow without reach, darkening the land around it, function inverted.

Father Gries took her arm and gently urged her on.

She said, "Do you see that fire, Father?"

He did not reply and she wondered if his lucidity had slipped from him.

He led her to the end of the corridor and through the wooden door that led to the offices. They entered a large, dark room, the only light coming through three stained-glass windows at the far end, so little that the room remained plunged in midnight and the windows glowed like bits of color suspended in the darkness.

As her eyes grew accustomed to the gloom, she saw that the floor, of wood, was highly polished and that the walls too, panelled in wood, picked up the dull shine of the windows. Over in one corner, behind a glass cubicle, the school's telephone operator sat in a contained circle of green light, her face, her hair, picking up the color as their own. Miss Jackson thought of death.

It was only as they approached the Dean's door—closed, its existence marked only by a brass knob—that Miss Jackson's eyes picked out the figure sitting hunched over on a chair at the far side of the door. At their approach he raised his head and in the instant before he lowered it again she caught the profile: the springy hair tightly patted down, the long forehead, the finely shaped nose sloping to thicker lips than expected and flowing then into the full chin, the muscled neck defined by the collar of the blue shirt.

She stopped, her mind momentarily emptied. Father Gries's grip tightened on her arm. He said, "We didn't spy. I want you to know that. It was the boys. They told us. It was their hatred."

She turned to face Father Gries, and she realized that the power of his grip came from his own discomfort, had nothing to do with her. It was neither aid nor restraint: it was his own fear.

The dense light from the window reflected off the white of

his gown onto his face: she could see his skull sheathed in spotted skin.

And she felt for him a fathomless loathing.

2.

For a moment, locking the door behind her was like salvation. Yet, as quickly, she knew it was but reprieve.

Home: the familiar mustiness encrusted itself around her. She closed her eyes and let herself go limp against the door, the washboard edges of the jalousied frame pressing into her back.

A bar of bleached sunlight, maintaining a solid cohesion, fell through the open window, illuminating only the fibrous dust that floated in it and a patch of faded carpet. The room was as she liked it: in twilight, a domestic arrangement of shadows. It offered the illusion of coolness and the sense of the airtight she'd come to associate with comfort. The clock, invisible in hulking bookshelves, clicked with monotony, the sound—like that of a stick striking tin—echoing dully through the walls, the floorboards.

She straightened up. It took effort, she felt as if she had no bones. She opened her eyes sharply and sparklers filled the darkness like shooting stars. She froze and, briefly, felt panic. She thought: Steady, remember who you are. Then she went empty, an internal evaporation, and she felt nothing. The clicking of the clock seemed to echo within her.

She let her handbag and umbrella fall to the floor, a single wooden thud, went over to the dark bulk of the armchair and fell into it. She thought: I just want to fade.

She let her eyes, now accustomed to the gloom, wander around the room: everywhere there was shadow, shadow imposed on shadow, grey on grey, black on grey, depth deepened by obscurity. The room looked larger than it was, felt smaller than it was.

From the bookshelves, a rectangle of black, the dull gleam of silver: a spoon: *To Miss Jackson with Gratitude—Spoonfeeding at its Best. Upper Six Genii.* So, once, she had been useful, once appreciated. Once, safe. It seemed to her now that that spoon, that inscription, were the relics of another.

She closed her eyes and all was dark, inside, outside. She had no face, she had no hands, she had no feet. The physical was no more. Still the clock ticked, echoing like a vaulted metronome, no longer marking time but distance too, taking her not forward but back. Faces: father, mother, aunts, uncles. Voices:

"Why do you want to go to that godforsaken place?"

"You are a Judas. You will kiss me goodbye and that will kill me."

"Promise you won't forget us, Victoria, dear."

"Have you had all your shots, Victoria?"

Control: she wished them away.

Blackness once more, and lightness too. It was sweet. She thought: I have joined with death.

And she was grateful.

The tapping was soft and it mingled with the regular click of the clock like the sound of a gentle drum.

She had slept. The bar of sunlight was gone and the darkness now was total: no dust, no glimmer, the stillness solidified.

The tapping, faster but no louder, overlapping the clock, was like fast water on aluminum: muted but sharp, subtly cutting.

Her body sagged heavily in the cloth-covered armchair and warm perspiration filmed her skin like membrane. She reached out and she couldn't see her arm; but the string of metal beads, tasselled at the end, was where she knew it would be. The light scrape of metal on metal, the clink of metal on hollow glass. The light, dancing with the swing of the bulb, came on in a circle of hard yellow, illuminating the chair, a side table of dark wood and, on the floor, one corner of faded Persian rug.

The tapping stopped. The clock and spoon glinted dully from the bookcase.

She stood with difficulty, muscles stiff, like weathered rubber. Her name was called softly from the door, the whisper disguising the voice.

She said, "Who is it?"

A whisper came in reply: "Open the door, Victoria."

"I said, who is it?"

"It's me. Sayed."

"Sayed?" It took her a moment to place the name: Mr. Rahim. Then she felt irritation. "What do you want?"

"Open the door, Victoria."

"Mr. Rahim, please go away."

"Victoria, open the door."

She said nothing, did not move. On her right the clock ticked out its monotony.

The rapping started once more, sharper and more rapid this time, racing the clock, resounding like the shocks of a hammer. Then it stopped. "Open the door, Victoria."

"What do you want?"

"I want to talk."

She approached the door. "There's nothing to talk about."

"Open up, Victoria." He rapped twice.

She thought: He's using the ring. And she hated it with passion.

She was in the front bedroom of a house she didn't know and the light, of the clarity of seized lightning, so bright that it glowed with a blue tinge, was on overhead, showing a neat, spare room: large bed tightly encased under a patterned blue bedspread; in one corner a wooden closet with a mirror, in the other a sink—stopper, soap, glass carefully positioned—and above it a small mirror pimpled with the dark spots of degeneration. The walls were of a light green and the air held in suspension baby powder and age.

She knew that she was not alone. She sensed another: her father maybe, or her mother. But, she thought, weren't they both dead? Yet, somehow, it didn't seem important. He, or she, was there and that didn't seem very important either. The presence was like a mathematical fact that existed in a realm of its own, parallel to hers, but that held for her no direct consequence.

Through the window, like a tableau painted on a sheet of black gauze, blazed the lights of the house across the street: a dining room, three people seated around a table, a game of cards, mouths agape in speech and laughter. The scene, hanging in the blackness of the surrounding night, was at a remove that went beyond the presence of the blacked-out road.

This blackness, this nocturnal infinity of the country, so total, as enveloping as the interior of a sealed casket, terrified her. It offered threat, suffocation. It wiped out all beyond the grope of electric light, it nullified the physical, it made spectral the world. And its power seemed to lick at her too.

In the house across the darkness, they continued to play cards, a man to the right, a man to the left, and a woman, blonde, facing her way. The table at which they sat was of a thick, dark wood, heavily polished, the wall behind the woman of an uninspired cream bare of decoration.

There was a roar in the night, of engine pushed to excess. It came from the left with a shattering suddenness, filling the room. A flash of movement from the darkness; a motorcycle with rider in silhouette against the light of the card-players;

the growl of a distressed engine; the vehicle, airborne, throwing the rider, entering the house, crashing across the table, front wheel crushing into the chest of the blonde woman pinning her to the wall, the men standing, shouting: "Fuck you! Fuck you! F-u-c-k y-o-u!", recognizing in obscenity the futility of protest, helplessness. Into the light ran two little girls, crying, chased by a woman with arms outstretched in a vain attempt to capture.

Victoria, unnerved, feeling the terror, wondered why the little girls sought to evade comfort.

She said, "Go away."

The rapping increased, the door shaking with each blow, the shadows on the slats lengthening and shortening with the movement, the heavy bolts at the bottom rattling in their holes.

She depressed the door handle and the door was flung open with violence. She stepped back. Mr. Rahim, in silhouette but for the folds of his white shirt, stepped slowly into the room. She could hear his breathing.

He said, "So. It's over."

She said, "It's over."

"At last."

"Why did you come here?"

He took two steps forward, so that the edges of the light caught the shine of his face. His eyes, puffy, looked tired. "So this is what you've done with the place. A tomb. No wonder you never invited anyone here. Or almost no one."

She said, "Please sit down." She felt the strangeness of the civility.

"Where?"

She indicated the armchair.

"Did he sit there, your student?"

"Is that what this is all about? Jealousy? After all these years?"

She carried a picture in her head: a small backyard of fragile shrubs and discarded cartons, a fence of crowded wooden slats. Above the rounded tops of the slats and repeated to distant extinction, the weather-worn backs of the duplicates of the house she knew to be to her left and just out of the picture. A simple house, a box-like affair of three-storeyed hollow walls stamped down the length of the street into a parody of architecture.

The sky above the fence was grey, with a uniformity of color and depth that denied the natural. The picture, so complete within the folds of memory, thrust at her even the acrid bite of factory emission.

At times there were people in the picture: father, mother, aunts, uncles. The faces, after twenty years recalled only in outline, appeared of their own volition. They came, they went, they shifted, they melted into one another. They stood stiffly, squinting into the low sun, their paleness fuzzily crystalline against the dark fence. Their flesh, their clothes, shared, in the frame of her mind, the quality of the shrubs: fragile people, fading, substance drained, so that they were, like a coterie of ghosts, but an arrangement of shadows.

They had not been a picture-taking people. At her departure, they had possessed no image except an unfocussed, heavily framed photograph of her freshly wed parents: father in army uniform, mother—stern, always—in concealing white. That white, a rebuff: it explained, she felt, her memory of the solitary, a girl alone with dolls in a house guarded by maternal impulse.

As with pictures, so with letters. They were a family that preferred as little of a record as possible, a self-effacement by omission.

So that twenty years before, as she had boarded the rusting ship for the island, there had been rupture, unremarked, unfaced, unadmittable. The telephone, crackling, stripping the voice to tin, had grown into the annual link: the birthday calls, greetings followed by the litany of recent familial death. As the years passed, the litany had grown longer, the voices to respond to—always the same expressions of congratulations and concern, like people reading from the same cue card—steadily fewer.

He snickered. "Don't be stupid, Victoria." He became casual, hips slackening, hands sliding into pants pockets. "Shut the door." He went over to the chair, heels sharp on the wooden floor, then cushioned to dull thumps by the Persian rug. He studied the chair, shrugged, lowered himself into it. Elbows on the arms of the chair, he stared through steepled fingers at her. Slowly, turning her back to him, she closed the door. The lock clicked softly.

He said, "How can you stand that damn clock?"

"What do you want, Mr. Rahim?"

"Sayed."

"What do you want?"

"You don't seem upset."

"Maybe I'm not."

"It's dark in here, Victoria. Put on some more lights."

"I like it like this."

He lowered his hands, folded them on his lap: the ring glowed red in the light. He leaned his head against the back of the chair and closed his eyes. "Why did you come here, Victoria? What's the meaning of all this?"

It was an impertinent question. She wanted to mock him. "The meaning of what? Life?"

"Why not? It's been your life."

"My life?" She repeated the words slowly, to herself, as if

searching them for a meaning beyond the obvious, for something more. "My life? There's been no meaning, no purpose. Not really. There never is, I don't think. It's just one of the little lies you have to make up from day to day, to keep going. You have to invent; and then you have to believe: that's the hard part."

"What did you invent?"

"I told myself I wanted to come here to help. To teach."

"To bring civilization to the colonies." Now it was his turn to mock.

"Then I changed my mind. I told myself I wanted to do a few watercolors."

"And you've stayed twenty years." He clasped his hands, fingers interlacing, thumbs rubbing hard one against the other. "You came to take, Victoria. Like any tourist, only worse. You stayed for a lifetime."

There had never been a place to play. The house imposed a rigorous silence. The backyard, small and junked, offered no scope: clouds of grey and electric blue pondered above the fence like a lid. She thought she could feel the reek of the factories brushing against her cheek. The streets of the neighborhood, twinned houses declining as one into a disreputable greyness, were alien. In protecting her from them, her mother had made her a stranger to them.

It was here, wandering around this backyard, crushing beneath foot the sparse, unhealthy grass, resting her leg for a moment on a rusted garden tool, a rotting crate, that she formed her earliest memory of boredom.

And it was from here not long after her ninth birthday—around the time she found out about her father's other women; her mother's reclusive indispositions so simply, so brutally, explained—that she first sought adventure.

A foot on a wooden box, a leg over the rounded top of the fence: she recalled neither fear nor excitement, just an urge.

The neighboring yard was a disappointment, was like a reflection of her own: the same sparse grass, the same rusting garden tools, a neighborly dereliction. The house too could have been her own but for the orange lace curtain hanging in the kitchen window.

She had taken a step beyond and it had left her without change. And with a kind of horror she decided that the yard beyond this fence, and beyond the next, and the one beyond that, would be the same: a rectangle of lost color and rusted metal, with a curtain that was like a spark.

"Well, the little snot from next door."

The boy, older than she, stood at the back door of the house. His dirty blond hair, too long, covered his ears and hung in strands across his eyes. He said, "I know you." Behind him the door opened and another boy, of his size and age but with darker hair recently cut, came out and stood beside him.

The first boy said, "You shouldn't be here. What are you doing here?"

She reached for the fence, but here, in the alien become familiar revealed suddenly again as alien, there was no box.

Then she knew terror: their hands were on her. A hand covered her mouth, pressing the flesh sharply against the front teeth. She was pushed to the ground: her bare arms kneaded the cool softness of the grass as they were pulled above her head and pinned down by hands more powerful than hers. Her dress was pushed up and other hands probed at an intimacy that had been, until then, as personal as breath. Her legs were kicked apart. Hot flesh tapped at her stomach, the insides of her thighs, as if in search.

Then, pain.

The hand on her mouth tightened. Now the thumb was pressing against her nostrils: air became precious. Her thighs, stretched and supporting a weight she had never known, felt as if they were being ripped.

The boy gasped. His movements slowed. And quickly, taking her by surprise, the weight, the fingers vanished. She was pulled to her feet. Her pain kept her doubled over; her legs trembled.

One of them said, "Get the ladder."

Presently she was pushed towards the fence. The ladder, of metal, was brought and set next to the wooden slats. They urged her right foot onto the first rung, working in silence, their breathing audible. Their rage was spent and she knew their fear now to be greater than hers.

Her legs would not work. The blond boy, his fear mounting, ran up the ladder, jerking at her arms while the other pushed at her from behind. The blond, one foot on the ladder, the other on the fence, got her to the top and then, with a final effort, pushed her over.

The house, the grass, the fence, the sky: her sight registered blurred glimpses as she fell, limp, her right elbow scraping painfully on the wooden box.

She lay still. She could not isolate her pain: it was everywhere.

At last, strength gathering, she arose and crept into the house.

Later, the wooden box provided the story of the cut and the soiled dress: she had been climbing on the boxes, she had fallen.

The next day her father threw out the boxes.

But something essential—she didn't know what—had been altered. Her mother, distant always, grew further away. She felt that her mother had known the truth; or that if she hadn't known it, she should have guessed it. In refusing to acknowledge it, in failing to come to her, her mother had abdicated the right to emulation.

It was the water that was greener on the other side: the translucent green of a clouded emerald, with patches of sandy brown here and there where, deep below, a rogue current stirred the sand.

From the deck of the ship the island had struck her as being large, of a greater bulk than she had expected: mounds of olive green folding beyond the harbor, lightening into banks of grey, mingling there with clouds of a darker grey. One hill, rising steeply from a narrow coastal plain, formed a backdrop to the bruised buildings of the port. Its green was flecked, beyond and just above the buildings, by the red triangular roof of what she took for a clock tower. Its summit, abraded by cloud, was being licked by crinkled threads of lightning.

A light drizzle sprinkled the deck, speckling her suit, a proper outfit whose weight she could already feel.

Some of the town came into view: red roofs dulled by rain, treetops of unfamiliar foliage, tiny houses pinned as if by miracle to the lower slopes of the hill. The clock tower, now definable, showed a face dissected by arms of brass.

Above the large sheds of the port hung limp Union Jacks. On the docks stevedores lounged around stacks of wooden crates while white-suited sailors of military bearing made their way to and from the low grey hulk of an American warship docked at a neighboring berth.

She had secured a teaching position at a high school of repute on the island, an institution run by Catholic priests, Englishmen and Irishmen, seeking to pack their staff with the foreign and the trustworthy before the expected independence of the island imposed a demand for the local. She was to teach English literature to the upper forms, Shakespeare, Chaucer, Austen, James, and the Brontës, preparing what she perceived as simple island minds for the challenges of Cambridge University examinations. It struck her as an awesome task, and she came, after a while, to think of it as a sort of mission.

Now, faced with the island—greener than she had thought; she had pictured dust and defoliation—her sense of mission diminished. The air had a stifling quality, was heavy with moisture. It was air you could drown in.

She had a fantasy. She would stay on board, she would return as she had come and it would all be as if it had never been, just a few weeks lost in a lifetime.

Then she imagined sun: the red top of the clock tower against the green of the hills, the huts out of a child's imagination, the trees. She thought: a few weeks, at least, a few watercolors.

She reached into her purse and felt her passport. It was a comfort.

"But the truth, Mr. Rahim. Sayed. You see, I was running. That's the truth about people like me. We're usually running from one thing or another. Someone, boredom, the place we come from. People like me who want to help, we're just runners looking for rest, protection. We help because of self-ishness, nothing more. We need to help in order to survive, to camouflage our fears." Her forehead was cool with perspiration. Her hands felt clammy. Now, a truth that she had known but never acknowledged came clear to her, in a rush of precision. The words surged with thoughts, visions, that were new to her. "Like Father Gries. That dried-up old man, what was he running from? The war? Hitler? A woman? I wonder what they're all running from, those cassocked cowards. Gries was lucky, though, he got away from whatever he was running from. He'll die here, safe."

"And you?" He opened his eyes and stared directly at her: light glinted from the shadows of his eye-sockets. "You can't stay here."

"I can't go back."

"Why not?"

"There's nobody left."

"Your mother?"

"She's dead."

"When?"

"Three days ago. Or is it four now? I don't remember any more."

"I'm sorry."

"Don't. I don't need condescension. Especially not from you."

"What was she like?"

The ordinariness of the question—as if her world hadn't shattered, as if he weren't a man she disliked with intensity—surprised her, offered relief. She thought, and then she said, "I don't really know. She always kept to herself."

"But you were her daughter."

"So what?" She raised her hands to her face and traced her features with her fingertips. "I look like her, you know." The too-high forehead, the too-rounded nose, the too-wide cheeks, the too-thin lips. "Plain." She thought: Nothing seems to fit together. "Sometimes when I look at myself in the mirror I wish I could remold things, a little more here, a little less there."

"I don't think you're plain, Victoria."

"You're a fool, Mr. Rahim."

"You've still got me."

"Don't be stupid."

"You're the stupid one, Victoria." Then his voice hardened. "Why a student, Victoria? Why a little black boy?"

"What are you interested in? His age or his color?"

"What do you think? Yes, I'm racist. You have to be, here. If you don't know that, you don't know anything about this place. Indians hate Blacks and Blacks hate Indians. That's the way it is."

"And whites? You just want to screw them, right?" Her eyes moistened. "I'll tell you why a student. Because he's the kind of person we look for when we come here. He's simple and uncomplicated. He can't create problems."

"And controllable, too. You're always in charge."

"Why not?"

"You know it was the students who gave you away?"

"I know."

"You're a fool, Victoria. But you're right about one thing. There's nothing here for you, you'd better get out."

"Why are you so concerned?"

His eyes moved to his interlaced fingers. Then, with a slow movement, he cracked them and grimaced, as from fatigue. "I guess I just want to see if you'll really go."

"You bastard."

Mr. Rahim, slim in a compact, fragile way, as if underfed in childhood, came on board from the police launch with the customs officials. He was full of a nervous confidence, with the assurance, she thought, of the initiate. His welcome—stiff stance, crooked smile, slight incline of the head—was practised, and his nervous bustle as he led her through the landing formalities touched her. She was being treated like precious cargo, too important to be held up by stamps and papers. He badgered the officials, thrusting her papers at them, assuring them that all was correct, demanding stamps, stamps, stamps. No one seemed to pay any particular attention to him but he got the stamps, of a cheap purple ink that smudged on the papers.

She said, "Please, Mr. Rahim, I've been on this ship for almost three weeks. A few more minutes won't matter. Please slow down."

But he bustled on ahead, his arms seemingly elongated by the weight of her bags. She followed, clutching her purse, stepping with care down the narrow metal gangway of the ship. He waited for her at the bottom, looking up as if in triumph. She thought with surprise: But he's showing off.

As she reached the last rung he said, "Careful," and she saw that the ground was dark and wet with oil. Everywhere there were little puddles of black water, shiny slicks of oil bubbling on the surface.

He led her through one of the large sheds, empty except for a high stack of boxes over in one corner and a clutch of fat men in ill-fitting clothes, shirts unbuttoned to reveal sweaty black chests, haggling over stacks of different-colored papers.

Perspiration trickled down her back, caught on the clasp of her brassiere, then continued on down, finally soaking into the waistband of her skirt. It had been cooler on the deck of the ship; here, the air was boiled, viscous. She thought: It would be easier to take it intravenously. She was pleased with the line and decided to remember it for a letter.

He drove her out of the dockyard in a small grey car—"It belongs to the school," he said with an offhanded pride—manoeuvring the vehicle with an exaggerated casualness, steering with the fingertips of the left hand, right arm crooked through the open window. She noticed on the middle finger of his right hand a large gold ring with a fake ruby set in the middle. It was much too big for the finger and was prevented from slipping off only by the knobby joint. She recognized it as a failed attempt at style, adornment, and she thought it attractive in its very ugliness.

He took small roads, past uninterrupted concrete fences painted white or cream over the tops of which showed thick green trees, red roofs, glimpses of intricate wood carvings decorating small houses. It struck her as being shuttered, with a tightness, a sense of the enclosed, she hadn't expected.

Mr. Rahim too struck her as being enclosed, tight. In the car his compactness became more evident. He was small and neat behind the wheel, so that even his economical manipulation of the car appeared expansive, overdone. He concentrated fiercely on the road, lips compressed, eyes moist at the corners, slightly squinted.

She said, "Are you the school's driver?"

The side of his mouth jerked; smile or grimace, she couldn't tell which. Like the Mona Lisa, she thought, but without the delicacy.

He said, "No, the history and geography teacher."

"Oh, I'm sorry."

He nodded, and she couldn't tell whether or not she had hurt him.

She said, "What is Father Gries like? I've received all these letters from him but they're all so official. No hint of the man."

He considered the question, sounding the horn once to warn off a stray dog. Then he said, "He's a priest. They sometimes forget they're men too."

The sarcasm surprised, pleased her. She waited for him to go on.

"He's the Dean of Studies. A German. A mathematician. He's been there as long as anybody can remember. Had a hard time during the war. I was a student here then. We liked to think of him as a spy. Sort of made us feel closer to the great effort. Until the Americans arrived, of course. Then we didn't need Father Gries any more. The uniforms, the jeeps, the MPs were enough for our imaginations." He grinned, showing a full set of prominent teeth, white at the front, yellowed at the side. The skin on his face wrinkled on the skull, emphasizing his thinness. "He's a reserved man, and severe. Don't expect warmth."

She said, "You don't like him, do you?"

He turned to face her, for the first time taking his eyes off the road. He smiled.

They turned onto a wider street lined with small stores and

shops. Ahead she saw the clock tower she had spotted from the ship.

He said, "That's the school."

Cream two-storeyed buildings with grey roofs surrounded by a high wall, this too cream cropped by grey. As they drove past the gate—the wall, she noticed, thick, as of a prison—she thought: A few watercolors.

Mr. Rahim noticed her tension. He reached out and put his hand on hers. She made to take her hand away but he grasped her fingers: he had a warm, light touch. He said, "Don't worry. You'll be all right."

"He wasn't the first, Mr. Rahim. You see, there's a fear in me. And a need. A fear of all men, and a need of them. To try to find what I don't believe exists. A man I can trust."

"So you slept with students? And what did you think you'd find with them? Trust? Maturity? You're talking nonsense, Victoria."

"Who are you to tell me that?"

"I'm the one you slept with once. Once, and that was all you ever gave. But you weren't giving, you were taking. You're a selfish bitch."

"Yes." Her voice was a hiss. "That's right. And what are you? A na-tion-al-ist?" She dragged out the word in the island way, to give it bite.

He laughed, his derision theatrical. "No, Victoria. I'm just another island boy you slept with. And I'm getting old." He laughed again, and the sound, less controlled now, conveyed a hint of the maniacal. "I want to see how much you've changed. Take off your clothes."

"You bastard. Get out."

"I'm getting old, Victoria. And you too. The hairs on my chest—you remember the hairs on my chest?—they're getting grey. And I've been wondering if you've been getting grey too. Raise your dress and open your legs."

"Get out!" she screamed, and the scream echoed throughout the house.

"Bitch. You open your legs for a student though."

He pushed himself up from the chair and she rushed across the room at him. He leaned back into the lamp; light danced with shadow. She felt the ring bite sharply into her chin and she fell backwards, to the floor, head banging onto the wooden boards. His hands grappled at her dress, pulling at the fabric, ripping at the panties, and finally she was exposed, knees held apart by sweaty palms. She heard his breathing, felt her chest tighten, prepared for the pain, the weight.

He undid his zipper with a quick movement and she felt him rub against her: he was soft. He pressed hard, rubbing himself on her flesh, but still he remained soft.

And then she knew that more was beyond him.

He raised himself from her and pulled back, his hands yet forcing her legs apart.

Then laughter: loud, echoing, endless. Saliva sprinkled lightly on the insides of her thighs. The hands were removed. The laughter went on and on.

Spluttering, he said, "Grey, Victoria, grey."

His footsteps knocked rapidly across the floor. The front door opened, slammed. And still his laughter echoed, fading into the click of the lock.

        3.

The sky was a mass of congealed blackness: she felt its pressure in the air, in the wet darkness of the night around her. The rain, sudden and hard, cleansing nothing, had brought up the smells of the gutter. A dull putrefaction clotted the air: she thought of day-old blood.

The school was in darkness. Here and there a straining

light-bulb threw a greyed light, an ineffective illumination. The school unanimated was a new sight to her; it slumbered, rising and falling in slow respiration. The clock tower, a slab of black reaching upwards from the bulk, was sharpened by the glow of the main street on the other side.

The gates were locked. She grasped the bars, still wet, the paint slick, the metal beneath pitted by corrosion. They had begun locking the gates two years before, during the riots; and their distrust of place, tangible at the time, had never ceased.

She walked the length of the sidewalk, following the wall. The pavement, unlit, glistened green then yellow then red from the flash of traffic lights changing a bit further down the street. She came to the door the priests used at night, a slab of grey sheet-metal tucked unobtrusively into the wall at the far end. It had been shown to her during the riots in a moment of panic when it seemed that salvation lay only in sudden flight to the American and British warships that had anchored in the harbor. She bent over and felt in the wetness of its base for the spring-latch that operated it. The door clicked open.

The courtyard in darkness was like ocean at night: an expanse that was more than endless, that was enveloping. She felt swallowed. The white lines of the parking spaces glowed faintly, giving the illusion of whitecaps, regular and frozen.

She walked quickly across the vastness, her sense of familiarity growing as she approached the building. She noted abstractedly that her feet were bare: the scratch of wet concrete was new and she let her soles drag along its roughness, a tickle and a pain.

Up the stairs to the lower corridor, tiles smooth and slippery underfoot; up the stairs to the upper corridor, the deadness of abused wood meeting her feet with a dry shock. She gazed down the corridor to the hooded light above one of the doors to the staff-room: the doors locked, panes of glass and white stripping. She thought of Mr. Bain and she thought of Mr. Rahim's photograph and she was amused.

She turned to the left, to a narrow stairway to the third floor, the priests' floor. She had always thought it strange that there was no door: authority—feared, resented—was its own barrier. And even as she placed her foot on the first step she felt its power, like paralysis. She pushed against it and, in a rush, was at the top of the stairs facing a long corridor, narrow and carpeted, subdued light revealing cheaply panelled walls and, at regular intervals, recessed doors of dark wood, each labelled with a small strip of white cardboard: Father K. Huggins, Father R. Reginald, Father P. Rodriguez, Father H. Lebrun, Father H. Gries. She stopped at Father Gries's door and took hold of the door-knob, twisted it slowly. It opened to a small, windowless chamber: unmade bed, littered desk, bookshelves, books, papers, a large crucifix, photographs of a man in uniform. The room, stuffy, cluttered, spoke of a life in great disorder.

Father Gries was not there. She wondered where he might be, and then she knew: the closest companions of the dead were those who themselves felt the brush of a cold wind.

She left the room, the door remaining open behind her, and made her way to the end of the corridor. Around the corner, ahead of her, she looked through the open doors to a large room where a bank of candles threw a steady glow, deepening the surrounding gloom to impenetrability.

She strode to the doors, emboldened now, sure. Father Small's casket, large and lidless, creating by its size and function a presence of its own, was hoisted before the candles. A statuette of the Virgin Mary, hands clasped in solicitation, stared down into its sombre depth.

At first Victoria could see nothing but the candles, the Virgin, the coffin: a work of light and lines suspended in the obscurity. She thought she had been wrong, that Father Gries had sought not the company of the dead but his own, nursing the pains of the past, paving the short, short road of the future.

Then, from her left, a movement, a flash of white, and she knew him to be there. Lurking, she thought. And, for a brief moment, so brief that the thought came not in word but in image, she wondered if he was sitting there, rosary wrapped tightly around hand, Bible on lap, seeing himself in the coffin beseeched by a plaster-of-Paris Virgin.

She said, "Father Gries."

He stood, approached slowly, and in the candlelight appeared grotesque. He said, without surprise, "Miss Jackson."

She said, "I have come to pay my respects."

He nodded, and his calmness, his acceptance, were like attack. He watched her, lips parted in the way of the aged, jaw slackened, his gown white and roomy hanging on him like badly pleated drapes.

She went to the coffin and looked in on a face, unrecognizable, of yellow and grey, shadowed hollows for eyes, unremarkable nose deflating into the flesh, lips clamped together as if against pain. She saw a mask, nothing more, a mask of a face she had never known in animation. She saw her mother.

She turned. Father Gries was still staring at her. But she saw that now he was not seeing her, that his eyes, focussed on the gloom beyond the coffin, were marking out infinity.

She said, "Father Gries," and a flicker of his eyes told her that she had his attention; she felt the master of that sudden lucidity. "I have something to show you." She took a step away from the coffin, towards him. "Look, Father Gries." With deliberation she pulled the strap of her dress down her right arm, then the strap of her bra, pulling the cup free of the clinging flesh. His eyes followed the movements, holding finally to the bared breast. "Yes, look, you old fool, have you ever seen a woman's breast? Have you dreamt of it? Wanted it?" She strode up to him, his eyes locked on the exposed whiteness. "Touch, Father Gries, go on." She took his hand, unwrapped the rosary, and brought the cold, stiff fingers to her breast. She held the hand there, felt his skin grow warm against her.

He stared still, now at her hand holding his. His face was unchanged, the lips still hanging apart, the eyes distant and glassy.

Then his hand moved. Slowly, the tips of the fingers pressing first, it closed over the breast with a gentle pressure, a hand testing the ripeness of fruit.

She released his hand. The muscles in her face contracted, upper teeth bit harshly down on lower teeth.

The pressure on her breast increased, the nipple ached. As his hand moved on her breast, fingers tracing the fullness of it, her judgement of him was confirmed, and her disgust was complete. They were one.

Her hand went to his neck, thick gristle, loose flesh roughened. Her fingers tightened around the ball of the Adam's apple.

He doubled over, hand to his chest, clutching.

In supplication, she thought. For forgiveness.

Then she thought: The old bastard's having a heart attack.

She examined him, fascinated. He might have been bowing exaggeratedly; there was even a kind of elegance in his pose.

She thought: How long is he going to stay like this? Will he fall?

She reached out to the back of his head, gave a light push. He groaned, sucked for air; the sound frightened her. Then he fell over, slowly, lightly, still with that surprising elegance. On the floor, he went into a frightened fetal pose, the hand tightened still against the chest. Then the arm went slack, he made a choking sound, and was as if frozen into shadow.

She knew the stairs to be short but the climb seemed to go on forever. The darkness was total, each step high, the flight itself steeply angled. Her thighs burned, the joint at her knees grinding as if rusted. Rough concrete walls pressed in on her, compressing the air, soaking it up, infusing the rest with a wet mustiness. Perspiration tickled her forehead, her neck, her back, her breast, like spiders running races on her skin. She no longer knew where was up, where was down, felt herself rock in a dreamy sensation of falling. She lunged for the wall, for solidity. Her palms met the concrete and it was like caressing sandpaper.

She pressed herself to the wall, hugging equilibrium, cheek and breast bitten by indentation. She continued up. Then her hand touched metal, the works of the clock, and she knew herself to be close to the top. For a moment she held the metal, cool and hard like rejection, then pulled herself past it, in a hurry now, to where there were no walls, to where the little red roof sat on four corner pillars like that of a rudimentary hut, to where at last there was light.

But at a distance only. No glow penetrated to the tower. The gleam of the main street illuminated the exterior, shot past the little room, and on every side there was but a twinkle here, a dull glow there, as of stars fallen and dying. Through the lacy silhouette of a tree she glimpsed the broken arch of a ship's deck lights, festive close up, from here incomplete and wretched.

She said, "Burnt out." The words echoed, and they were like those of another.

Of her father. Of her mother.

"Why do you want to go to that godforsaken place?"

"You are a Judas. You will kiss me goodbye. And that will kill me."

"Promise you won't forget us, Victoria dear. . . ."

And yet, they were the ones who had turned into, had always been, shadows.

The picture came to her: the small backyard of fragile

shrubs and discarded cartons, the fence of crowded wooden slats, the duplicated houses, the sky of grey radiating factory emission.

To return to it: a horror.

In disgrace: a greater horror yet.

To return to nothing, from nothing, with nothing; to return with but a handful of shadows. It was the greatest horror of all: to prove them right.

The clock below her struck once and the sound, sharp, lingering, scraped her mind to blankness, leaving the pure knowledge of devastation curled like a reptile in her stomach.

Here though was comfort, her mind unencumbered, the clutter gone. She felt pure; she felt she could fly. She wanted to capture it, to possess it forever.

She heaved herself up, threw her legs over the wall and sat, feet dangling into the darkness. She tugged her skirt up, uncovering her legs, relishing the wet thickness of the air.

Mr. Bain, young, smiling, sat with her. He said, "We are shadows, Victoria. That's our problem. Yours, mine, Gries's. Our time is long gone. We are of a different age. We are not, none of us, wanted here. We are not required. We don't belong."

She looked around once more. The blackness, the broken lights: a complete vision of nothingness. And in this, a scene of the limitless, of a world without scope, she found a pleasure without memory.

She rocked herself forward in an easy, natural motion, thinking nothing, sensing instead the rightness, moving with thrill beyond the point of recovery. The night, the lights, the wall of the tower swung before her vision: movement blurring sight, movement downwards without speed. Her right arm, flung by the twirl of her body, cracked loudly into metal and the clock struck once. Then twice.

Her breath stuck in her throat. All went black.

And the clock struck again, and again, and again . . .

CONTINENTAL DRIFT

The room, a rectangular hole between two slabs of building, has the feel of an elevator shaft. The dull light from the lamp on the reception counter shows walls of a scuffed sky-blue; a stairway off to my right leads upwards to shadow within which, with concentration, I make out the outlines of a large door. In front of me, talking with the concierge—a big man with tired eyes, rounded shoulders, and a voice theatrical with studied patience, or weariness—are two Spaniards, a man and a woman, young, equally ragged, as if they have been travelling on foot for days, but barely. The woman, eyes alternating between rabid, uncomprehending attention and desperate fatigue, says nothing, stands just a little off to the side, their packs, bound with belts and pieces of string, leaning against her legs.

The concierge says, "Fifty francs each. Bedding deposit."

The Spaniard is fidgety. His French is bad. "But we are leaving in the morning. Four o'clock. We do not have much money."

"It is a deposit. You will get it back tomorrow morning."

"But we have little money." He is pleading now, in low tones.

"No deposit, no bedding. That's all there is to it."

"You think we steal your bedding?"

The concierge says nothing, patiently rolls his pen between his fingers.

The Spaniard says, "But how I am sure you give me my money in the morning?"

"And how can I be sure you'll give me back my bedding in the morning?"

"We're not thieves." A stridency enters his voice.

"You give me fifty francs, I give you the bedding. And in the morning we exchange once more. It's the rule, it's simple. Fifty francs each please." He maintains his evenness of tone without effort: he knows he has won.

The man turns to the woman and mumbles rapidly in Spanish. She digs into the pocket of her jeans and hands him bills rolled as tight and as flat as a stick of chewing-gum. With difficulty he tugs out two fifty-franc notes and tosses them onto the counter, a flick of the wrist that implies both disdain and resignation.

The concierge takes up the money and, with neither comment nor glance, showing only an impenetrable passivity, hands over two stacks of white bedding. He gestures with his thumb towards the shadow at the top of the stairs. "Par là," he says to the man; and to the woman, "Toi, de l'autre côté."

The woman, uncomprehending, flustered, looks at her friend with a kind of desperation. He explains, indicating the stairway across the room from the one he is to take. She grabs him by the shoulders; clearly, she does not like being separated from him. But he pushes her off, mumbling, scoops up his bedding, shoulders his pack, and sets off up the stairs without looking back. She follows him with her eyes, then looks wildly at the concierge.

He says, more softly, "Par là, mademoiselle," pointing her to her stairway.

Suddenly meek, with eyes fearful, she takes her bedding, drags her pack to the stairs, and disappears up into the webby darkness.

The concierge, neutrality unperturbed, says to me, "Passeport, s'il vous plaît, monsieur."

I hand over my passport along with a fifty-franc note, take up my bedding, and make my way up the stairs into the darkness, the shoulder-straps of my pack pressing like two weighted hands into my tensed flesh. The Spanish woman's face, her terror at so simple a thing, remains vividly with me. It seems to hint at the precarious, as if—in her vision, along with what is before her—she senses herself at the crumbling edge of a precipice. It is not that this look is new to me; it is, rather, that I have seen it before, many times in many places, this look that is a new version, more tragic, of continental drift. The Arabs in England, the Turks in Germany, the Gypsies in Spain, the swarming lost of the bars, backrooms, and alleys of Amsterdam. And everywhere, in the streets, the subways, the hidden corners, are the hippies—so strange a word, so dated, evocative of an era before my own—balding men and greying women with beads, bangles, and backpacks, guitars strung on their shoulders, like refugees lost in time, aging people stuck in a past that clings only to them, like the dust and soot that cloak the buildings, famous, infamous, and nondescript, of Europe. There flows from their eyes the melancholy fear of those adrift, travel imposed not by desire but by habit and circumstance, in what I have come to think of not as wanderlust but as wanderlost.

They fascinate me, those faces, those looks, those eyes. They attract me; for they seem to harbor truths that will always lie well beyond the reach of my security.

The mattress—on the lower bunk of a double-decker, the upper bunk littered with the jumbled jetsam of another traveller—is, as usual, thin and bare, a meagre slab beneath me. The pillow, of even more desperate dimensions, is barely distinguishable from the sheet I've thrown loosely on. Four high-wattage bulbs make sleep impossible; the light, rejected almost with violence by the sky-blue walls, seems to gather in the middle of the room and explode out into every corner, stifling shadow.

Lying here in my jeans so faded they are nearly white and socks mended in the crushed, haphazard way of the inexperienced, I feel the drain of my six months of wandering: little town after little town to big town after big town, from train to bus and bus to train. faces and languages switched from one day to the next as easily as switching channels on a television. Faces, styles, cars, buildings, landscape in ungraspable array. And the cathedrals! Lord, the cathedrals! Endless miles of flying buttresses, crowds of spires and gargoyles: boundless piety in carved stone. And then the museums. I gave up on them early on, all the paintings and statues, centuries and a continent on display, when I began to feel that all of Europe was a museum, and all the men and women merely caretakers; when it began to seem to me that no sooner had Europe lived a passage of its life than it put the relics on display behind glass sombrely labelled, the past—remote and recent—neatly packaged.

And now, lying on the barely realized mattress, feeling the boards of the bed pressing in on my back, the question that first occurred to me a couple of weeks ago once more presents itself: what, in all this time, after all these miles, have I learnt?

I have had fun, at times. Have been angered, irritated, stunned. And, often, merely bored. I have seen many things, encountered many people. But all in passing, experiences less complete than dreams, visions fraught with the insubstantial, footnotes forming of themselves no whole, offering but image and sensation as recompense for endless motion. Lessons? But there has been commitment to nothing; so, whence the lessons?

I reach down with my right arm to the backpack beneath

the bunk, find the side pocket, unzip it, and take out my diary, a small hardcover book shut with a brass clasp. On the cover, of a tan felt soft and warm to the touch, is my name stamped in gold cursive script: *J. T. Farrell*. James Timothy. An ordinary name, it suddenly occurs to me; there seems to be something distinctly unprecious about it.

I haven't written in the diary for a while. Much time has passed without anything worth noting. But, as I flick through it, I am surprised to see that it has been a full two months. It depresses me to read my last entry, a brief description—so brief, with subjects and prepositions dropped, that I think I detect the incipient boredom—of a run-in with a persistent prostitute in Munich. "Cheap fuck! Cheap fuck!" she had shouted in heavily accented English stumbling after me in the street. I had ended up running through the crowds on the sidewalk, pursued by her screams: "Sauhund! Con! Fag! Hijo de puta!" All the spitting language of an international side-show.

And after Italy I had scrawled, "No more church doors please, no more altars, no more crosses."

Instinctively I reach for the pen encased in the binding of the book but as my finger touches it I decide that there is nothing to write, that, still, I *feel* like writing nothing. I want instead to withdraw to a cafeteria, to order a coffee in a language that requires of me no linguistic calisthenics, and then to hop the subway home, to shower, dinner, bed. It is, I realize, the same sensation that comes to me after a few hours spent in the Royal Ontario Museum or the Art Gallery: enough of the old and the captured; time needed to assimilate it, store it; and time, then, to breathe the fresher air of things yet uninvented.

I put the notebook beside me on the bed and close my eyes, turning my face to the wall to escape the light.

Voices, loud and British, echo down the hall and into the

room. In irritation I open my eyes and turn towards the door. Two men, young but with faces aged by thick, weathered skin, enter together. Towels are draped wetly over their shirtless shoulders. Their hair, still damp from the shower, is uncombed, and their skin—an underlying greyness drawn out by the probing light of the room—recalls the color of marble statues greyed by exposure.

They pay no attention to me, walk to the far end of the room to bunks, top and bottom, burdened with weathered army backpacks and satchels. One busily towels his back, as if scratching with the towel, while the other, less concerned, throws on a white shirt that quickly grows spotty with dampness.

The toweller says, "Remember the Dutch one? What was 'er name?"

"Hildie? Tildie?" his friend replies, untidily sticking his shirttails into his jeans.

"No-no-no, Hildie was the German. Battle a Britain all over again. Only *I* was doin' the bloody bombin' this time."

His friend, pulling a comb with difficulty through his dirty-blond hair, laughs. "You shoulda heard the noise you two was makin'. Enough to raise the dead."

The toweller sits on the lower bunk caressing the memory. "More than the dead, 'enry. She was a good one."

"How many times that night? Three? Four?"

The toweller grins, then gives a raucous laugh. "Don't bloody remember. But she performed miracle after miracle that night."

"Rise, Lazarus. Again and again and again."

The toweller flings his towel at 'enry, knocking the comb from his hand, and they both double over in exaggerated laughter.

I cover my eyes with my forearm, listening with growing reluctance to the conversation. I wish they would leave, for they bring back to me my own two spells of sexual adventure early on in the trip, quick, unhappy trysts that engendered in their embarrassed aftermaths a dissatisfaction and a loneliness such as I had never before known.

But they won't leave, begin discussing the varied abilities of the girls they bedded in Italy. I suddenly get a vision of them as semen machines leaving deposits wherever they go, like male cats in uncontrollable heat, followed, in respite, by this savored inventory of technical details, public boasts of pubic circus tricks.

My stomach hollows at the thought, and my mouth goes sour. With a quick movement I roll out of the bed, slip into my hiking boots—scuffed and dusty, red laces frayed at the ends—and make my way from the brightness of the room and corridor to the darkness of the entrance hall where the concierge, almost somnolent, is reading a book in the yellow circle of his lamplight, and out into the febrile air of a quiet dusk.

The sky, clouded, is of a grey uniformity that seems to throw its color onto the cobblestones of the wide street. Trees, in the last of their full green, line the opposite sidewalk, the stores and cafés beyond their thin trunks already darkened, shuttered. The sidewalk is deserted and the silence itself, so unrelieved, seems to whisper in unseizable tones.

Suddenly a small car squeals around a corner, shoots past me, and disappears down the street. I think, with envy, of people hurrying home. The fading whine of the car engine is replaced by a silence gone inert and an almost perceptible quickening of the multiplying greyness. It is as if the town is sinking into itself, sucking all life indoors in the small-town fashion I know so well, the descent of dusk bringing a retreat that is like desertion.

I walk the length of the street, to where it opens out into a large square in the middle of which rises a monument, a column of concrete surmounted by a bare-breasted woman in dramatic posture. Graffiti and posters, visible but unreadable in the dying light, cover the base of the monument. The buildings enclosing the square are in darkness but for two places on the far side: an unpeopled bar fronted by white chairs and orange tables, and a garishly neoned hotel. Neither is inviting, and for a moment I wonder what to do next. Eat? But I'm not really hungry. Continue my walk? But exploration, unkindled, now takes effort. I am tired, I know, of continually going nowhere.

Beside me on the sidewalk is a telephone booth and I suddenly wish I could call someone, but no one is within easy reach, familiarity distant. Then I notice that the phone lacks both receiver and cord. It is like a sign.

A light drop of rain lands on my face. Without a thought I turn around and, with hurried step and a sense of relief, make my way back to the hostel, to its threadbare bed and piercing light and voices that bring distress.

"Excusez-moi."

Shouts echo through the halls. Boots pound up and down stairs.

"Excusez-moi."

My shoulder-blades hurt and the pain, with a kind of determination, begins creeping its way slowly up my neck.

"Excusez-moi."

I open my eyes and look up into a face shadowed by the light. "Yes?"

"Ahh." The man straightens up, shoulder-length hair, thick and black, picking up the light and breaking it into sparks. He has a strong, square face with generous features, a face that inspires both instant trust and distrust, the kind of face, laughing eyes, open smile, that can disarm. "You are American?" he says. The accent is British, but the pronunciation, careful and delicate, as if each word is being stroked before spoken, clearly comes from a gruffer, more solid language.

"No, Canadian." His question and my answer, repeated enough in the last months to become a kind of litany, irritate me; they bring to mind the American girl—tanned, Californian—who, on the train last night, said to me with sarcastic bite, "And do you have a Canadian flag on your backpack, like *all* the Canadians?" I wanted to hit her but, instead, simply said, "Yes. We don't have to hide our nationality." I then fled her, pushing my way through the crowded corridor to another car.

"Please forgive me for disturbing you," the man continues, "but do you have a . . . ?" He doesn't have the word. "For beer. To open the bottles." And his hands, large, with soiled fingernails, mimic the action of taking the cap off a bottle.

"A bottle opener."

"Yes, that's it. A bottle opener."

"No, I'm sorry." I close my eyes, hoping he will go away.

"You said you are Canadian?"

"Yes." My irritation grows.

"Are you from Montreal?"

"No. From a little town you've never heard of. In Ontario. But you've probably never heard of there either." I keep my eyes closed but as I hear myself speak my irritation lessens. "I go to university in Toronto."

"I knew a Canadian once. In London. Very nice. Very kind."

"You're not . . . are you British?"

"No-no." He gives a resounding chuckle, drawing it out in such a way that I realize the question has brought images to his mind, images he wants to savor, if only for a second or two. "No, I'm Spanish."

I open my eyes and sit up. "You speak very good English."

"I spent a year in London. I wanted to learn the language."

His eyes look directly at mine; his posture—slim, solid body clad in black jeans, dark-blue shirt, and black vest—reflects a relaxed confidence. There is nothing tentative about him.

"My name is Enrique," he says.

"James." I put out my hand. Enrique grasps it briefly, but with strength. The roughness of the skin surprises me. There is contrast between the clipped precision of his language and the knotted hardness of his hand: each seems to suggest a different background.

"I am with a friend in another room. We are going to have dinner. Would you like to join us?"

"Thank you, but I'm tired."

"We don't have much. Sausage, bread, apples, a few bottles of beer. But we would be pleased if you would share it with us."

There is in his invitation a kind of old-world sincerity, an elegance of the kind that, at the beginning of the trip, I had expected to encounter daily but that, more often than not, has presented itself only in artifacts, in carved wood and chiselled stone, as if petrified. His words, his manner, are almost anachronistic, but at the same time attractive. "Thank you," I hear myself saying. "I'd like that."

We walk down the hall to a much larger, dormitory-like room crowded with single beds, some sheathed in white, others grey rectangles of thin mattress. Enrique leads the way to the far corner. Half-reclining on one of the beds is a tall, thin man, scraggly blond hair uncombed and badly cut, face drained of blood in the way of the ill. Enrique introduces us: "This is Carlos. Carlos does not speak much English." Then he speaks rapidly to Carlos in Spanish and I hear my name. Carlos smiles thinly, with a reticence that is somehow not distancing, as if it contains its own apology, establishing a kind of disinterested neutrality. We shake hands, a weak, brief motion, and before I can sit, at Enrique's urging, on the edge of the bed, Carlos is already gazing through the ceiling at stars years distant.

As Enrique busies himself laying out the meal—unwrapping the sausage, slicing the apples with a pocket knife, hooking the bottle caps on the edge of the metal bed-frame and banging on them with the flat of his palm, the beer fizzing and flowing out from beneath the partially twisted caps—I wonder at the contrast between the two friends: the one dark and strong with full, expressive lips; the other fair and fragile, with thin, bloodless lips that fade inconspicuously into his face; Enrique overflowing with a vitality that works at the food with a certain relish; Carlos languishing flaccidly, and this with effort, the blue of his eyes paled almost to extinction. Had I just seen them on the street, without contact, I would have thought Carlos British, undernourished and adrift. Enrique, Gypsy-like, I would have instinctively mistrusted.

And yet it is Enrique who, with a distracted fussiness that is like warmth, now hands me half an apple and a thick slice of sausage, who wipes the spilled beer from the bottle before passing it to me.

"Are you guys travelling?" I automatically take in Carlos with my gaze although I know my words to be incomprehensible to him.

"Yes, but not for pleasure." Enrique places a beer in Carlos's hand, practically wrapping his fingers around the bottle. "We are looking for work." He hoists himself onto the neighboring bed, crosses his legs, and slips a piece of sausage into his mouth. He speaks as he chews. "There is much disemployment in Spain now."

"Unemployment."

"Unemployment, pardon me. My English is not perfect. I could not stay in London as long as I had wished. Money was the problem. As always."

"You ran out of money?"

"My father died, very suddenly. He left many debts. The lawyers got rich. And my family passed from not very rich to not very poor."

"So you had to leave England."

"My mother has five other children, all younger than I. She needed help to support them." He breaks his slice of apple into two and pops a half into his mouth. "But there are no jobs in Spain now."

Carlos, still reclining, sipping slowly at his beer, ignoring his food, speaks rapid Spanish to Enrique. Enrique replies, as rapidly, and breaks out into a raucous laugh punctuated with cries of "Eyyy, Carlos! Eyyy, Carlos!"

To my surprise I recognize the elements. The laughter a bit forced, the tone teasing yet aimed, clearly, at reassurance. Still laughing, Enrique says to me, "Carlos worries. He was reminding me that we must go to the train station tonight."

"Are you leaving?" It surprises me that I find the thought distressing. People coming, people going. It all ceased, after a while, making any impression. Encounters, like everything else on this trip, are little more than brushes with vapor.

"Not this evening, no. There are no trains, and we need to rest. No, we are going in search of others like us. It is sometimes the best way to find out where the jobs are."

"What kind of jobs are you looking for?" Relief comes as a physical sensation, a deflation of the sudden tension.

"Picking grapes."

"Can you make money doing that?"

"Some. A little. We keep what we need in order to continue, the rest we send to our families. It isn't much but it is better than nothing."

"And when there are no more grapes?"

"We'll see. We will worry about that later." He turns to Carlos and they converse in Spanish, the voices retaining their particular cadences: Enrique's urgent with a suppressed energy, Carlos's a slowly rumbling whisper from between stretched, drained lips.

I finish my apple and take a bite from the sausage, a red spicy meat, solidly packed, that floods my mouth with a warm oil. As Enrique and Carlos speak, building around themselves the spare exclusivity engineered by a private conversation in a language not possessed by the others around, I empty my mind, eyes flitting around the room. Blue walls, bared lightbulbs throwing shadows into the corners, beds made and unmade. My ears enjoy the soft, rolling music of their conversation, the sounds of the language, by themselves, a poetic device. Their voices alternate, the sharp urgency of Enrique followed by the meditative sleepiness of Carlos. At times their voices run into each other, interrupting, sounds dodging and skipping, energetically seeking supremacy, Carlos's whisper spurting into the gaps of Enrique's urgency then retreating before its growing timbre, lapsing into a silence that is a tensed expectation.

With the sounds of their conversation in the background, my mind goes back to the beginning, to the three of us, John, Grady, and me, backpacked, booted, and moneybelted, abandoning university midway, seduced by thoughts of Europe, attracted by the romance of a greater acquaintance with the past. John, the engineer doubtful of his vocation, more attracted to his guitar than to structural theories; Grady, bored with political science, unable to see importance in anything; and me, James, growing insensitive to the finest of fiction, distanced, unexpectedly, from the printed page.

Much has changed in the six months since our late, cramped charter flight. John was left behind in London, our first stop, for treatment of a disease picked up from a young prostitute. In Amsterdam, Grady floated off to the ingested comforts of outer space, deciding quickly that he had found something of importance. And I continued on alone to the museums, the churches, the streets grim with the dirt and dried blood of history. When the time came, later, to link up, Grady failed to arrive and John, changed, had already inserted himself into another group.

Where was the mistake? I wonder. Was it in the departure itself? Or did it come later, in the damp alleys of Venice or the street of prostitutes—a Hades more substantial in the flesh—in Frankfurt? Or was there even a mistake? From where this emptiness and boredom alleviated only by a quick irritation? It came rapidly to John, and he sought relief and distraction in bartered sex; Grady, I feel, had always borne it within him, and he found his outlet in the tax-subsidized concoctions of a drug bar. I remember with distress Grady's fascination with the discarded syringes that littered the back streets of Amsterdam. It was a fascination I could not and still cannot understand. In our little Ontario town, swollen in August by summer residents, anything could be bought, alleys could be found littered with discarded paraphernalia. Amsterdam was little more than a larger, more extended version of our little town, a passage of adolescence, institutionalized, converted into a way of life.

The conversation ends and the sudden silence brings me back to the room: the lights, the walls, the beds, Enrique sitting crosslegged, Carlos lying limp.

Enrique says, "We should go to the train station. Would you like to come with us?" After the Spanish, the English sounds duller, cooler, the British accent distant and controlled.

"Has it stopped raining?"

Enrique speaks to Carlos in Spanish and, with effort, he hoists himself onto his left elbow and peers out through the window above him into the perfect darkness of the night. Finally, rolling over and sitting up, he says, "No rrain."

The street is still wet, the trees dark and heavy with dripping

leaves, the cobbled pavement black and rutted like the back
of a great, wet alligator. The lights that shine from buildings—
few, mere hints of red or white sparkle here and there, the
retreat of the town complete—fail to light the darkness, seem
rather to emphasize its depth and the impenetrability of the
shutters and doors that exclude so totally the outside world.

We walk in silence down the middle of the street, Enrique
and I with hands stuffed into our jeans, Carlos, thin and tall,
seemingly huddled into himself, head almost crouching between hunched shoulders.

I enjoy the darkness and its blanketing hush. It offers a
freedom, a retreat from the rush that has caught me up in the
past months. See this, see that. Do this, do that. Here, in this
little French town late in the evening, there is nothing to see,
nothing to do. It is as if I owe nothing, own nothing, feel
obligation to no one, not even to myself. And as I relish the
sense of lightness, I feel a new vein of energy working itself
into me. My eyes fall to my boots and I think I can almost see
the new energy moving them along, marching in leisurely
time with the battered shoes of Carlos and Enrique. I breathe
deeply of the moist air and think with pleasure that, tonight,
with a mind suddenly unencumbered, I will sleep well.

We come to the end of the street, to the square I saw
earlier this evening. As before, only the bar—from the distance, empty—and the hotel offer signs of life. The rest of
the buildings and the monument in the middle have been
absorbed by the dark so that the two snatches of light, glaring
without reach, are like clutches of glow tossed into a nocturnal
countryside emptiness.

We pause at the edge of the square, looking, examining the
totality that seems to rock us, to unhinge our sense of balance.
Carlos mumbles to Enrique, who thinks for a moment then
mumbles in reply. It is a worried exchange, quietly spoken,
desperation not far beneath the surface, a conversation of the

night and the quiet. Then they step together into the square.

I make to follow them but a hesitation, abrupt and un-expected, holds me back. I am, I notice, suddenly nervous. My hands, relaxing in the pockets of my jeans, go cold with sweat. The muscles in my upper back hunch and tense.

Enrique turns and calls, "James, come on. You are dream-ing?"

I step forward towards them, thighs reluctant. They wait for me, then take up once more their leisurely pace into the darkened, deserted square.

I examine my nervousness and find questions: Why, of all the people in the hostel, did they choose me to share their meal? Why me to invite for a walk far from the company of others? My hand goes uncomfortably to my moneybelt. They are moneyless Spaniards with impoverished families back in Spain. I am a Canadian, not rich but not poor, travelling to my fill in Europe. I begin to see a kind of fateful logic con-structing itself around us all, and a vision comes to me of falling, slowly, with pain and confusion, into the darkness. I wish a car would come squealing at us, its whine and its lights cracking the hardening cocoon.

The night air, undisturbed, no longer seems merely fresh, the dampness penetrating now, coating my bones with a chilled moisture. An uncontrollable trembling seizes my right arm.

We leave the pulsing darkness of the square and take the road, almost as dark, to the train station. This is relief, but of the slightest degree. My distrust of my companions, un-warranted, I know, a distrust that I am, at the same time, ashamed of, has grown beyond the range of my logic. As I watch my boots, left, right, moving reluctantly forward over the cobblestones, I search for a reason to return to the hostel. But another vision, of a swift knife and a falling into the shadows, presses itself in on me, spurts of panic, barely controlled, like surging lava restrained by the frailest of membranes, thrusting insistently at the outward calm I am still, somehow, able to maintain.

On we walk, in silence still, the only sound the soft fall of our shoes on the street.

Carlos lights a cigarette, the head of the match rasping into flame, and for a moment in the flickering light everything gleams, his face a floating spectre.

Darkness comes again and with it the acrid, almost acidic smoke of the cheap tobacco. Enrique mumbles and Carlos passes him the cigarette. He pulls heavily on it so that a red glow casts itself onto his face, the features—the full nose, the deeply furrowed brow—thickening to what strikes me as near-caricature.

Soon, sooner than I expect, just ahead at a bend in the road stands the train station, dully lit by lamps embedded at intervals into its walls. It looks shuttered and abandoned, no one to be seen. Enrique and Carlos speak quietly, anxiously, to each other and pick up the pace.

At the barricaded main door of the station the sense of desertion is even greater. I feel the quiet desperation that has seized Enrique and Carlos: if there is no one to ask about jobs, what will they do tomorrow morning? Where will they go?

We stand for a moment in the weak light of a lamp, peering into the darkness. Then, without a word, Enrique hurries forward and disappears into the obscurity of an unlit corner.

Carlos, hunched and withdrawn, hands stuck into the pockets of his jeans, cigarette dangling from between his lips, stares away into the night. I suddenly feel sorry for him. He is like an overgrown boy with resources inadequate to the situation, resented, in which he finds himself. I want to reassure him, to offer a word of encouragement, to squeeze his shoulder with the message that the world is not as empty, as rejecting, as it must seem at this moment.

But Carlos, almost as if sensing my thoughts, steps away, claiming for himself a greater space.

I wonder where Enrique has gone and move cautiously towards the corner. My nervousness, I note, has of itself disappeared. In the grip of the shadow the darkness lessens. I make out human forms silhouetted against the greater night behind them, two people sitting huddled on a bench under what I guess to be a blanket, another—Enrique—leaning over them, supporting himself with an outstretched arm against the wall of the station. They are talking quietly, in whispers less conspiratorial than intimate, with affection, as if they know each other.

Enrique offers cigarettes, strikes a match, and in the weak glow of the leaping flame two female faces—young, weary, each framed by straight, black hair—hungrily reach out their cigarettes. Then the light is gone and all that remains are two glowing ends floating, bobbing, before faces once more effaced.

Enrique says, "Buenas noches, adios," and his voice, louder now, is generous with warmth. He turns and walks towards me with energetic steps, takes my arm familiarly, and calls to Carlos. "Let's go," he says.

"Do you know them?" I ask, looking one last time into the darkened corner.

"No, we only just met."

"The way you were with them, as if you knew them."

"They have very little money. They must spend the night here. They are taking a train early in the morning. To jobs. So will we." He tells Carlos the news and Carlos, for the first time this evening, laughs, even becomes expansive, but still with a reserve.

Carlos talks all the way back to the hostel. Enrique, exuding energy, hums a tune to himself, laughing occasionally at something Carlos has said, the sound of his voice, authoritative, confident, at ease, ringing into the empty night, beating back the darkness, filling the blackened square, running along the street ahead of us, into the alleys and shuttered doorways. He speaks with relish of life in London, of the women he has known, the women he has loved. And he laughs, a sound unrestrained, a joy unbridled. I recognize the laughter as the sound of a freedom I have never known, an internal unshackling, and I engage the sounds, savor them, marvel at them. And I know that I want to have for myself that sense, that sense of life suddenly electrified.

When we get back to the hostel the concierge is asleep, his head on the counter. He stirs only slightly as we make our way up the stairs to the rooms.

We stop outside the door to my room. "Will we meet in the morning?" I ask.

"We must leave very early," Enrique replies. "Before dawn."

"In that case, good luck. And thank you." I put out my hand.

Carlos shakes it briefly and pulls back. He is anxious to get to bed.

Enrique wraps my hand in both of his, a solid grasp, enveloping. "Maybe one day," he says. "In Canada."

"You never know. Maybe." I know it to be a lie, as does Enrique, but a satisfactory lie. Images, incomplete and fragmentary, a trip of torn edges. But this one image, of life momentarily peaked, will remain with me, will form of itself a glittering whole, will give value to an experience until now unsatisfactory.

Enrique claps me once on the shoulder and then they hurry down the corridor to their room.

As I enter my room, darkened, the other bunks occupied with bodies wrapped in white, I think: I'd like to go with them. But I know the urge to be absurd.

I undress, get into bed, and pull the sheet up to my neck.

From the far end of the room a voice whispers, "Too bloody good, that's what *they* think they are." The tone is one of hurt, of complaint.

Another voice replies, "All talk and no action. Bloody frustrating."

"Goddam Frenchwomen. This town's a dump anyway."

I laugh quietly. The voices go silent. And in the moments before I fall asleep I contemplate with more relish than regret the security that is mine.

CHRISTMAS
LUNCH

The little house was on a dingy street just off Bathurst and I was appalled at the thought of having Christmas lunch here, in this area through which I hurried late every Thursday night after doing my wash at the laundromat. The hosts were strangers and I had allowed my friend to drag me along only because I had nowhere else to go, nothing else to do, and it seemed wrong to spend all of a blustery Christmas day in a cold room with only a book for company.

The door—paint peeling and the wood visibly damp—was opened by a pot-bellied, middle-aged man wearing a white T-shirt and brown polyester pants, the kind which, at the merest hint of humidity, chafed the skin and gave a general feeling of discomfort.

"Merry Christmas," he said, taking my friend's hand. "Come in. Give me your coats."

My friend introduced me.

"From Trinidad too?" Raj, the host, inquired.

"Yes."

He had the look of a cane-cutter, gaunt of face but corpulent lower down. His handshake was shy and he looked strangely misplaced. He draped our damp coats over his arm and offered a drink.

My friend took a soft drink. "My stomach can't take anything hard, man. Still messed up."

"And you?" Raj nodded at me.

"Whatever you have," I said, still contemplating flight. "Rum and Coke?"

"Okay. Have a seat." He disappeared through a door from which flowed the almost viscous smell of sizzling curry and burnt garlic.

My friend introduced me to the others in the room. There, lounging barefooted on the floor next to the stereo, was side-burned Moses. Next to him, in an easy chair amateurishly covered in red vinyl, sat his wife, Pulmatee, a tiny woman of such anonymous aspect that she spent the entire afternoon disappearing into the background. On the red couch which squatted at right angles to Pulmatee's chair were the host's wife, Rani—a dour-faced woman who nodded at me and wrung her hands dry on a rag—and a young girl, a cousin of Rani's, who wiped a scowl from her face and flashed two prominent gold teeth at me.

The silence in the room was charged. It was clear that our arrival had interrupted a family dispute.

Rani, dabbing at her hands with the rag, said to Moses, "Anyway, is his business if he want to invite her. Let him feed her since he's the one who feeling sorry for her."

Moses shrugged and sipped his sweating beer.

Raj brought the drinks and, muttering, made me sit on the couch, scrunched between the perspiring Rani and the cold metal frame.

I thanked him and he mumbled an embarrassed "You're welcome", as if he had little occasion to say the words and was out of practice.

I lit a cigarette and Rani, heaving herself up with a grunt, ran to bring me an ashtray.

"Nothing like Trinidad hospitality at Christmas time, eh

boy? Especially when you away from home." Moses flashed his white teeth and, unaware that he'd been addressing me, I got only an aftertaste of possibly unintentional sarcasm.

"Right," I said, fiddling with the cigarette, "nothing like it."

My friend said, "How the job going, Moses boy?"

Moses said, "Is not easy, man. You work from morning till night, you break your back, and these people never happy."

My friend said, "They don't know how to take it easy, you see, Moses. Everything for them is work, work, work. And the work never finish. I tell you, not only woman's work never done, eh. Back home, if you didn't want to work, you didn't work and that was that. But here . . . how you could be happy living like this day in day out, eh? Tell me."

Moses couldn't tell him. They shook their heads sorrowfully.

I looked around the room, sensing a certain chaos, a disorder of things, that made me uncomfortable. In one corner stood a home-made stand, two wooden orange crates nailed together and painted a leery oak; on top of this had been placed a gaudy statuette of a woman, breasts exposed by the casual draping of her robe, entwined in plastic vines and topped by an artificial rose. In the opposite corner slouched a small tinsel Christmas tree which had seen several joyous seasons too many. Around its base was a plastic nativity scene: blue Mary, red Joseph, purple Jesus, green cow, and orange donkey. A faded red carpet covered the floor. The green walls had been haphazardly decorated with Christmas cards, some salvaged from past years, and incongruous framed postcards of the Hindu religious hierarchy. It was as if decoration meant less beautifying than simply filling up space, a dash of color here and there.

Moses was still explaining to my friend why he found life in Toronto so terribly difficult when the front door opened and a fat woman of about twenty-six with pale, blotchy skin sauntered in singing at the top of her voice. All eyes fixed on her and, surprised, she broke off the song. "Why isn't anyone dancing?" she asked.

Moses, staring her in the eyes, grinned. "We waiting for you to start, Ann. Where your husband?"

"He's getting ready to go to his parents for dinner."

"You not going?"

She shook her stringy brown hair. "No, I don't want to see his parents." She spoke in a voice which told of an ongoing bitterness, a voice which asserted fact and discouraged further questions.

Rani and her cousin sighed pointedly and went into the kitchen.

I nodded at Ann.

"What's your name?" she asked in a manner so familiar it was unsettling.

I told her and she gazed momentarily at me, as if trying to read my mind. Her eyes were tiny, and so dark it was as if they reaped an extra measure of shadow from the world. The circles under her eyes might not have been bags; they had the appearance of carefully applied mascara, but it was their very neatness that gave them away. The rest of her—from her unwashed hair to her scraggy silver evening shoes—was so rumpled, her rouge applied in so slapdash a manner, that the darkness under her eyes couldn't have been artificial: it was more instructive than an amused glance allowed.

She dropped herself onto the couch and crossed her legs, striking a masculine pose. Her powder-blue slacks gathered in folds of fat at her thighs and her unclean feet, encased in the thick straps of the evening shoes, wriggled to some private rhythm.

"What work you does do, Ann?" Moses asked in a leading voice.

"None," she replied. "I don't want any man to be my boss.

Except my husband. If I have to go to work, I'll go into the oldest business. Prostitution. Because any other job is a kind of prostitution. You're still selling your body and what it can do."

"You want to work for me?" Moses asked mischievously.

Raj, standing next to him, blushed, embarrassed.

Ann, emotionless, said, "My husband knows some pimps who can break you in two." She sucked her teeth and looked away. Unexpectedly she said, "I'm from Newfoundland. I dream of going back there."

It was a strange declaration, offered almost in confession. It hung limply in the air; not even Moses knew what to do with it.

"You have any brothers or sisters?" Moses said at last.

Ann brightened visibly. "Eight brothers and seven sisters," she said proudly.

There were gasps of incredulity.

Moses said, "All-you never hear about birth control or what?"

"Newfoundland women don't like contraceptives, they think they're unnatural. And out there there's—or at least, there wasn't—no TV or cinema or anything. Nothing. All you could do in the evening was screw." She erupted into raucous laughter.

My friend snickered, embarrassed. Raj pretended to examine the stereo. Moses guffawed. I lit another cigarette. Rani and her cousin came to the door and listened; they were grinning.

"I mean, you wouldn't believe how beautiful it is," Ann continued, striking a match for her cigarette. "I love the country. Hunting. Fishing. When you pull in your lobster traps, you have fresh lobster. You don't have to buy anything. Everything's free. It's not like in this concrete hell full of lost souls."

The sudden bitterness took us by surprise. Again there was

a silence, the shuffling of feet, the clearing of a throat.

Moses said, "But it must be a hard life out there, not so?"

"No, it's not," Ann said softly, studying her fingers which lay interlaced on her lap. "It's beautiful. Imagine, getting up at ten, eleven o'clock in the morning, sleeping as late as you want, then going out to cut one or two cords of wood for your stove, a wood stove, of course. I dream of going back there. I hate this place. . . ." Her eyes filled with tears.

"Why you come here then?" Moses demanded, brushing aside Raj's restraining arm.

Ann passed her white knuckles across her eyes. "When I was fourteen, my parents tried to make me marry my uncle's son. I ran away."

"They wanted you to marry your first cousin?"

She nodded, and a tear dripped from the tip of her nose. "Oh God, I want to go back," she moaned. "I hate living in Toronto. Everybody's so cold, nobody cares about you."

"I care about you," Moses smirked.

"Whenever I think I'm getting adjusted to the place, something happens to make me sad again."

"Like what?"

"Like my husband brings somebody home," she sniffled.

"Another woman?"

"No. I have to entertain his friends." Then she shook her head, signalling she'd say no more. She said, "I've got to feed my baby," and rushed out the door.

"She lives upstairs," Moses said to my friend.

Rani wordlessly reached for the cigarette Ann had abandoned in the ashtray and stubbed it out. Rani was not a smoker and the crushed cigarette continued to smolder.

Raj said, "Moses, you shouldn't . . ."

"Oh Gawd, Raj man, just having a little fun, is all."

My friend, leaning against the wall, grunted non-committally. We exchanged glances; I couldn't read his face.

"I know," Raj whispered, "but don't push she too hard, she have a lot of troubles."

Moses laughed. "Like she giving you something or what, boy? How you sticking up so for she, eh? Ey, Rani, keep your eye on Ann and your husband, you hear, girl?"

Rani sucked her teeth, gave him a harsh look, and disappeared once more into the kitchen. Raj shook his head and looked at Pulmatee. Pulmatee avoided his eyes; she was less unmoved than removed.

"Anybody want a beer?" Moses asked, standing and dusting the seat of his trousers.

"Come and eat," Rani called from the kitchen. "It getting late."

It would have been a good time to leave and I was about to ask Raj for my coat when he took me roughly by the arm and half pulled, half led, me into the kitchen.

It was a large room, three times the size of the living room, with a large window looking out onto the snowed-in backyard. There were few cupboards and the appliances—stove, fridge, both dappled with rust—appeared to have been inserted at random. Next to the fridge was an open closet in which several coats were hanging: a coat closet in the kitchen? Then I understood: in some inexplicable way, the rooms had switched purposes, the house had switched sides: what had once been the front was now the back, and vice versa.

The air, warm and damp, smelled strongly of curry, garlic, and burnt oil. Water condensed on my skin and a drop of perspiration tickled down my chest.

The table, standing in the middle of so spacious a room, seemed covered in a solitude strangely heightened by the knives and forks and plates that had been placed neatly in front of each chair. Raj directed me to a seat. I said, "Thank you," and this time he elected not to reply; he simply nodded, but still shyly.

When we were seated—Moses, muttering, managed to introduce a note of confusion into even so simple an act— Rani's cousin placed a platter of hot roti on the table. Then she giggled, covering her mouth with her hands. Moses, laughing, pointed to the platter: "That's a hot one, boy." Raj and my friend also laughed, as did Rani and, with restraint, Pulmatee. I didn't understand. Moses explained: "Look at the picture on the tablecloth." I saw an apple tree, a nude man retaining modesty with a leaf, a nude woman, breasts hidden by the hot platter, holding a half-eaten apple in her hand: a jaded Garden of Eden. "A real hot one," Moses giggled, creating the sound of someone choking.

Rani brought me a plate of curried chicken. She smiled the sugary smile of a grandmother and said, "We have plenty, so just ask if you want more, okay? Don't be shy."

The others had already started eating. No one spoke and for a long time the only sounds were those of violent mastication and heavy breathing, as if the meal were a tedious chore. Pulmatee, Rani, and her cousin stood in front of the stove, looking at us eat and talking lowly to each other. I concentrated on my food, blocking out Raj's slurping and—after having witnessed the first—blinding myself to the periodic splashes of saliva from Moses' yawning munches.

I thought about Ann, wondering about the performance we had witnessed, about her husband and her baby, and the horrors of her life which I could in no way conjure up. I wondered how long she'd lived in Toronto: she spoke with no accent. I would never have guessed she was from Newfoundland.

As if willed, the front door scraped open and Ann's voice, powerful yet weak and painfully theatrical, boomed into the kitchen: " 'Bye, darling. Love you. *Love you*."

Moses sneered, "He's a Chink."

Rani and her cousin cleared the dishes away. Raj belched

three times and rubbed his stomach. We returned to the living room. It was the women's turn to eat and we left the kitchen to them.

Ann was still at the open door, waving to her husband. Moses gave me a look which said that it was all for our benefit, a role conceived in mockery and executed in pantomime. Hearing us, she turned around and closed the door.

Moses howled: the zipper of her slacks was undone.

Ann, nonplussed, said, "Oh, how'd that happen?" She took hold of either side of the opening and, pretending to free the stuck pull, parted the zipper, revealing a pink panty. "Ooooh," she said in feigned horror.

Moses, grinning, offered to help. She accepted. He tugged gently at the zipper, taking his time, and after a few seconds of struggle pulled it up.

"Thank you very much," Ann said airily.

"You're welcome," Moses replied.

Ann indicated a wet spot on her T-shirt. "I have to change, the baby puked on me."

Raj, opening a door which had remained shut until now, said, "You can change in the bedroom, Ann."

Moses said, "Need more help, Ann?"

"Not this time, thanks." She looked offended.

Raj said, "The baby okay alone up there?"

"Yes, I can hear him if he cries." She closed the bedroom door behind her.

My friend laughed and said to Moses, "You better wash your hands quick, boy. You never know what she have inside them pants."

Rani came into the living room. "And you better throw away that glass you drinking from," she giggled.

Raj laughed weakly. I lit a cigarette.

Ann came out of the bedroom and headed for the kitchen. Moses stopped her and indicated the drawing of a rum bottle on her clean T-shirt. "Is the rum good?" he asked.

She looked puzzled and then said with a naive twitter, "Yes, very."

"Let me see," he said.

"It's good." Her voice hardened: she was losing control of the situation.

Moses said, "I want to feel it."

"No, I'm married."

"So what? I'm married too."

"You don't know my husband. If you knew him, then you could." She gave a hollow laugh and tried to walk past him. He seized her wrist. Without a word she slapped his hand and he released her. Looking hurt and irritated, she hurried into the kitchen.

Raj said, "Cool it, Moses. She gets angry sometimes. You harassing her too much."

Moses guffawed. "Like she really giving you something or what? What is it? You like big breasts? Where you does do it, up there or down here?"

"Oh shit, Moses." Raj gestured helplessly.

Suddenly Ann hurried out of the kitchen, a smile on her lips and tears in her eyes. She strode to the door and left the flat.

This time she didn't return.

I had another rum and Coke and then, faking illness, fled the house. A sense of dereliction arched through my head and switches of tension twitched down my back.

As I hurried away through the falling snow, I glanced back at the house with its walls of mismatched red brick and collapsing porch. Ann's flat on the second floor was in darkness. In the living-room window of Raj's flat, I saw Pulmatee. She was looking through the window at the snow. She looked sad.

MAN AS PLAYTHING, LIFE AS MOCKERY

It had rained earlier that morning. Then a wind had arisen and driven away the clouds that had made a rumpled grey sweater of the morning sky. Aspect changed dramatically: the wind, cold and with a bite, brought in its own cloud, low, white, rapid with the urgency of a miracle sky. There was a play of light and shadow that altered the view more rapidly than the eye could seize it. It was like viewing, in rapid succession, the positive and negative of the same photograph: the vision was tricked, the substantial lost, so that even the angular concrete of the airport carpark across the way was emptied, became unreal.

His stance, feet apart, hands clasped behind his back, was casual. It was an attitude struck, a pose. Only the fingers could give him away: even intertwined, they were in motion, playing with one another, rubbing at one another, dissipating energy in small spurts, like dust. They held a scrap of paper that might have been a large theatre ticket, or a grocery list. But a closer glance revealed more history, its creases and lines filled in with the luminous brown that comes not from dirt but from years of handling.

He unclasped his hands, taking the paper in his right palm.

He raised it but didn't look at it immediately. A lengthy darkening of the outside view caused his reflection to be etched in the glass wall in front of him and for a moment he studied his face: square, pudgy, with inexpressive eyes caught in the middle of thick, circular spectacle frames, hair so thinned that in the muted light he looked bald. Then his body: a raincoat of unarresting cut, an impression of bulk compressed onto a small frame, a sturdiness that surprised him.

The sun flashed suddenly and his image was effaced. Outside, a man in white coveralls, carrying a broom and a garbage bag, shuffled by chasing a wayward paper cup. The absurd figure, a tragi-comedy on legs, irritated him. He turned his lips down, deepening the hollows that defined his cheeks, and finally, as if in anger, looked at the paper in his hand.

It was a photograph, the outlines of black, white, and grey blurring through time into a desperate fuzziness, so that there was no distinction, no sharpness to the image, like an ink drawing on cheap paper. But his memory sharpened the lines, defined the contours, and to his practised eye a youthful female face came clear. Her smile was thin, not hesitant but threadbare, a gesture, he could tell, summoned for the camera from a carefully rationed reserve.

The photograph produced no effect in him. It had become too familiar over the years and he searched it now only for the way things might have gone: how the cheeks might have sagged, the eyes bagged, the forehead crinkled. But the effort was beyond him. The image was too static, had replaced the vivid elasticity of memory so that the face was no longer a face but a frozen combination of features.

The woman, his wife, had almost ceased to be real.

He slipped the photograph into his coat pocket, half-turning to glance at the arrival monitor that hung from the far wall behind him. There had been a change: the letters ARR now commented on her flight number.

Something within him jumped.

It was not that he had hoped to avoid memory. That would have required an effort beyond his resources.

And he had recognized that, for him, it could never be myth. The transformation would have depleted him, would have used him up; and that depletion, that sense of a life gone by, would have been bequeathed to their daughter, an unfair inheritance. So that what for him could never be myth had, for their daughter, quickly taken on atmosphere. She was denied perspective, save for that of the novel. He saw this as strength: it was a way of moving forward.

She was now twenty-seven. Then she had been five.

He was now fifty-four. Then he had been thirty-two.

Twenty-two years: it was a lifetime.

Still, he remembered. The rain, the mud turning the night into a glutinous surge: the thunder of heavy guns, seeming always close, gouging then dulling the senses; the banks of black smoke for days on end defining the sun into a circle of red-hot metal; the corpses and pieces of corpses backing up in the ditches by night, rotting in the ditches by day; and the flow of people—in front, beside, behind—men, women, children, faces blank with misery, possessions abandoned, moving without urgency, like people stripped of all but the automatic, offered nothing now but a knowledge of loss and a numbing sense of violation, victims of a mass rape. Even terror, then, had been beyond them.

And yet no memory was as vivid as the warmth that had filled his hand, that had pressed limply against his chest, exuding exhaustion.

He had shielded his daughter from nothing. She saw, as he did, the severed head of a neighbor lying beside the road; had helped him fight off the dogs driven crazy by hunger; had foraged for roots in soil long dredged; had watched, with him in a torpor, as a mother prepared to carve her husband's body so her children, hollow-eyed approximations of themselves, could eat.

He was grateful that none of this had remained with her. She recalled only playing with sand, playing with dogs, faces and movement; memories edited of carnage.

He himself had lost none of it. But he had retained too the memory of her warmth, a warmth that held its own terror, of night, of contemplated infanticide, of horror of his own hands, of utter senselessness. And yet, in an unfathomable way, it was a positive memory.

It had been a grey, violent time, a time in which the rules of human life had been usurped by human madness, an experience of images that formed no whole, that took no shape, an experience without parentheses. It was history in the making, episodic, he and his daughter particles insignificant in the upheaval of event. None of the usual prejudices applied. It was an extraordinary time, requiring extraordinary responses, eliciting extraordinary ends. The centre had been lost, all had become unpredictable.

So they had trudged, father and daughter, across the bridge of black iron that offered an unrelieving safety, separated from the wife, the mother, by hundreds, by thousands of miles of chaos, just another attenuated refugee family among countless other attenuated refugee families, misery blending them into a whole for the news photographers who scurried around, absorbed, flashbulbs popping.

Attenuated: by profession, by civil war. The wounded needed a doctor; his right hand was bulbous with pus from a wound by an infected scalpel. His wife, a surgeon more skilful than he, went off into the night with her bundle of instruments. He knew the horrors that awaited her: amputations without anaesthetic, stomachs that spilled their contents, bodies with more rips than pores, blood less precious than water. The images, red, gleaming, startling in their intensity, had come to him through a feverish haze as he watched her retreating back, her bundle. He knew he had felt pain; he had retained the knowledge of it. Pain, he had learnt, could not be a memory; the mind resisted, and only the absence of well-being could be submitted to review, in a withdrawn, intellectual way.

Hours, days, weeks: he didn't know how much time passed. Night and day switched places, and back again. His wife didn't return. He didn't know where she had gone, which of the many groups she had left with. Heavy artillery blended dusk with dawn as the fight closed in. Still she didn't return. And when the guns caused their town to split in two, spilling its guts like an overripe corpse, he fled with his daughter, following the tide.

No one talked of safety. No one talked of direction. No one talked. They trudged, through a landscape overturned.

He remembered the first evening of safety, a night spent in a churchyard, in a rain that couldn't cleanse. The church had been crowded, the pews, the altar, the corners disappearing under black, heaving bundles of sighs. He had found a spot against an outside wall, had sat, his back to the wall, his raised knees covered by a piece of cardboard, his daughter asleep on the ground under the cardboard.

Sleep had eluded him on that night: around him thin chests collapsing in an oblique light, apparitions of limp bodies, arms, legs dangling, being carted away by shadowed figures. A night of death in mime.

Just before dawn, the man lying next to him—a stranger of familiar clothes and unfamiliar dialect—very quietly pressed a six-inch knife into his own side, up to the wooden hilt and then beyond. He made no sound; there was little blood. He sighed as if in satisfaction and a thin trickle of red crept from the left corner of his mouth, slashed rapidly down across his cheek, like a wound opening itself.

He had watched, had made no attempt to interfere, had offered a mute compassion which, he knew, denied his profession. It had been a private act, silent, relieving, like the swallowing of a pill.

He had watched as the rain eased, then stopped, and the sun, creating steam, sliced more deeply into the churchyard, the ground black with people stirring tentatively, in disbelief of life.

His neighbor, drained, already shrunken, one hand still clutching what was left of the knife hilt, attracted no attention.

Safety. It provided no answers. They had to be made.

He remembered, but no longer really cared to, the trek through the city solidified with refugees in search of further flight. Papers, stamps, signatures; documents newly printed, crackling with the fresh and the official he could have believed no longer existed; tiny pleasures that surprised him, like being asked to sign his name and discovering that once more, in some miraculous way, it counted for something beyond the simplest of identification. He was asked for his medical papers. He didn't have them. But he was a doctor, he had a profession. It struck him as extraordinary, and he wondered, but only for a moment, that he could have watched with equanimity the suicide of his churchyard neighbor. That this could be construed as a denial of his profession seemed to him now only a passing fancy.

He managed, through contacts, to get the necessary papers. Everything could be managed somehow, even from a country still convulsed against itself—everything but his wife. Paper, if not destroyed, stayed put, could be traced, retrieved; but a person moved, was driven by spasm beyond human control like a piece of meat moving through intestine. Her rescue was the one thing he couldn't manage. She was too distant, out of his reach.

Wait, they said, wait for the war to end.

Wait for things to settle down. Settle yourself first.

Here's your visa. Take your daughter. Go. Wait.

One man, an official in a white shirt with sleeves rolled stylishly, incongruously, to his elbow, meaning to be kind but in the hurried way survival demanded, said, "You've lost everything. You've lost your wife. Count her for dead. Take your daughter and go."

And he had thought: Yes.

So he had emigrated, got himself accredited, begun to build a base in a land alien to him. Here, the war was remote, a small item on the world-news page of the local newspaper. Then the war ended and the land he had left, quickly grown alien, withdrew into itself, became hermetic. It sealed his wife in.

He noted the withdrawal with calm. He was building his base. Much of the period he recalled only through a haze, as of fatigue, and it was this eviscerating effort that now offered itself as myth to him. His wife, the memory of her, began to evade him and after a while—he didn't know how long; time revealed its man-made fragility, divested itself of context—he stopped the unconscious calculation of time's breach. It had become pointless in every way.

His daughter grew quickly and, in a way that he found inexplicable, began to slip from his grasp. She was, he realized one evening, no longer an asexual being. She was becoming aware of differences, and his clumsiness only increased her apprehension. He was a doctor, he knew the technical details. But how to explain them to his daughter? For a time, he thought of his wife, as of a stranger, with blame. And then he thought of her no more.

Back then, the city which had become his had been grey and stolid. Nothing sparkled. The foreign was distrusted. People kept to themselves. They worked and, afterwards, retreated to family, to a privacy that was itself hermetic.

So it surprised him when, at the hospital, Marya began seeking him out to talk: about her flight from Soviet armies at the end of the war, about the family she had had to abandon, about the man who had brought her here then discarded her for a middle-aged artist who promised mothering and an Oedipal sexuality. She went, from the first, to the heart of the personal.

No reply came to him; he felt a sense of caution, a wariness. He asked, with unmerited rudeness, why she had singled him out.

It was, she said, because she recognized in him someone who might understand: they shared a quality, a quality of absorption. In the grey city, it marked him.

He remained guarded.

She talked, and as she talked, weaving images, conjuring horror, his reserve broke.

He told her about his flight, his daughter, his problems, his wife, too, but almost incidentally: she was just another element.

Marya offered to help with his daughter.

He hesitated; he was a doctor, she a floor-cleaner. He often passed her in the corridor, he clasping a chart, she a mop, each acknowledging the other only by the merest of pauses, the way a bee might react before an artificial flower, with surprise and a mild confusion. Then, after a night of thought, he accepted her offer.

At first, his daughter resisted, but Marya was persistent. Over time they grew close, Marya, his daughter, and him. And the first time he slept with Marya he was surprised at the warmth and pliability of her flesh. Every day at the hospital he touched patients, but with her his fingers trembled, lost their professional edge, offered a thrill without memory, and culminated in an act that was, to him, startling in its exclusiveness. He discovered in his hands a set of abilities he thought he had lost. It was like a gift.

When, eventually, Marya moved in—she had only two suitcases and a box of assorted papers, pictures, mementoes, knick-knacks that assumed value only to an attenuated life—it seemed the natural thing to do, even, yet especially, in the grey city.

One evening he took a mental step outside his life and gazed back at it with what he thought was objectivity, and he was struck by what a perfect family they made. He thought with a gentle awe: I am happy.

I am happy. Yet, with lucidity, he refused to indulge the thought. It was an attitude not only of the present but also of the future; it reached beyond the graspable to the uncertainties of hope, dream, and expectation. He had seen too much, been through too much, been too much the pawn of the unpredictable. He would deal with what he could see, feel, smell, touch, hear, understand. He rejected the nebulous; he would not speculate.

His life then, to his relief, became uneventful. He worked. He bought a house. Marya became a housewife. His daughter grew. Years passed in an unthinking contentment. His base expanded. His hair thinned, he took on a squat appearance.

When the letter arrived bearing stamps of a familiar style, yet less lyrical than those he'd known, extolling now the virtues of trains and pick-axes, it was as if some unexplored part of his mind had always known it would. He was not surprised. He was angered. Not at his wife: that she was alive after so many years was just a fact. His anger was, rather, at the unpredictable, at those elements that fitted no pattern, that came at random to disrupt. For his wife he felt no sorrow, no pity, a little relief. It had been too long.

Her letter told of hardship and distress, of years of physical labor on the farm to which she had been banished. Her words, unadorned, shorn of stylistic flourish, impressed him as would a relic. The country in which she was caught remained so remote; the letter was like a communication from the distantly dead.

His reply was passionless. He could not pretend. He gave her, briefly, the details of autobiography. He sent her some money, as he would continue to do every month for years even as the country, sealed, convulsed once more unto itself. He didn't mention Marya; there was no point. The two would never meet, they could never affect one another. To mention her might simply have caused an unnecessary distress.

Her letters—fragments of self, in the style of the memo—continued to come, if infrequently. He replied, also in the style of the memo, communication of the flimsiest kind, reminders of existence rather than exchanges of thought.

His daughter grew. Marya continued to live as his wife. The letters, with their intricate, colorful stamps, continued to come. He sent her money, automatically, as if paying the telephone bill; it was no hardship, he saw it not as duty but simply as something that had to be done, like a household chore.

Sometimes he would read the letters to his daughter, translating from the language of which she had, over the years, retained only a few words. The daughter never made a comment, just asked at the end for the stamp. Once she said, "I wish she'd use different stamps, I have lots of these red ones already." He felt her attitude was correct.

After his daughter had moved into her own apartment, he continued ripping out the stamps for her. She never asked to hear the letters. After a while she stopped collecting stamps.

Marya took over the collection.

Of course, in the end, it had all been a matter of choice. "You had no choice": the words formed of themselves in his mind.

But he'd wanted to avoid such preparation. It hinted at

self-defence, at justification of action in a time that had made thought, will, decision absurd.

He sought distraction. A crowd had gathered at the exit of the Customs Hall. In front of the doors—of an opaque glass that revealed the movements of shadowed ghosts—was a small old man in a casual blue and white uniform that lent him little air of authority. He faced the crowd, his blue peaked cap pushed to the back of his head. What was he? A guard? A guide? A porter? He joked with people in the crowd, he looked stern, he stood at attention, he leaned loosely on the wrought-iron rail that marked off the path from the doors; he was like a man who couldn't decide on a function, on an appropriate image, as if, despite himself, he was infected by those around him.

He felt sorry for that little old man in his anonymous uniform: he looked lost.

"You had no choice." The words formed once again, like a chant of response in the church he had attended for a time every Sunday morning twenty-two years before in order to improve his comprehension of English. And the thought pursued itself: "You had no choice. I did. For myself. For our daughter. Should I have refused? What is this loyalty that would deny life? To what does it aspire?" Words. Forming in his mind, they thickened the saliva in his mouth: he wanted to spit. Words now could only confuse.

He had long accepted that he would never again see his wife, and that she was here now affected him only in that it revealed his essential insignificance: man as plaything, life as mockery.

He had had no hesitation in bringing her out, not, he knew, from love but from duty, unquestioned, unquestioning, the way one lays flowers on the grave of a relative dead twenty years. His action carried no moral weight; the automatic never could. It had just been, just was.

He slipped his hands, suddenly cold, into his coat pockets.

Nervousness: he caught it, slipped momentarily into confusion. In that eternity of seconds he lost his name, his memory, his place in the world; his very existence seemed to slip from him. His fingers, grasping at the rough cloth of the coat pocket, seeking stability, brushed the picture. He took hold of it between two fingers, withdrew it.

But then a face that had changed little in its essence, much in its detail, slid past the little old man. His mind took a step backwards so that, observing her advance towards him, he observed himself and, on yet another level—not that of the observer of self but of another, less photographic, more judgmental—he remarked on his composure. She was here, he was greeting her, like an appointed official fulfilling duty.

The second level of his mind persisted, observing her with what the third level thought an interesting dispassion. She wore a plain coat, light grey, with no pretension to style. She was smaller now than before but less soft, with a rigidity in her forehead, her eyes, her mouth. Her skin was bronzed and a single thought—the picture, the past, the present—fused the levels of his mind: she used to be proud of her pure, un-blemished skin, her only vanity.

In her left hand, the arm crooked at the elbow to accommodate a cheap plastic handbag, she held, like an amulet, a blue air-letter, his own, he guessed, probably the last he had sent, the one in which he had told her what to do, what to expect, on arrival at the airport. He supposed she made a touching sight.

With a tremor of panic, he clutched the photograph into his left fist, now gone moist.

Then she was before him, looking somehow tragically short.

They shook hands.

Hers was small, dry, rough, with a strong grip, a hand that no longer knew the syringe, that had been transformed by plough and hoe and shovel. He held it for a few unthinking seconds while her eyes—revealing a reserve, a puzzle, blank yet questioning, signalling a sense of betrayal yet a compassion he couldn't grasp—looked frankly into his own.

He knew, then, that she knew about Marya. And he knew, too, that he felt no guilt, no shame: relief, rather, and an enigmatic gratitude.

She took her hand away with a masculine briskness.

He said, "How are you?" After twenty-two years, in a language so long unused, the words, simplistic, meaningless, without weight, offered a measure of himself: he couldn't pretend.

"I am well, thank you, and how are you?"

"I am well."

"And how is our daughter?"

"She is well." Then: "She is longing to see you."

He had sensed her unasked question and was grateful for her tact. Or was it fear? No, he decided, she was not a weak woman, she was a survivor in a way that he had never been. Could he, a doctor, who took a pure pride in the intellect, have survived those years in the fields as she had? Millions had died; starvation and execution had raked the ranks of their generation. Survival demanded a skill that was not his. He needed to see a future. He could build, but merely to survive: for this, strength evaded him.

"She had to work. She couldn't come with me." Transparent, he knew: this too revealed his weakness. But she said nothing, in no way acknowledged his lies, and once more he was grateful. He said, too hurriedly, "We have a lot to talk about."

"There is nothing to talk about."

"I have rented an apartment for you. I will take care of all your needs." Like an invalid, he thought, regretting his words.

"You owe me nothing."

He took her suitcase—of cheap plastic, like her handbag—tipped the porter, led her in silence to the exit. The doors slipped open. Outside, the air was cool, given bite by the wind. The sky was once more grey. There was no sun: the carpark across the way took on the aspect of monolith.

"Is she beautiful?"

His calm pleased him, but he couldn't look at her: "No, but she is a good woman. She has been a good mother to our daughter."

"I meant our daughter." Her voice did not change, was neutral.

Stupid, he thought. He had answered the two unstated questions, had revealed all in a manner more abrupt, more crushing, than he'd intended.

But she was a survivor.

"Yes," he said, "our daughter is beautiful."

The wind fingered down his neck, struck his chest. He shivered. The suitcase in his right hand was light, the photograph in his left a more onerous weight. With an effort of will, he opened his palm. The photograph fluttered out. The wind picked it up, flung it into a gutter. He picked up his pace: there were things to do.

Presently, not long after they had driven off, the old man in white coveralls, carrying a broom and a garbage bag, came along on yet another turn past the carpark. He saw the photograph, the outlines of black, white, and grey blurred into a desperate fuzziness, so that there was no distinction, no sharpness to the image, like an ink drawing on cheap paper. His mind couldn't sharpen the lines, couldn't define the contours.

He swept it into the garbage bag and went off in his unsteady shuffle after a fluttering candy-wrapper.

DANCING

I was nothing more than a maid back home in Trinidad, just a ordinary fifty-dollar-a-month maid. I didn't have
no uniform but I did get off early Saturdays. I didn't work
Sundays, except when they had a party. Then I'd go and wash
up the dishes and the boss'd give me a few dollars extra.

My house, if you could call it a house, wasn't nothing more
than a two-room shack, well, in truth, a one-room shack with
a big cupboard I did use as a bedroom. With one medium-size
person in there you couldn't find room to squeeze in a cocka-
roach. The place wasn't no big thing to look at, you understand. A rusty galvanize roof that leak every time it rain,
wood walls I decorate with some calendars and my palm-leaf
from the Palm Sunday service. In one corner I did have a old
table with a couple a chairs. In the opposite corner, under the
window, my kitchen, with a small gas stove and a big bowl
for washing dishes. I didn't have pipes in my house, so every
morning I had to fetch water from a standpipe around the
corner, one bucket for the kitchen bowl, one for the little
bathroom behind the house. And, except for the latrine next
to the bathroom, that was it, the whole calabash. No big
thing. But the place was always clean though, and had enough
space for me.

It was in a back trace, behind a big, two-storey house belonging to a Indian doctor-fella. The land was his and he always telling me in a half-jokey kind of way that he going to tear down my house and put up a orchid garden. But he didn't mean it, in truth. He wasn't a too-too bad fella. He did throw a poojah from time to time and as soon as the prayers stop and the conch shell stop blowing, Kali the yardboy always bring me a plate of food from the doc.

The first of every month the doc and the yardboy did walk around with spray pumps on their back, spraying-spraying. The drains was white with poison afterward, but I never had no trouble with mosquito or fly or even silverfish. So the doc wasn't a bad neighbor, although I ain't fooling myself, I well know he was just helping himself and I was getting the droppings. People like that in Trinidad, you know, don't let the poojah food fool you. You could be deading in his front yard in the middle of the night and doc not coming out the house. I count three people dead outside his house and their family calling-calling and the doc never even so much as show his face. We wasn't friends, the doc and me. I tell him "Mornin" and he tell me "Mornin" and that was that.

I worked for a Indian family for seven, eight years. Nice people. Not like the doc. Good people. And that's another thing. Down there Black people have Indian maid and Indian people have Black maid. White people does mix them up, it don't matter to them. Black people say, Black people don't know how to work. Indian people say, Indian people always thiefing-thiefing. Me, I did always work for Indian people. They have a way of treating you that make you feel you was part of the family. Like every Christmas, Mum—I did call the missus that, just like her chilren—Mum give me a cake she make with her own two hand. It did always have white icening all over it, and a lot of red cherry. They was the kind of people who never mind if I wanted to ketch some tv after I finish my work. I'd drag up a kitchen chair behind them in the living room, drinking coffee to try to keep the eyes open. And sometimes when I get too tired the boss did drive me home. Understand my meaning clear, though. They was good people, but strick. They'd fire you in two-twos if you not careful with your work.

Nice people, as I say, but the money . . . Fifty dollars a month can't hardly buy shoe polish for a centipede. I talked to the pastor about it and he tell me ask for a raise. All they gimme is ten dollars more, so I went back to the pastor. You know what he say? "Why don't you become a secketary, Sister James? Go to secketerial school down in Port of Spain." Well, I start to laugh. I say, "Pastor, you good for the soul but you ain't so hot when it come to the stomach." Well, I never! Me, who hardly know how to read and write, you could see me as one of them prim an proper secketaries in a nice air-condition office? Please take this lettah, Miss James. Bring me that file, Miss James. Just like on tv! I learn fast-fast servant job was the only work for somebody like me.

That was life in Trinidad.

Then I get a letter from my sister Annie up in Toronto. She didn't write too often but when she set her mind to it she could almost turn out a whole book. She talk on and on bout Caribana, and she send some pictures she cut out from the newspaper. It look so strange to see Trinidadians in Carnival costumes dancing and jumping in them big, wide streets. Then she go on bout all the money she was making and how easy her life was. I don't mind saying that make me cry, but the tears dry up fast-fast. She write how Canadians racialist as hell. She say they hate black people for so and she tell me bout a ad on tv showing a black girl eating a banana pudding. Why they give banana to the Black? Annie say is because they think she look like a monkey. I couldn't bring myself to understand how people so bad. Annie say they jump out of the stomach like that. I telling you, man, is a terrible thing how people born racialist.

Anyways, Annie ask me to come up to Canada and live with she. She wanted to sponsor me and say she could help me find a job in two-twos. First I think, No way. Then, later that night in bed, I take a good look at myself. I had thirty years, my little shack and sixty dollars a month. Annie was making five times that Canadian, ten times that Trinidadian. I did always believe, since I was a little girl, that I'd get pregnant one day and catch a man, like most of the women around me. But the Lord never mean for me to make baby. I don't mind saying I try good and hard but it just wasn't in the cards. I thought, No man, no child, a shack, a servant job, sixty dollars a month. What my life was going to be like when I reach sixty? I think hard all night and all next day, and for a whole week.

After the Sunday service, I told the pastor bout Annie's letter. Quick-quick he say, "Go, Sister James, it is God's doing. He has answered your prayers."

I didn't bother to tell him that I didn't pray to God for help. I figure he already have His hands full with people like the doc.

Then it jump into my head to go ask the doc what to do. He was always flying off to New York and Toronto. So I thought he could give me more practical advices.

I went to see him that morning self. He was in the garden just behind the high iron gate watering the anthuriums. Kali the yardboy was shovelling leftover manure back into a half-empty cocoa bag. I remember the manure did have a strong-strong smell because they did just finish spreading it on the flowers beds.

The doc was talking to himself. He say, "A very table masterpiece of gardening." Or something like that. That was the doc. A couple of times when I was walking home I hear him talking to his friends and it was big and fancy words, if you please. But when he talk to me or Kali or we kind of people, he did start talking like us quick-quick. Maybe he think we going to like him more. Or maybe he think we doesn't understand good English. I always want to tell him that we not chilren, we grow up too. But why bother?

I knock on the gate.

The doc look up and say, "Mornin, Miss Sheila."

"Mornin, doctor."

"Went to church this mornin, Miss Sheila?"

"Yes, doctor."

"Nice anthuriums, not so?"

"Very nice anthuriums, doctor. Is not everybody could grow them flowers like you."

He shake his shoulders as if to say, That ain't no news. Then he say, "Is hard work but they pretty for spite, you don't think so?"

I remember the day a dog dig up one of the anthuriums and the doc take a hoe to the poor animal and break his head in two. There was blood all over the place and the dog drop down stone dead. The owner start to kick up a fuss and the doc call the police to cart the man off to jail. But that was just life in Trinidad and I didn't say nothing. But ever since then those pink, heart-shape flowers remind me of that dog, as if the plants pick up some of the blood and the shape of the heart. It was after that that the doc put up the brick fence with broken bottles all along the top and a heavy iron gate.

I say, "Doctor, I want to ask you for some advices."

He say, "I not working now, Miss Sheila, come back tomorrow during office hours."

"I not sick, doctor, is about another business." But still he turn away from me, all the time spraying-spraying with the hose.

Kali stop shovelling and say something to the doc.

The doc say, "What is this I hearing? Miss Sheila? You thinking bout leaving Trinidad?"

Kali start to laugh. I see the doc wanted to laugh too. He turn off the hose and drop it on the ground. He walk over to the gate. He say, "Is true, Miss Sheila?"

"Yes, doctor." And I get a strange feeling, as if somebody ketch me thiefing something.

"Canada?"

"Yes, doctor."

"Toronto?"

"Yes, doctor."

"So what you want to know, Miss Sheila?"

"I can't make up my mind, doctor. I don't know if to go or if to stay."

"And you want my advice?"

"I grateful for any help you could give me, doctor."

He start rubbing the dirt from his hands and he stand there, thinking-thinking. Then he lean against the gate and say, "Miss Sheila, I going to tell you something I don't say very often because people don't like to hear the truth. They does get vex. But you know, Miss Sheila, people on this island too damn uppity for their own good. They lazy and they good-for-nothing. They don't like to work. And they so damn uppity they think they go to Canada or the States and life easy. Well, it not easy. It very, very hard and you have to work your ass off to get anywhere. Miss Sheila, what you could do? Eh? Tell me. I admire you for wanting to improve your life but what you think you going to do in Canada? You let some damn stupid uppity people put a damn stupid idea in your head and you ready to run off and lose everything you have. Your house, your job, everything. And why? Because of uppitiness. Don't think you going to be able to buy house up in Canada, you know. So, I advise you not to go, Miss Sheila. The grass never greener on the other side." He stop talking and take a cigarette from his shirt pocket and light it.

I didn't know what to say. I was confuse. I say, "Thanks, doctor. Good day, doctor," and start walking to my house. Before I even take two steps, I hear Kali say, "Them nigs think the world is for them and them alone."

And he and the doc start to laugh.

There I was, hands hurting like hell from suitcase and boxes and bags and I couldn't find the door handle. My head was still full of cotton wool from the plane and my stomach was bawling its head off for food. I just wanted to turn right round and say, "Take me back. The doc was right. I ain't going to be able to live in a place where doors ain't have no handle." But then a man in a uniform motion me to keep walking, as if he want me to bounce straight into the door. Well, if it have one thing I fraid is policeman, so I start to walk and, Lord, like the Red Sea parting for Moses, the door open by itself.

This make me feel good. I feel as if I get back at the customs man who did ask me all kind of nasty questions like, "You have any rum? Whisky? Plants? Food?" as if I look like one of them smugglers that does ply between Trinidad and Venezuela. I thought, I bet the doors don't open like that for him!

As I walk through the door I start feeling dizzy-dizzy. Everything look cloudy-cloudy, as if the building was just going to fade away or melt. I was so frighten I start to think I dreaming, like it wasn't me walking there at all but somebody else. It was almost like looking at a flim in a cinema.

Then I hear a voice talking to me inside my head. It say, Sheila James, maid, of Mikey Trace, Trinidad, here you is, a big woman, walking in Toronto airport and you frighten. Why?

I force myself to look around. I see faces, faces, faces. All round me, faces. Some looking at me, some looking past me, and some even looking through me. I start feeling like a flowers vase on a table.

Then all of a sudden the cloudiness disappear and I see all the faces plain-plain. They was mostly white. My chest tighten up and I couldn't hardly breathe. I was surrounded by tourists. And not one of them was wearing a straw hat.

I hear another voice calling me, "Sheila! Sheila!" I look around but didn't see nobody, only all these strange faces. I start feeling small-small, like a douen. Suddenly it jump into my head to run headlong through the crowd but it was as if somebody did nail my foot to the floor: I couldn't move. Again like in a dream. A bad dream.

And then, bam!, like magic, I see all these black faces running toward me, pushing the tourists out of the way, almost fighting with one another to get to me first. I recognize Annie. She shout, "Sheila!" Then I see my brother Sylvester, and others I didn't know. Annie grab on to me and hug me tight-tight. Sylvester take my bags and give them to somebody else, then he start hugging me too. Somebody pat me on the back. I felt safe again. It was almost like being back in Trinidad.

Sylvester and the others drop Annie and me off at her flat in Vaughan Road. Annie was a little vex with Syl because he didn't want to stay and talk but I tell her I was tired and she let him go off to his party.

Annie boil up some water for tea and we sit down in the tiny living room to talk. I notice how old Annie was looking. Her face was heavy, it full-out in two years. And the skin under her eyes was dark-dark as if all her tiredness settle there. Like dust. Maybe it was the light. It always dark in Annie's apartment, even in the day. The windows small-small, and she does keep on only one light at a time. To save on the hydro bill, she say.

She ask me about friends and the neighbors and the pastor.

It didn't have much family left in Trinidad to talk about. She ask about the doc. I tell she about his advices. She choops loud-loud and say, "Indian people bad for so, eh, child."

She ask about Georgie, our father's outside-child. I say, "Georgie run into some trouble with the police, girl. He get drunk one evening and beat up a fella and almost kill him."

She say, "That boy bad since he small. So, what they do with him?"

"Nothing. The police charge him and they was going to take him to court. But you know how things does work in Trinidad. Georgie give a police friend some money. Every time they call him up for trial, the sergeant tell the judge, We can't find the file on this case, Me Lud, and finally the judge get fed up and throw the charge out. You know, he even bawl out the poor sergeant."

Annie laugh and shake her head. She say, "Good old Georgie. What he doing now?"

"The usual. Nothing at all. He looking after his papers for coming up here. Next year, probably."

Annie yawn and ask me if I hungry.

I say no, I did aready eat on the plane: my stomach was tight-tight.

"You don't want some cake? I make it just for you."

I say no again, and she remember I did never eat much, even as a baby.

"Anyways," she say quietly, "I really glad you here now, girl. At last. Is about time."

What to say? I shake my head and close my eyes. I try to smile. "I really don't know, Annie girl. I still ain't too sure I doing the right thing. Everything so strange."

Annie listen to me and her face become serious-serious, like the pastor during sermon. But then she smile and say, "It have a lot of things for you to learn, and it ain't going to be easy, but you doing the best thing by coming here, believe me."

But it was too soon. With every minute passing, I was believing the doc was righter.

Annie take my hand in hers. I notice how much bigger hers was, and how much rings she was wearing. Just like our mother, a big woman with hands that make you feel like a little child again when she touch you.

She say, "Listen, Sheila," and I hear our mother talking. Sad-sad. From far away. And I think, Is because all of us leave her, she dead long time but now everybody gone, nobody in Trinidad, and who going to clean her grave and light her candles on All Saints? I close my eyes again, so Annie wouldn't see the tears.

She squeeze my hand and say, "Sheila? You awright? You want some more tea?"

She let go my hand, pick up my cup, and went into the kitchen. She say, "But, eh, eh, the tea cold aready. Nothing does stay hot for long in this place." She run the water and put the kettle on the stove. When she come back in the living room I did aready dry my eyes. She hand me a piece of cake on a saucer, sponge cake, I think, and sit down next to me.

She take a bite from her piece. "You know, chile," she say chewing wide-wide, "Tronto is a strange place. It have people here from all over the world—Italian, Greek, Chinee, Japanee, and some people you and me never even hear bout before. You does see a lot of old Italian women, and some not so old, running round in black dress looking like beetle. And Indians walking round with turban on their head. All of them doing as if they still in Rome or Calcutta." She stop and take another bite of the cake. "Well, girl, us West Indians just like them. Everybody here to make money, them and us." She watch me straight in the eye. "Tell me, you ketch what I saying?"

I say, "Yes, Annie," but in truth I was thinking bout the grave and the grass and the candles left over from last year and how lonely our mother was feeling.

"Is true most of them here to stay," she continue, "but don't forget they doesn't have a tropical island to go back to." And she laugh, but in a false way, as if is a thing she say many times before. She look at my cake still lying on the saucer, and then at me, but she didn't say nothing. "Anyways," she say, finishing off her piece, "you see how I still talking after two years. After two years, girl, you understanding what I saying?"

"So I mustn't forget how to talk. Then what? You want me to go dance shango and sing calypso in the street?"

"I don't think you ketch what I saying," Annie say. She put the saucer down on the floor, lean forwards and rub her eyes, thinking hard-hard. "What I mean is . . . you mustn't think you can become Canajun. You have to become West Indian."

"What you mean, become West Indian?"

"I mean, remain West Indian."

I think, Our mother born, live, dead, and bury in Trinidad. And again I see her grave. I choops, but soft-soft.

Annie say, "But eh, eh, why you choopsing for, girl?"

"How I going to change, eh?" I almost shout. "I's a Trinidadian. I born there and my passport say I from there. So how the hell I going to forget?" I was good and vex.

She shake her head slow-slow and say, "You still ain't ketch on. Look, Canajuns like to go to the islands for two weeks every year to enjoy the sun and the beach and the calypso. But is a different thing if we try to bring the calypso here. Then they doesn't want to hear it. So they always down on we for one reason or another. Us West Indians have to stick together, Sheila. Is the onliest way." Again her face remind me of the pastor in the middle of a hot sermon. You does feel his eyes heavy on you even though he looking at fifty-sixty people.

My head start to hurt. I say, "But it sound like if all-you

fraid for so, like if all-you hiding from the other people here."

I think that make she want to give up. I could be stubborn when I want. Her voice sound tired-tired when she say, "Girl, you have so much to learn. Remember the ad I tell you bout in my letter, the one with the little girl eating the banana pudding?"

"Yes. On the plane I tell a fella what you say and he start laughing. He say is the most ridiculous thing he ever hear."

Annie lean back and groan loud-loud. "Oh Gawd, how it still have fools like that fella walking around?"

"The fella was colored, like us."

"Even worser. One of we own people. And the word is black, not colored."

It almost look to me like if Annie was enjoying what she was saying. And I meet a lot of people like that in my time, people who like to moan and groan and make others feel sorry for them. But I didn't say nothing.

All the time shaking her head, Annie say, "Anyways, look eh, girl, you going to learn in time. But lemme tell you one thing, and listen to me good. You must stick with your own, don't think that any honky ever going to accept you as one of them. If you want friends, they going to have to be West Indian. Syl tell me so when I first come up to Tronto and is true. I doesn't even try to talk to white people now. I ain't have the time or use for racialists."

I was really tired out by that point so I just say, "Okay, Annie, whatever you say. You and Syl must know what you talking bout."

"Yeah, but you going to see for yourself," she say, yawning wide-wide. "But anyways, enough for tonight." She get up, then suddenly she clap her hands and smile. "Oh Gawd, girl, I so happy you here. At last." She laugh. And I laugh, in a way.

She pluck off her wig and say, "Come, let we go to bed, you must be tired out."

Before stretching out on the sofa, I finish off my cake. To make Annie happy.

Next morning Annie take me downtown in the subway. It wasn't a nice day. The snow was grey and the sky was grey. The wind cut right through the coat Annie give me and freeze out the last little bit of Trinidad heat I had left in me.

I don't mind saying I was frighten like hell the first time in the subway. Annie, really playing it up like tourist guide, say, "They does call it the chube in Englan but here we does say subway." I was amaze at the speed, and I kept looking at the wall flying past on both sides and wondering how I ever going to learn to use this thing. I kept comparing it to the twenty-cent taxi ride to Port of Spain, with the driver blowing horn and passing cars zoom-zoom. The wind use to be so strong you couldn't even spit out the window. But the subway though! The speed! But I couldn't tell Annie that. When she ask me what I think of it, I just shake my head and pretend it was no big thing. To tell the truth woulda make me look like a real chupidy. Annie wasn't too happy bout that. A little vex, she say, "You have to learn to use it, you can't take taxi here."

I doesn't remember a lot from my first time in Yonge Street. Just buildings, cars, white faces, grey snow. Everything was confuse. It was too much. The morning before I was still in my little shack in Mikey Trace, having a last tea with the neighbors—not the doc, of course, but he send Kali over with twenty Canadian dollars as a present—and this morning I was walking bold-bold in Toronto.

Too much.

We walk around a lot that day. We look at stores, we look

at shops. She show me massage parlors and strip bars with pictures of naked women outside. In one corner I see something that give me a shock. White men bending their back over fork and pickaxe, digging a hole in the street. They was sweating and dirty and tired. Is hard to admit now, but I feel shame for them and I think, But they crazy or what? In Trinidad you never see white people doing that kinda work and it never jump into my head before that white people did do that kinda work. Is only when I see that Annie didn't pay no attention to them that I see my shame. I turn away from them fast-fast.

By the end of the day my foot was hurting real terrible and my right shoe was pinching me like a crab. Finally we get on the subway again and I was glad to be able to rest my bones, even with all kinda iron-face people around me. We stop at a new station and Syl was waiting for us in his car.

It was a fast drive. Syl did always have a heavy foot on the gas pedal. I remember trees without leaf, big buildings, a long bridge, the longest I ever see, longer than the Caroni bridge or any other bridge in Trinidad. By the way, that was one of the first things I notice, how big and long everything was. And when somebody tell me that you could put Trinidad into Lake Untarryo over eight times, my head start to spin. It have something very frightening in that.

Finally we get to Syl place, a high, grey, washout apartment building. The paint was peeling and the balconies was rusty for so. I say, "Is the ghetto?" I was showing off. I wanted to use one of the words I pick up from a Trinidad neighbor with a sister in New York. But Syl and Annie just laugh and shake their heads.

Annie point to a low building across the street. "They does call that the Untarryo Science Centre."

"What they does keep in there?" I ask.

Annie say, "I hear they does keep all kinda scientific things, but I really don't know for sure."

"You never go see for yourself?" I ask.

Syl cut in with "And waste good money to see nonsense?" He laugh short-short and tell Annie to stop showing me chupidness.

We went in the building and Syl call the elevator. That was my first time in a elevator but I used to seeing the prim an proper secketaries going into one on tv, pushing a button, nothing moving and they come out somewhere else. Is a funny thing, but you ever notice that elevators doesn't move on tv? Is as if the rest of the building does do the moving up and down.

I look at Syl and I say, "Eh, eh, boy Syl, it look like you grow a little. You ain't find so, Annie? He not looking taller?" Annie didn't reply but Syl blush and close his eyes, just like when he was a little boy. He did always like to hear people say he grow a little because he don't like being shorter than his sisters. He like to say he grow up short because we did jump over his head when he small, but I doesn't believe that. "And I see you still like your fancy clothes." He was wearing a red shirt which hold him tight-tight at the waist and green pants as tight as a skin on a coocoomber. I notice his shoes did have four-inch heels and I realize that was why he was looking taller, but I didn't mention it. Syl have a short temper when it come to his shortness and his fanciness. I didn't talk about his beard neither. Annie tell me he was growing it for three months and it still look as if he didn't shave yesterday.

We get off at the eight storey and walk down a long-long corridor. Same door after same door after same door. Annie say, "I could never live in a highrise. It remind me of a funeral home, with coffin pile on coffin." We turn a corner and I hear the music, a calypso from two or three carnivals back.

Syl didn't have a big apartment, only one bedroom. All the furniture was push to one side, so the floor was free for dancing. The stereo was on the couch, with a pile of records on the floor next to it. There was a table in one corner with glasses and ice and drinks on it.

Somebody shout from the kitchen, drowning out the calypso, "Syl, is you, man? Where the hell you keeping the rum?"

Syl say, "You finish the first bottle already?"

The voice say, "Long time, man. You know I doesn't wait around."

Syl say, "Leave it for now, man, come meet my sister Sheila."

Annie, vex, say, "Fitzie hand go break if he don't have a drink in it always."

A big black man wearing a pink shirt-jac come out from the kitchen. Syl say, "This is Fitzie. He with the tourist office up here."

A pile of people follow Fitzie from the kitchen and more came out of the bedroom. Syl wasn't finish introducing me when the buzzer buzz and more people arrive. The record finish and somebody put on another one. People start to dance. A man smelling of rum grab on to my waist and start to move. It was a old song, stale. I didn't feel like dancing. I push the man away and went to get some Coke. The Coke didn't taste right, it was different from the one in Trinidad, sweeter and with more bubbles. It make me burp. Fitzie pat me on the back.

The front door open, a crowd of people rush in dancing and singing with the record before they even get inside properly. I couldn't believe so much people was going to fit in such a small room. Somebody turn up the music even louder. Syl give up trying to tell me people's names. It didn't matter. The music was pushing my brain around inside my head, I couldn't think straight, couldn't hardly even stand up straight.

Fitzie say to me, "Is just like being back home in Trinidad, not so?"

I ask Annie where the bathroom was and I went in there and start to cry even before I close the door.

I don't know how long I stay in the bathroom. I kept looking in the mirror and asking myself what the hell I was doing in this country. I was missing my little shack. I wanted to jump on a plane back home right away, before the doc could break down the shack and put up his orchid garden. It was probably too late, the doc wasn't a man to wait around, but all I wanted was that shack and my little bedroom. I kept seeing the pastor saying goodbye, and the neighbors toting away the bed and dishes, the palm-leaf on the floor, the calendars in the rubbish.

Somebody pound on the door and I hear Annie saying, "Sheila, you awright? Sheila, girl, talk to me."

I hear Fitzie say, "Maybe she sick. You know, the change of water does affect a lot of people."

I wipe my eyes and unlock the door. A man push in, looking desperate, and Annie pull me out fast-fast. She say, "What happen? You feeling sick?"

I shake my head and say, "No, is awright. Is only that it have too much people in here. But don't worry, I awright now."

"You want to go home?"

Fitzie say, "I'll drive you."

"No, really, I awright now."

We went back into the living room. It was dark. People was dancing.

West Indians always ready for a party to start but never ready for it to end. It didn't take long before the air in the apartment was use up. Everybody was breathing everybody else stale air, the place stinking like a rubbish dump. Curry, rum, whisky, smoke, ganja and cigarette both. And the record player still blasting out old Sparrow calypso.

I start to sweat like cheese on a hot day. Somehow people find enough room to form a line and they manage to move together, just like Carnival day in Frederick Street, stamping and shuffling, stamping and shuffling, and shouting their head off. Syl, in the middle of the line, grab on to my arm and pull me in. I feel as if I didn't have no strength left, I just moving with the line, Syl pulling me back and pushing me forwards.

Finally the song end and the line break up, everybody heaving for air, some people just falling to the floor with tiredness. I couldn't breathe. It was like trying to pull in warm soup through my nose. I push through the crowd to a open window. A group of people was standing in front of it, drinking and smoking.

Fitzie was talking. "These people can't even prononks names right. They does say *Young* Street when everybody who know what is what know is plain an obvious is really *Yon-zhe*. Like in French. But that is what does happen when you ain't got a culcheer to call your own, you does lose your language, you does forget how to talk."

A young man with hair frizzy and puff-out like a half-use scouring pad say, "At least we have calypso and steelband."

"And limbo."

"And reggae."

"And callaloo."

Fitzie spot me listening. "Eh, eh, Sheila man," he say, "but you making yourself scarce tonight. All-you know Sheila, Syl sister?"

Everybody say hello.

Fitzie ask me how it going and I say it very hot in here.

The young man with the scouring pad hair laugh and say, "Just like Trinidad."

Everybody laugh.

Fitzie say, "Yeah, man, just like home."

The young man say, "Is the warmth I does miss, and I not talking only about the sun but people too. Man, I remember Trinidad people always leave their doors open day and night, and you could walk in at any time without calling first. Canajuns not like that. Doors shut up tight, eyes cold and hands in pocket. They's not a welcoming people."

I was going to tell them bout the doc, with the big house and the fence and broken bottles. I wanted to say even me did always keep my shack shut up because if you have nothing worth thiefing, people will still thief it, just for spite. But I didn't want to talk, I just wanted to breathe. Besides, Syl done tell me he don't like people talking at his fetes. He only like to see people dancing and eating and drinking. Seeing people sitting around and talking does make him vex. He say is not a Trinidadian thing to do.

I manage to get to the windowsill and I look out at the city. The lights! I never see so much lights before, yellow and white and red, line after line of lights, stretching far-far away in the distance, as if they have no end. That was what Port of Spain did look like from the Lady Young lookout at night, only it was smaller and it come to an end at the sea, where you could see the ships sitting in the docks. But after looking at this, I don't think I could admire Port of Spain again. This does make you dizzy, it does fill your eye till you can't take any more.

Fitzie the Tourist Board man say, "You looking at the lights?"

"Yes."

"They nice. But can't compare with the Lady Young though."

I didn't say nothing. I felt ashame, but I couldn't say why.

He ask me to dance. Reggae music was playing. I not too partial to reggae. It does sound like the same thing over and

over again if they playing "Rasta Man" or "White Christmas". So I say no, next song. He grab my arm rough-rough
and pull me. I say, "Okay, okay, I give up." Then he hold me
tight-tight against him, so that I smell his cologne and his
sweat and his rum and his cigarettes and he start moving,
pushing his thigh up between my legs. I try to pull away but
he was holding on too tight, doing all the moving for the two
of us.

About halfway through the song somebody start shouting
for Syl. The front door was open and a white man was
standing just outside in the corridor. My heart start to beat
hard-hard. The voice call for Syl again. Fitzie stop moving
and loosen his grip on me. Everybody else stop dancing. They
was just standing there, some still holding on, staring through
the door. All the talking stop. The music was pounding
through the room. A cold draft of air from the window hit
my back and make Fitzie hands feel hot-hot on me.

I take a long, hard look at the white man. His face was a
greyish whiteish color, like a wax candle, and all crease up.
He was pudgy like a baby. He was standing hands on hips
trying to look relaxed but only looking not-too-comfortable.
I think his hair was brown.

Fitzie say, "I bet I know what that son-of-a-bitch want."

Annie come up to me, put her arm around my shoulder.

The man take a step closer to the door, as if he want to
come in. I feel Fitzie tense up, but it seem to me the man was
only trying to get a better look inside.

Fitzie say, "Like he looking in a zoo, or what?"

Then Syl appear at the door, shorter than the man but
wider, tougher looking. Syl say loud-loud, "What you want
here?"

I couldn't hear what the man was saying but I see his lips
moving.

Syl lean on the door frame, shaking his head. Then he
choops loud-loud.

The man take a step backward, waving his hands around in the air.

The song come to an end, the turntable click off. I could hear myself breathing.

Syl choops again and say, "You call the cops and I go take you and them to the Untarryo Human Right Commission. Is trouble you want, is trouble you go get."

The man put his hands in his pants pockets and open his mouth but before he could talk somebody else push himself between Syl and the man. It was a short, fat Indian fella by the name of Ram. He did arrive at the party drunk. A white girl was with him, drunk too. Annie tell me she wasn't his wife, she was his girlfriend. His wife was home pregnant and vomiting half the time.

Ram say, "What going on here, Syl boy?"

Syl say, "This son-of-a-bitch say the music too loud. He complaining. He say he going to call the police."

Ram say, "The music too loud?"

The man say, "I just want it turned down. I don't want to have to call the police."

Ram laugh loud-loud, put his arm around Syl shoulder and say, "Syl, boy, the music too loud. It disturbing the neighbors. So what we going to do bout this?"

"Ram, boy, it have only one thing to do, yes."

"Yes, boy Syl, only one thing."

Ram put his hand to his nose, blow twice, rub the cold between his fingers and then wipe his fingers clean on the white man's sweater.

The white man pull back and push Ram away. Then he turn grey-grey and rush off, leaving Syl and Ram in the door.

I start to feel sick.

Ram and Syl, laughing hard-hard, hug on to each other.

The young man with the scouring pad hair run to the door and shout down the corridor, "Blasted racialist honky!"

Fitzie run up to Syl and Ram shouting, "Well done, man,

well done. All-you really show that son-of-a-bitch."

The young man say, "Nice going, man, you really know how to handle them."

Annie say, "Good, good."

Suddenly everybody was laughing. A few people start to clap.

Syl take a rum bottle and drink long and hard. He fill his mouth till a little bit run down his chin. Ram shout, "Leave some for me, man," grab the bottle and take a mouthful too.

Syl spot me and call me over. I was finding it hard to smile but I try anyways. He put his hand on my shoulder and Annie put her arm around my waist. Syl eyes was red like blood and he couldn't talk right. After some mumbling and stumbling, he manage to say, "Sheila, girl, you see what just happen there? Remember it, remember it good. Is the first time you run into something like that but it ain't going to be the last. You see how I handle him? You think you could do that? Eh? You think you could do that?"

I didn't know what to say. I was feeling I didn't want to treat nobody like that and I didn't know if I could. Finally I just say, "Yes, Syl," without knowing myself what I mean.

Ram say, "Screw all of them."

I say, "Maybe we should go back home?"

Annie say, "But it early still, girl."

I say, "No, I mean Trinidad." Our mother's grave, and the grass and the candles was in my head again.

Syl dig his fingers into my shoulder. "Never let me hear you saying that again. Don't think it! We have every right to be here. They owe us. And we going to collect, you hear me?"

I say, "Syl, I ain't come here to fight." I start crying.

Annie say rough-rough, "Don't do that," and it wasn't my Annie, it wasn't Annie like our mother, it was a different Annie.

Then Syl grab me and shout, "Somebody put on the music. Turn it up loud-loud. For everybody to hear! This whole damn building! Come, girl, dance. Dance like you never dance before."

And I dance.

I dance an dance an dance.

I dance like I never dance before.

VEINS VISIBLE

The illuminated hands of the alarm-clock showed one a.m. Vernon wondered why it had gone off—he'd set it for six-thirty—and he wondered too why its ring was intermittent and came from a far corner of the bedroom.

The room was dark. The window showed as a dully luminescent square. He could just make out the left edge of the dresser, a slash of icy mirror above it.

The alarm continued ringing. He reached for it, pressed the button. Still it rang, intermittent.

His wife stirred in the bed next to him: "Vernon, the phone."

He pulled the sheets back, lowered his feet to the floor, toes searching the rough carpet for his slippers. They weren't there.

The ring, identified now, seemed to grow louder, the pauses shorter, less patient.

He shuffled over to the phone in his bare feet. He thought: Like walking on an unshaved cheek. He felt old. He sensed Jenny sit up in the bed.

"Hello."

As he listened, his eyes searched the windowpane, seeking to pierce the grey glow. The glass was fogged over; along the bottom a thin sheet of ice had built up; he pressed at it with a fingernail, cleanly detaching a chunk. That part of him that was not engaged on the phone was surprised that the slab of ice seemed to float, that he could move it easily, whole. Then the warmth of his fingertips bored through the ice, touched the glass behind. He realized that the slab was melting and that, while it seemed to float, it was supported only by the liquefied part of itself. A convex pool of water had collected on the windowsill below, like a drop of smoky crystal.

"Where'd they take him?"

His fingers, damp, moved to the film of moisture that gave the glass the opacity of old plastic. In an ever-widening circle, he brushed the moisture aside, sending two runnels of water down the glass, creating a wet porthole through which he could see a distorted world clothed in white. Fresh snow hid even the streetcar rails, turned the street into an unfolded shroud. The unbroken stretch of red-bricked building on the other side of the street was shuttered, darkened. The restaurants, second-hand bookstores, and used-clothing shops that occupied the street level were dark and, in the yellow thickness of the street-lamps, gave no hint of their function. The flats above the businesses were also in darkness except for the dullest ochre in one small window, a night-light, maybe, or that of a cloistered bathroom.

"Where are you now? Who's with the kids?"

A streetcar, its one headlight showing with the diffused yellowness of a flashlight, trundled slowly past, leaving in its wake two thin, black stripes, like a trail. Vernon felt the floor tremble lightly under his bare feet.

"I'll be there as soon as I can."

Jenny said, "What is it? It's Hari again, isn't it."

She turned on the bedside lamp and the reflection of books filled his wet porthole. "Is he drunk again?"

Vernon didn't answer. He let the phone glide over his ear,

down across his cheek; let his arm drop, as if deprived of strength, the receiver, tightly grasped, seeming to radiate heat into his hand.

"Did the police pick him up or what?"

The porthole was fogging up once more. Slowly, the books disappeared.

"Vern?"

"He's in the hospital."

"And."

"An accident. The car ran off the road. The snow."

"So how is he?"

"Dying."

She was silent.

There had been no dawn. The sky had gone from ink black to watercolor grey, shutting out day, offering only a restrained approximation of twilight. The snow on the street had been whipped into a brown slush by salt truck and snow tires, had pooled in the gutters in a brassy sludge. The asphalt looked black and solid, fresh, and the buildings, neon and hand-painted signs now showing at every window, in every door-way, were heavy with the waterlogged density of wood that had travelled the high seas.

The smell of the hospital was still in Vernon's nostrils as he lowered himself from the streetcar, his boots, speckled gaily with paint, sinking into a ridge of slush. To his right, a car squealed to a halt, the driver startled. Vernon, feeling his fragility, acted as if he hadn't noticed; pride seized the scream, of terror, of anger, that had leapt to him.

As he made his way up the stairwell—narrow, walls of dulled ochre, red carpet frayed at the edges, rubbed away in the centre to the original matting—he heard the door to their flat opening, first the squeak of the upper hinge, then the more extended wail of the lower.

Jenny, in her Saturday outfit of jeans and sweater, stood in the doorway. "I saw you getting off the streetcar."

He pushed past her, kicked his boots off onto the doormat.

She followed him into the kitchen. "You were gone a long time."

"Peter was at the hospital. We were talking."

"What about?"

"Back home. How it was."

"Of course. What else."

He slumped into a chair at the small dining table. His eyes were reddened with fatigue; the skin around them, roughened now, no longer buttressed by crescents of fat, looked scaly. In the leaden haze that drifted thickly in through the window above the stove, age proclaimed itself; the light made plain those changes, each subtle in itself, that went unseen from day to day, that revealed themselves only in the stress of the intimate, vulnerable moment.

Jenny thought: He's getting old. And for a moment she panicked, not for herself but for him. Time had been abbreviated; it was as if this night had taken him years away.

"How's Hari?"

"I told you. Dying."

"What of? What's wrong with him exactly?"

"Everything. He's just breaking down."

"What are the doctors doing?"

"Nothing."

"Nothing?"

"There's nothing to do. I saw him. He's flesh. His skin was stripped away. It wasn't neat. You could see his veins."

"Did you talk to him?"

"You can't talk to meat," he said with an unexpected vehemence.

She said, "I feel sorry for him too, you know."

"Do you."

The words, of a spare brutality, spoken as if in conversation, took her by surprise; but she acknowledged to herself the fairness of the question. She said, "It's the changes, Vern, they're too many." She wanted to add: Look at you. But she said instead, "Look at me." And she held her hands out for him to see: the veins, distended, erupting sinuously from the skin; the bones sweeping to the unpainted nails, shorter now and imperfectly shaped; the rings—engagement, wedding, tableaux of a different world, a different time—askew on the finger no longer slender but merely thin.

He looked at her hands, but vaguely, as if part of him had retreated. Then he looked away.

He said, "We were men of substance."

She lowered her hands.

He said, "*We* hired people to paint *our* houses." And he looked at his own hands as if at a curio. He could not recognize them; with the toughened skin, with the speckles of paint trapped in the wrinkles, with the crescents of dirt under the nails, they were those of a stranger. "Men of substance."

She said, "Yes, Vern, substance. But only of a kind."

He clasped his hands, finger interlacing with finger in deliberate movement.

She said, wearied, "What's the point, Vern?"

He looked up at her, one eye cocked in accusation.

She said, "Don't do that."

He said, "You don't remember, do you."

"I do remember, damn you." She moved agitatedly to the sink, filled the kettle, and—in what still felt like an ancient gesture—lit the stove with a match. The flame leapt around the burner with a sharp, sudden groan, in a contained explosion. "You can't forget what used to be. I just wish you wouldn't push it. There's no point. You'll end up like Hari."

"Bullshit." He said it gently, like an endearment.

She let the kettle clatter onto the flame and turned to face him. "You talk about substance. Hari: what's substance?"

"He was. We were." He unclasped his hands and let his face fall into them in an indication of fatigue.

"Your substance. Your substance was money, things. It was the Japanese tea ceremony."

"Bullshit," he repeated. Yet he wanted to retreat, to plead fatigue. He was tired, but it was not sleep that he sought. The weight that gripped his body seemed to have anesthetized him, so that while one part of him wanted to run, the other remained indifferent, just as the mind alone revolts at the violence done by a dentist's probes to a frozen mouth. He said, "The tea ceremony," he gave a stiff chuckle, "it was just something outside our experience."

"It was something outside anybody's experience." The water boiled. She turned her attention to making coffee: the swish of jar lid, the tinkle of spoon on cup.

The Japanese couple visiting the island had been more exotic than the bare-breasted Nigerian dancers. People spoke of Japs and Nips, recalled the yellow peril and Pearl Harbor— events that had touched the island only peripherally, through the American soldiers stationed there during the war for rest and recreation, what little there was of it—and it was as if, in the twenty-five years between the end of the war and then, the Japanese economic miracle hadn't occurred, as if the people of the island couldn't connect these visitors, polite to the point of imbecility, with the cars and small trucks that clogged the roads of the island.

The Japanese, small and smiling behind wire-framed glasses, were said to be experts at the tea ceremony. No one in the island knew anything about the tea ceremony: tea was a tea-bag, boiling water, milk, sugar. The ritual, in a place without rituals, seized the imagination. The Japanese were invited into the most prestigious homes, lionized, televised. Vernon had provided a cocktail party and a dinner party.

Then, a month after their departure, the unravelling: the island's television station ran a *National Geographic* film of the tea ceremony. It wasn't the same thing. It was vastly different. The truth emerged: the Japanese weren't Japanese at all. They were Korean, they knew nothing about tea, they had taken an impressive bundle of money out of the island with them for "investment in Japan". The story had dragged on for weeks and was capped—insult on insult, this—by a picture of the Japanese couple, as they continued to be known, drinking Nescafé in the dining room of the ship that had taken them away.

At first it had seemed like a joke: simple people—simplicity viewed then as a virtue, when they were truly simple, playing at the world until the wider corruption inexorably attracted them—eager to be duped by a greater sophistication. Yet Vernon had always felt that more than a simplicity had been involved, more than an island naivety. A certain stupidity too had played a role, a stupidity easily camouflaged by a flippant self-derision, a self-caricature that turned the stupidity itself into a virtue.

Was this truly, as Jenny insisted, the substance to which he clung? He had always resisted a deeper examination and Hari, like Peter and his other friends, had long rejected the thought that what they had had might have been illusion, a mirage created by sea, sky, sand, and a moneyed circumstance.

And so, slowly, they were being unravelled by a life that demanded effort.

Jenny placed the coffee cup on the table in front of him. She said, "Are you hungry?"

He shook his head: No.

She said, "You know, Vern, you're not a weak man. Under the right circumstances."

He took her words as offered: without irony, without

sarcasm, as compliment even. He knew what she meant. He had spent the better part of his life providing, stabilizing, sheltering, practising with a certain gentility, as it seemed now, the art of being a man. But he had inherited his wealth in a place where wealth justified itself only in its very existence, where the acquisition of wealth created its own bars. And this money, inherited, had its own needs, created its own resources, its own talents. When stripped of all that he had taken for granted, all that had come so effortlessly to him, he found the lessons of a lifetime futile. Skills became useless, absurd, and life required a different kind of strength, a strength that could only be grown into, that could not be dredged up from under the collapsed experience of a lifetime.

Vernon had never doubted his ability to survive. But to go beyond survival? To practise once more the art of being a man in the way that he understood it?

Jenny, seated across the table from him, contemplated the coffee in her cup.

He said, "You're stronger than me. You've always been." He looked away to the kitchen window; the ice had melted, the steam turned to runnels and streaks. The sky showed like grey canvas. "When we had to run, you brought your jewellery, you were prepared. Me? I didn't want to believe. How can you accept a total loss? It's easier to turn away. Like me. That's why we live in a dump, that's why I have to paint other people's pretty houses." He was tired and he spoke the words as they came to him. A bubble formed in his stomach and began an upward movement; his head swirled in slow motion. He gulped at his coffee, stood up and walked over to the sink. The pressure of the bubble eased, his head steadied.

Jenny said, "You should go to bed."

"I don't want to." He turned on the cold water and splashed a palmful onto his face. His flesh felt inert, thickened.

"You remember how Hari used to joke about Noolan?" Jenny's voice cut above the dull thud of tap water hitting the aluminum sink.

"Joke? It was no joke." His hands clutched into fists, the veins bunched up from under the skin. He thought he saw the blood rushing through them.

He could hear Hari talking. He would move to Newfoundland—or Noolan, as Hari would say, tongue burdened by alcohol slurring the name into mythical obscurity—and he would buy a high ladder, he would climb that ladder and sit on the top and gaze over the ocean to the island so he could see the cricket games.

It had been no joke, no one had ever laughed; and it had turned grim the day Hari announced, with a belligerent seriousness, that he had worked out the southerly angle at which he would set the ladder in order to get an unobstructed view of the cricket grounds through a gap in the mountains.

Vernon said, "Best seat in the house, maan."

Jenny snorted. "He couldn't learn to leave that seat. That was his problem. He couldn't get away, not far away enough from what he was running from to see what he was running to."

Vernon clenched his fists on the counter. The spray of the water still thudding into the sink speckled his arm. "He wasn't running *to* anything." He gesticulated with one fist: the stained walls, the peeling door, the window framing grey. "This?"

She stood up, agitated, moved to the door, leaned against the frame, her arms folded across her ribs, lifting her breasts. "Yes. This." An expressionless voice: it struck him as odd, as a reproach.

He opened his mouth to protest; it took extraordinary effort. The sound caught in his throat, bubbled, popped.

The telephone rang in the living room.

Jenny went to answer it, leaving him with a sense of abandonment, of futility. He seemed to face an awesome void.

Still the sound bubbled in his throat. It filled his ears, mingling with the water crashing into the sink to form a roar.

The kitchen—the window, the walls with the cheap, unframed prints, the spare table with metal chairs—tilted upward, losing the horizontal, and it took an effort of lucidity to comprehend that his head was inclining to the left. He could feel the veins and tissue on the right side of his neck tighten, begin to strain. He thought: They must be bulging like cables.

Jenny appeared in the doorway. She spoke, mouthing words he could not hear. Her face tightened and then she was crowding him, reaching around the body he now felt incapable of moving to turn off the tap. The roar lessened, ended. The words no longer bubbled in his throat. His ears felt light, cavernous.

She spoke once more and her words echoed, seeming to come from a great distance. He had to seize on individual sounds to elicit a message from what she was saying.

"It's Peter. He's drunk, he's crying, and he wants to come over." Her voice was heavy with anger. "I won't have him here. Not again. No more. He and Hari were always drunk enough."

"Tell him, tell him . . ." He faltered, straightened his head, the tightened veins relaxed. "Tell him to go to bed. I don't want to see him. Not now. Not today." And, expecting guilt, he felt relief, as if freed from a burden he hadn't before recognized.

She said, "You're tired. Go to bed."

A vein began to pulse on his temple and, by instinct, she reached out and rubbed it gently with the tips of her fingers.

He was walking on a wide sidewalk. There was sun but no warmth, the air neutral. It was early in the day. People walked by singly, cars could be seen only in the distance.

He walked with a purpose. He was going somewhere but he was glad no one asked his destination. He would not have known what to reply and imagined acute embarrassment at the question.

He looked with a particular uninterest at the stores he passed—record stores, clothes stores, links of fast-food chains—dark interiors offering not mystery or enticement but gloom and the possibility of money ill-spent.

Then, as if it were the most natural thing in the world, he found himself lying on the sidewalk looking up at the sky, ink blue with curls of diaphanous white cloud. That something was not right he was fully aware, but only when he tried to get up did he realize that his torso had been severed diagonally from just under his ribcage to the small of his back. His hips and legs lay two feet away, beyond reach, like the discarded lower half of a mannequin.

People walked by. He saw the disdainful curve of women's jacked-up ankles, the well-pressed hems of expensive pants, shoes black and solid. No one took notice of him.

Curious, he examined his lower half. The cut had been clean. There was no blood. The wound appeared to have been coated in a clear plastic and he could see the ends of veins pulsing red against the transparent skin. There was, he knew, no danger.

He wanted to put himself back together again. He knew that all he had to do was get hold of his legs, put them to his torso, and all would be fine. Maybe he would need a little glue, he reasoned, curiously proud of the practicality of the thought, but surely he would be able to keep his parts together until he could get to a hardware store.

He tried to reach for his legs but balance eluded him and he rocked back and forth like a toy rocking-horse, his legs approaching then retreating, approaching then retreating, without ever getting any closer, seeming instead to gain distance so that he became afraid of losing sight of them.

Embarrassment: what a fool he must appear to the passers-by. But surely someone would see he needed help. Surely they understood: didn't this happen to everyone? It had occurred so mildly, so finely, this separation.

A man wearing a grey hat and grey overcoat stopped. He bent down towards Vernon.

It was Hari. Then it was Peter. Then Hari again.

Then it was no one. Just a man.

The man had no arms.

Despair.

It was hot under the covers. He could feel Jenny's body, her warmth, her curves, rising and falling rhythmically next to him. The room was dark, the window luminescent. The left edge of the dresser had the solid angularity of a casket and the slash of mirror above it, white, icy, glowed in the dark. The clock showed a few minutes before one.

His clothes—not his pyjamas, his street clothes, thick and heavy with seams that seared patterns into his skin—enclosed him like a body cast, gripped at him with a glutinous wetness.

He threw back the covers and met the gratifying chill of the air. He eased off the bed, the roughness of the carpet cushioned by his socks, and stood for a minute, uncertain, tasting still the dregs of the despair that had forced him into wakefulness.

The window offered the only light. Changed perspective redefined that corner of the dresser, that sliver of mirror, made them ordinary, graspable. He walked to the window and, in the darkness, it was like gliding: he had no sense of control over his legs, it was as though he were being conveyed.

The glass was fogged over, the moisture thickening the light of the street-lamps and lavishing it over the surface like another skin, more substantial than even itself. Vernon rubbed at it with his fingertips and he noticed, with an interest that struck him as a kind of strength, that tonight there was no ice.

His fingers created a wet porthole, the moisture collecting at the edge like a rim.

A light snow was falling. The buildings across the street were shuttered and dark. The street-lamp revealed once more a white shroud, the streetcar tracks and slush of the day camouflaged by a fresh, new skin.

The bed creaked behind him. Jenny said, "Vern?"

He said, "Yes."

The telephone rang. He reached for it with deliberation, as if he had been expecting it.

"Hello."

As he listened he continued to finger the porthole, creating patterns in the water, watching them disappear into the whole, then creating new ones.

"When?"

His hand moved in circles, enlarging the porthole, causing the rim of water to thicken and bulge.

"Now, look here, Peter."

The rim broke. The water, channelling itself along the bed of the rim, flowed down the windowpane in a single, thick runnel, pooled on the wooden frame, swelled, tumbled over the side, and exploded like a dark stain on the windowsill.

"Screw you, Peter."

He hung up, still with deliberation, and reached for the porthole, already clouding over.

He said, "Hari's dead."

Jenny sighed, got out of bed and went over to him.

He said, "You know, Peter's dead too."

She put her arm around his waist. He felt her warmth and realized how cold he'd grown. He thought: The whole world, everybody's a refugee, everybody's running from one thing or another.

And then another thought chilled him: But it's happening here too. This country around him was beginning to crack. The angry words, the petty hatreds, the attitude not of living off the land but of raping it. He had seen it before, been through it before, and much more, more that was still to come, until a time when, even from here, the haven now, people would begin to flee.

He saw the earth, as from space, streams of people in continuous motion, circling the sphere in search of the next stop which, they always knew, would prove temporary in the end.

Through the porthole the snow grew heavier, the flakes bloated and ponderous. The street-lamp blinked once, twice, then went out. All that remained of the world was Jenny's arm, her warmth, her weight pressing against him. And the vein that pulsed in his temple.

He thought: Where to next, Refugee?

COUNTING
THE WIND

.   This morning as usual, as I come out of the bedroom
for breakfast, I say to Grandmother, "Good morning,
Grandmother, how are you today?"

And this morning as usual, sitting in her rocking chair
staring out the window, Grandmother replies, "Quiet, son,
quiet, for I am counting the wind." But this morning, not as
usual, she adds: "They are many this morning."

The extra comment, so unlike her, startles me. "Begging
your pardon, Grandmother, what did you say?" The new
words are more than unexpected, are like a scar suddenly
materialized on a face long unblemished. I look at her, a little
figure in black sitting up rigidly, eyes clear and intent reaching
out into the cloudless blue. She says nothing more, is lost in
her concentration.

"They've taken the town," my wife says, putting my bread
and coffee on the table.

"Who?"

"They."

"Who are 'they'?"

"Does it matter?"

I go to the window and look out to the town on the distant
hill. Houses, white walls, red-tile roofs, clustered in great

disorder. At the top, the tower of the fortified church, brown, of stone never whitewashed. At the bottom, skirting the old Roman city walls, the river of liquid emerald spanned by two bridges, one stone and ancient, the other steel and recent. We are too far away and the town too dense, its streets narrow and tight, to reveal any activity. The only discernible difference this morning is a column of black smoke rising from somewhere in the centre like a storm cloud billowing from the earth.

Grandmother had begun her vigil at the window just over twenty years before, the day after the night Grandfather died while on his way home, a robber's knife opening his back like a melon split for eating. Emilio was the one who found him lying cold, wet, and dead in the middle of the dusty, unpaved road that led through the fields, dry and bald, to the little farm where they lived at the time.

He remembered the night well. The thinnest crescent of moon, stars, behind them as backdrop a sky so dark it offered but its immensity. On either side of the road along which he walked more by instinct than by light in search of Grandfather, the empty, hilly fields rolled away in shadow, filling the dry night air with the odor of dead earth desiccated by the sun and that vague, peculiar smell of distant fire. He could see nothing beyond the most general of shapes, bulks of darkness lesser or greater than the drowning night. Unable to see, looking without hope of finding, he tripped over Grandfather, fell directly onto him, felt the stickiness of his blood wash onto his face and chest, smelt the pungency of freshly cut meat.

Grandfather was too heavy for Emilio to carry, so he dragged him back to the farm holding him by the feet—bare, bereft of even socks, for it was these plus the little money he had had on him that they had stolen—over three miles of gravelled road, through the darkness that absorbed his cries, through the darkness that gave him at one point of uncontrollable grief the thin, absurd hope that this was not Grandfather he was dragging: he had not seen his face, there was not enough light.

When he came within sight of the lights of the farmhouse, he screamed and screamed. For long minutes, minutes lengthened by his exhaustion, his grief, his terror, no one appeared. Then the door opened slowly and a head, his father's head, looked cautiously out. Emilio screamed: "Papa!" His father flung the door open and ran out, his movements jerky and grotesque from the lame leg that kept him in immobilizing pain much of the time. He looked wildly around, confused, not knowing from where in the night the cry had come. Emilio screamed again.

His recollections after that were confused: voices, hands, people scrambling in the night, being lifted. And a scream, a long, pure, and piercing scream which, in its pain, quickly lost all resemblance to Grandmother's voice and became an appeal to the heavens, an appeal issued from a throat gone savage.

It was from the next morning, when Grandmother seemed to function better than he, boiling her clothes in black dye in the huge vat normally used for stewing, that she lost her language and began, in her nearly total silence, counting the wind.

This too was how he came to his job. The cemetery in which they buried Grandfather had just lost its caretaker. The job was offered to Emilio's father and when he didn't want it—his bad leg, which would cause his decline and eventual death, a hindrance—Emilio accepted it. Caretaker of a cemetery! The thought appalled even then. It seemed a post for someone decades older than his eighteen years. But he saw it as a way out of the farm, an enterprise dying in the grip of drought, and as a way, too, of fulfilling the responsibility he felt towards Grandfather for having grated his head through to the skull.

His first view of the cemetery remained with him, for it was the only thing in those days of stupor that offered a startling sparkle. He had always been aware of the cemetery but had never really paid attention to it, in the same way that, always aware of death, we never really contemplate it until such a moment as it places itself squarely before us, revealing in a sudden divulgence the hideous infinity of its unknowns. As they made their slow way that hot August morning towards the cemetery, bearing Grandfather in the box that seemed too small to contain all he had been, the windows of the rectangular, five-storey tombs shone at them from the gentle hill they covered, hundreds of panes of glass shooting off sun from the buildings of dark stone, tomb-buildings forming of themselves a town, a little city of the dead.

In the years since, first his mother then his father died. The farm was abandoned and Grandmother came to live with him at the cemetery. He married. It was years before his wife conceived and, when she did, the baby, unexpected, so long no longer hoped for, was like a second breath, a sudden infusion of purpose and ability in their marriage.

Their life out of the shadow of the distant town had been a quiet one, at most two or three funerals a month and, in between, the undemanding tasks of his charges: some gardening, some patching, some neatening.

But that day, the column of smoke rising from the town told him that changes were in the wind, changes that should have had nothing to do with them. They had never paid attention to the worries of the world. Yet, he never forgot, those who had killed Grandfather had had nothing to do with him either. They had come at him out of the dark, wielding knives that struck indiscriminately, with a terrifying neutrality. So, as he watched that tall column of thickening smoke, he worried.

To get here from the town you have to follow a long unpaved road that runs through the bare hills. When a funeral procession begins its final journey towards us, it is easy to follow its progression by the dust that it kicks up. In this landscape even a single man stands out like a cockroach on a whitewashed wall.

I am almost finished breakfast, my usual meal of bread, butter, and a mug of thick, black coffee with two heaping spoons of sugar, when my wife, our baby feeding at her breast, calls to me from Grandmother's window: "Who is being buried today?"

"Nobody."

"Well, someone's coming."

"Who is it?"

"I don't know, it's a car."

I push back my chair and, wiping my chin on my sleeve, go to the window. At my approach Grandmother, feeling crowded, shifts impatiently in her rocking chair, her Bible gripped tightly in her hands. I do not recognize the car. "It's not for a funeral," I say, "he's driving too quickly. People never hurry when they're on cemetery business. No, it's something else."

"Quiet, quiet," Grandmother hisses, slapping at her lap once with the Bible.

My wife glances at me, puzzled, then shrugs in the gentle, dismissing impatience she has built up over the years for Grandmother. She takes her breast from the baby and goes into the bedroom with him. I gaze once more at the speeding car, the only movement but for the column of smoke in the baking expanse before me, and my anxiety rises.

"The wind," Grandmother says, "the wind."

I squeeze her shoulder gently, with an affection that she, in her absorption, fails to notice; and, as so often in the past, I wonder for a brief moment or two what it is that she is seeing.

He began work that morning on the tomb on the far side of the cemetery, just across from the ossuary. It was a building long neglected, almost two hundred of its two hundred and sixty crypts—five up by twenty across on the front and back, five up and six across on the sides—having remained untended, some for months, some for years. Most had not been fitted with glass panelling at the aperture, had been simply sealed with a concrete block stamped with the words FUNERARY PROPERTY OF . . . or HERE IS DEPOSITED THE BODY OF . . ., as if families had buried their loved ones with dispatch and a businesslike dusting of the hands. They were crypts left un-decorated: no framed photograph, no vase with flowers, no rosaries left on the narrow sill, not even an offering of words beyond the cryptic cemetery labelling. The problem was, he knew, that these crypts were mostly rented. There would be, at one point or another, a time for each of them to be opened up, cleaned—the bones going to the ossuary only feet away—and made ready for the next occupant. Over time, weeds had sprung up on some, roots working their way into the cracks, eating away at the cement that held the concrete blocks in place. Others had simply begun to crumble at the edges, letters fading, concrete dark and pitted.

He began the clean-up at the fifth and highest level, ladder well grounded in the gravel. First he pulled out the weeds and let them drift, spinning, to the ground; then, with a piece of thick wire, he dislodged the cracked and crumbled cement from around the edges, blowing the grey dust away until the cavity was clean. It was, he reflected, a bit like cleaning a wound and it made him think back to the morning years before when, younger, in too great a hurry to go to the town to visit the woman who would become his wife, he had fallen from the ladder and struck his forehead on a stone. He had had to clean the wound himself, brushing away sand, picking out tiny pieces of gravel from the exposed flesh: this was how he had learned gentleness. The wound, when healed, had left a bright pink patch the shape of an exploding star on his sunburnt skin.

He worked quietly, taking his time partly, he knew, in deference to the long-forgotten dead who lay within feet of him, and also because it was easy, pleasant work. The sun, not yet too hot, warmed him just enough to bring a light sheen of perspiration to his forearms.

He was working on the second crypt, one of the nameless ones, time having left nothing but the faintest outlines of the first two letters of his or her name, when he heard heavy footsteps crunching along the gravel towards him: boots, and a rapid, measured pace that was a mixture of controlled urgency and determination.

"Cemetery keeper," a man's voice shouted.

"Here."

I remain at the top of the ladder, my mind noting a sudden surge in my anxiety. I wonder where my wife and baby are. The footsteps come closer and presently, from around the corner, appears a man in a dirty blue uniform and black riding boots. Hanging at his side from the black belt strapped around his waist is a large pistol. He hasn't shaved in several days. "Cemetery keeper," he says, looking up at me through eyes squinted against the sun, "come down, I want to talk to you."

I climb down, taking my time. He is not a tall man, but solidly built. His eyes are red with fatigue and the bushy eyebrows above them seem to weigh heavily on his forehead. What I took from the top of the ladder for dirt on his uniform are, I now see, patches of dried blood.

"Cemetery keeper, I need some of your space."

"Well, we're almost full here. How many crypts do you need?" It is business. My anxiety lessens, confidence strengthens.

"No crypts. I need ground, a place where we can dig."

"For how many?"

"I don't know yet."

"Very many?"

"Just show me the ground, cemetery keeper. The rest doesn't concern you."

"And what about the records?" It is part of my job to enter in the cemetery log every burial, the name, the date, the cause of death. "I must write everything down."

His tongue licks at his lips as, thinking, he eyes me. "We will give you a list," he says finally.

"All right, come with me." I take him to the only open ground left in the cemetery, a plot of land on which the town council had promised, years before, to build another tomb but had never found the money to do it.

He nods in satisfaction. "It'll do. For now."

I walk him back to his car and he drives off without a word, without a glance.

I go into the house. My wife, on her knees washing the floor, looks worriedly at me, questions in her eyes. I shrug. Over at the window Grandmother, leaning forward in her rocking chair, looking now not up at the sky but down at the burnt fields, mutters to herself. Through the window I see the car speeding back to town, dust billowing in its wake. Grandmother mutters again. "Pardon, Grandmother?" I say.

"The wind," she says, "the wind."

And I see that her eyes are locked with a great intensity on the speeding car.

He was wakened early the next morning, the sun was not yet up, by the growl of a truck pulling up at the side of the house.

Low voices gave orders. Metal clinked on metal. Pulling on his pants, he peered out the window to see figures of men, still shadowy in the pre-dawn, jumping down from the high-backed tray of the truck. In the cast of the dim headlights he recognized the soldier who had come to see him the previous morning, an officer, he saw now, from the way the others deferred to him, in where they stood, how they stood.

Behind him, in the darkness of the bedroom, the baby began to cry and he heard his wife, awoken with him in a sudden spasm of fear, scramble from the bed over to the crib. Through the anxiety clutching at her voice she tried to soothe him with sounds that, in their urgency, only caused him to cry more. Then he was silent and Emilio knew she had given him her breast.

He made his way through the darkened house and out the front door into the cool morning air. In the sky the last of the stars were dying out against the dawn that was beginning to hint at itself. The lights of the truck glowed in a yellow haze from the side of the house. The soldiers, ten in all, were lined up in two ranks, each with a shovel in his hand and a rifle slung over his shoulder. At his approach, the officer, blood stains on his uniform looking once more like dirt or grease in the light of the truck, turned to him. "Good morning, cemetery keeper," he said in a voice that conveyed displeasure at seeing him.

"Good morning."

I look from him to the soldiers and back to him. "Is this not an early hour to be having a funeral?"

"Calm down, cemetery keeper, this has nothing to do with you. Go back to your bed and get your beauty rest."

"What happens here is my business. The cemetery is my responsibility."

"The books are your responsibility," he says curtly, reaching into his breast pocket for a sheet of paper that he holds out to me. "Here is your list, all the names."

I take the paper and hold it up to the light. Thirteen names, three of which, to my shock, I recognize. "How did they die?"

"Wounds received in battle."

"In battle?" Of the names I know, one is the schoolteacher, a thin, sickly man whose greatest exertion is his daily walk to and from the school; the second is little more than a boy, thick in the head but kind in a dim-witted sort of way, who spends most of his time helping his father in their grocery store; and the third is his father, a thin, tall man, ascetic in aspect, who considers himself something of an intellectual—he can, could, be seen almost every evening sitting conspicuously upright in a chair in front of his house, his nose stuck in a book—and whose only visible regret is the slowness of his son. These are not people to have died in battle. "They were fighting?" I ask.

"You heard what I said, cemetery keeper. Died of wounds received in battle. Write it." He turns from me and signals to his men to follow him. One man is left with the truck, on guard. As they march away towards the plot of open ground, the officer's voice rings out into the brightening dawn. "Go about your work, cemetery keeper, and we will go about ours." He does not look back at me and I stand there, cold in my thin nightshirt, holding the sheet of paper, knowing with a brutal certainty that the cemetery is about to undergo a change that is as yet too subtle for me to understand; and knowing too that I alone am no longer master here. For a moment my anger rises and I want to run after them, demanding death certificates, numbers, dates. I want to reassert my authority.

Then, from behind me, I hear my wife calling to me in a whisper. She is peering around the corner of the house, one fearful eye below dishevelled hair. We go into the house and she demands to know what is happening. What can I say? "The army is burying its dead."

Suddenly Grandmother, still in her nightdress, hair uncombed, eyes bloodshot and staring wildly ahead, shuffles out of her bedroom. She comes up to me, seizes my sleeve, and tugs harshly at it. "Do you hear it?" she whispers urgently, "Do you hear it building? My God, my God, the wind."

Four hours later, when they had left, he clambered down from the ladder and made his way among the tombs towards the open ground. With so many men to dig, it had taken them longer than it should have to bury thirteen people and Emilio was curious about what they had been up to. He walked past the last of the tombs beyond which, around the corner, he saw a small mountain of uncovered earth, light brown and rocky, in chunks large and small, more broken than shovelled out.

"Halt! Don't move," a voice suddenly called out, its confidence strangely tremulous at the end.

He looked around and at the far end of the tomb saw a soldier, rifle hanging uselessly by the strap from the crook of his left elbow, relieving himself against the marble plaque of one of the crypts.

"Wait right there," he said, struggling to hold on to the rifle while buttoning up his pants.

Emilio stood still, watching the soldier with growing amusement. He was not very old, sixteen or seventeen, and from the look of him had never shaved, had never even needed to. "I am just inspecting my cemetery," he said.

"Well, you can't." He approached, rifle cradled in his hands. "I have orders."

"I am in charge of the cemetery."

"Not this part of it."

"What's going on here?" Emilio swept his hand towards the mound of dirt.

"Get back. This is not for you." The soldier pushed at him with the rifle. "Go on. Get out of here." He displayed more nervousness than aggression.

"Take it easy, boy, calm down. Everybody has to take a piss some time, even brave warriors." He had meant it as a joke but he saw the boy's face darken and his right index finger curl around the trigger of the rifle. "All right," Emilio said, retreating. "I'm going."

He returned to his work on the tomb, his mind examining the picture that he had captured of the army's work. It didn't require much thought to realize that all that dirt couldn't have been from thirteen graves, that it could have come only from a pit, large and deep, preparations for the interment of far greater numbers.

"Open up, cemetery keeper, it's me."

"Who are you?"

"Isidro. The guard."

"It's two o'clock in the morning. What do you want?"

"Just open up. I want something to drink. My canteen's empty."

I open the door. The boy, rifle slung on his shoulder, hesitates on the threshold, then steps forward into the weak light of the single candle burning on the table. In the light, his face, open and unsure, appears fragile. I motion to him to sit at the table and he does so, stiff-backed, without removing the rifle, with a formality that shows his barely controlled uncertainty.

"Are you hungry?"

"No. Yes. Well, if you have some bread."

"And cheese?"

"Thank you."

"Please keep your voice down, the baby's asleep."

While I get the bread and cheese and a cup of water, he sits unmoving, the light from the candle highlighting certain of his features, the flat of the forehead, the jut of his nose and chin, the gleam of the buttons on his tunic. He does not look at me, stares ahead at the wall. He looks from here more than ever like a boy.

"You have been a soldier for a long time?"

"Long enough."

"You have killed?"

He turns his head towards me and, for a moment, is silent. Then, with an irritation in his voice, a sense of injury, he says, "Of course, many times."

I place the food before him and he looks at it, the hunk of bread, the cheese, the water, as if trying to decide what to do with it.

"Eat," I say and he bends protectively over the food, elbows to either side of the plate, and begins to eat. His manner, with its guarded quickness, is almost surreptitious. He eats in silence for a few minutes, the only sound that of his drinking, the water swallowed in audible gulps. I sit to his left, watching him, waiting for him to finish.

He finally straightens up, pushes away the plate, throws back his head, and finishes off the water. Then he turns and watches me, wordless.

"Are you still hungry?" I ask.

He shakes his head: no.

"Is there something else you would like?"

Again he shakes his head: no. But he makes no move to leave and, for a few seconds, we sit in mutual silence in the darkness of the candlelight. Outside the wind begins to blow, a low, quiet hiss.

"The wind is up," I say. "It must be cold out."

He nods, almost imperceptibly.

"Will you be warm enough?"

Again he nods, slowly standing up, his back remaining as stiff and as straight as his rifle. I follow him to the door, open it for him, and again, as on entering, he hesitates at the threshold, looking out now into the night. He glances quickly at me before stepping through the door and, in that second or two, I think I see tears in his eyes. Maybe it's the bad light, maybe his fatigue, maybe my imagination, but that quick look tells me that it is neither hunger nor thirst that has prompted this visit, just the simple fears of a boy left alone at night in the stark darkness of a cemetery. I suddenly know, too, that he has never seen battle, has never killed anyone. This is the closest company he has ever kept with death.

Before shutting the door and returning to bed, I listen for the sounds of the night. There is only the crunch of his boots on the gravel, and the swishing and hissing of the wind among the tombs swallowed by darkness.

Sleep does not come easily. I lie awake in the darkness, my wife under the blanket next to me pretending to sleep, for she knows that when she lies awake with worry I become agitated with worry for her. I know, however, that eventually her pretence will become reality and she will sleep deeply from her effort to spare me.

Time passes slowly in the dark. There is no movement of sun, are no shadows to lengthen then shorten then lengthen, marking for us the steady passage of the hours. Time in the dark is time frozen. Thoughts, unordered, come and go, unlikely hints of memories and fears. Faces, feelings, light and dark, each brushing lightly against me, nudging my emotions, tickling my soul.

My wife's breathing becomes deep and steady. I relax, knowing her to be safe in her dreams. The baby lies quietly asleep in his crib in the corner, my son whose mere existence offers me a satisfaction I cannot understand, a satisfaction that goes instinctively to the very core of all that I am. My head works its way into the pillow, fitting nicely into the hollow it has carved out for itself, a fold of material rising against my right cheek in a secure, comforting embrace. My eyes close in the pleasant grip of approaching sleep; to open them now would require effort, or shock.

Yet, a part of my mind remains alert, as if on watch, and it is this part that, some time later, detects the sounds of a slow movement in the living room, that in alarm pries open my eyes and directs them to the bedroom door, a black rectangle defined at its edges by the fuzz of a weak light beyond. A moment of quiet wonder is followed by a sudden tension and I fling back the blanket, freeing myself from its constriction. Not courage, this, but a simple urge to protection: my wife, my baby.

My wife stirs at my movement and, briefly, I freeze until she settles back down. Then I get up and walk slowly over to the door, open it slightly, and look out into the living room. The candle is lit and Grandmother, in her nightdress but with hair reassuringly brushed into place, a mug of coffee in her hand, is sitting in her rocking chair before the open window. I go out, closing the door behind me. "Grandmother, what are you doing up at so early an hour?" The clock on the wall shows that it is just past five a.m.

The air coming in through the open window is cool. I throw a blanket from the sofa around my shoulders, take a chair from the table, and join Grandmother. Through the window, darkness. The stars have gone but the sun has not yet begun its ascent. Grandmother, intense, does not seem to have noticed me. She is seeing something that I cannot. "Grandmother," I say, "what do you see? What is out there?"

"Shhh. The wind. I am counting." Her tone is not so much patient as removed, absorbed. Her answer, for the first time, irritates me, but I understand immediately that my irritation comes not because of her but because of myself, because of this unease I feel but do not understand. I pull the blanket more tightly around myself and sit quietly, looking out with Grandmother into the darkness, listening to the constant whisper of the wandering wind.

Not much later—the sky was just beginning to lighten—he heard the growl of a truck and the crunching of gravel beneath its wheels. He glanced at Grandmother. She was unperturbed, as if she hadn't noticed the arrival of the vehicle. "More dead," he said, getting up to dress. He would need to go get his list.

He found his wife awake in bed. He motioned her to stay where she was, hurriedly put on his clothes, and went outside. As he closed the door behind him he saw that Grandmother was now leaning forward in her chair, paying rapt attention to her private events.

He had barely taken two steps in the cool morning air when a familiar silhouette rounded the corner ahead of him and said in a conversational voice, "Hold it right there, cemetery keeper. I have your list." In the background he heard another truck pulling up, and behind it a third.

"Good morning, Captain."

"Sergeant. Here's your list." The sergeant stopped three paces away and tossed him a roll of pages bound with a rubber band. He caught it with both hands. The sergeant turned to go but he stopped, half turned. "Oh, by the way, for your information, they have all died of natural causes."

"All? How many are there?"

"I haven't counted them."

"Natural causes, you say."

"Yes. Like those from yesterday."

"Them too? Not battle wounds? I don't understand."

"Think about it, cemetery keeper. When a bullet enters

your body, it is natural to die, isn't that right?"

Emilio didn't know what to say. For a moment he thought the sergeant was making a grotesque joke.

"This is army business, cemetery keeper. There is nothing for you to understand. Natural causes, don't forget." He turned and walked off towards the trucks, a weary, lumbering silhouette in the morning half-light.

Emilio stood for a moment, the roll of names growing warm in his hand. Inside the house the baby began to cry. He knew his wife would be up, turned and went inside. Grandmother was still in her rocking chair looking out, hands gripping tightly at the arms of the chair. Behind her the sky showed a cool, light blue. His wife was in the bedroom sitting on the edge of the bed nursing the baby.

Reassuring her, he went and sat at the table. In the light of the candle he opened out the roll of pages, five in all. On each, scribbled hastily in a near-illiterate hand, were ten names. He recognized none of them, so he knew they were not of the town. They were bringing others here, strangers, probably from other towns in the region that the cemetery also served. He fetched the cemetery log from under the bed in the bedroom and was about to put pen to paper when he heard the first volley of shots.

The firing doesn't stop, goes on and on and on like a roll-call of thunder, only sharper, more piercing. The baby, frightened, cries. With every volley my wife groans as if she has been hit. Grandmother shows no reaction. And I sit frozen at the table, pen poised, aghast, thinking: Stop-stop-stop-stop—

And finally the silence. A silence that echoes. A silence more full of threat than the shattering that prompted it. A silence that brings to mind frightening images of impossibility and nightmare.

My jaws hurt. I become aware that I am clenching my teeth tightly, upper against lower, and that the strain, a dull pain, is reaching up past my temples to my forehead in a slow, heavy throb. I make an effort to open my mouth but it is difficult; it is as if the teeth are glued together. As they move stiffly apart, with pain, double screams come from behind me: my wife, my baby. In one movement I am up, around and in the bedroom, my chair crashing to the floor.

My wife, hugging the baby tightly, her head thrown back, is sitting on the floor beside the bed, her mouth open in an animal scream. I throw myself down next to her, reach for her head and pull her to me. Abruptly she stops screaming, makes a choking sound, whispers, "Monsters, monsters." Her breathing is labored. The baby sputters and begins to calm down. My wife pulls gently away from me, strokes the baby's head, returns his mouth to her breast. I brush the hair from her face, kiss her on the forehead and help her back up to the bed. When, after a while, she looks at me, it is with eyes large and glittering, fear and tears.

I sit with them for a few minutes, less to soothe them, I realize, than to assure myself that they are safe. It is dark and cool in the room but perspiration covers my skin, and when I run my fingers along my wife's neck and shoulders they come away wet. Soon, her eyes are closed and she is rocking slowly back and forth, the baby, feeding peaceably, almost lost in her arms.

I get up and leave the bedroom, closing the door behind me with care. Grandmother is snoring at the window, a soft morning light spreading over her and into the room. The sky, light blue and clean of cloud as if swept by the night wind, tells of great heat to come.

Peace: an old woman asleep before a window open to the sky and sun.

Peace: my wife nursing our baby.

Peace: the candle still burning on the table, flame steady and yellow.

My life goes through my head, presents itself to me like

painted reminders, and my anger surges at this intrusion by the sounds of active death.

Never again, I think, never again, making my way across the room and out through the front door. I will tell them to stop, I will tell them this cannot continue, I will tell them.

I hurry across the gravel to where the three trucks, large and olive green, are parked. From beyond the last truck come voices, low, brief, speaking words rather than sentences. A group of soldiers, blue uniforms almost grey with dirt, rifles slung on shoulders or held wearily in one hand, is standing around smoking. They look at me uneasily as I approach. None of them says anything. The crunch of my shoes on the gravel echoes against the metal of the truck. The sergeant is not with them. I ask for him. They look at each other. Still no one speaks. I ask again. Then a voice hoarse with threat says, "Go away, cemetery keeper. The sergeant is a busy man."

"Only a minute," I say.

"Not even a minute," the voice replies.

I cannot see the soldier. He is sitting somewhere beyond the group. "Please," I say, starting through the group towards his voice. The soldiers make way and I find myself staring at the barrel of a rifle. Holding it is the young guard, Isidro. His eyes, red, sparkle with insanity. There is a grey tint to his face.

"Go away," he says in a voice not that of last night, "go now before I take you for a walk too." His eyes are intense, with a blazing ferocity I have seen before only in dogs driven mad by thirst and hunger. I raise my hands in the air and back away. I know now all hope is gone.

He stayed inside the house all day. Grandmother, awoken, dressed, spent her day as usual in her rocking chair before the window. His wife, mute, sat curled into a corner of the sofa hugging the baby to her. Once, sitting at the table, he tried to inscribe the roll of names into the cemetery log but when it came time to enter the cause of death his fingers failed him, would not even hold the pen.

As the day wore on it grew hot in the house. In mid-afternoon, lulled by the stillness and heat, they all fell asleep, Grandmother in her rocking chair, his wife on the sofa with the baby on her lap, Emilio with his head on the table. When they awoke—all at the same time, the growl of approaching trucks shocking them into a wild, tensed wakefulness—the sun was already setting, the sky a deepening blue.

They sat listening in silence: heavy brakes, dying engines, countless boots thudding to the gravel, orders voiced, a sudden explosion of swear words, and finally the heavy, crunching shuffle of a crowd moving slowly across the gravel like the biggest of funeral processions.

There was a knock at the door. Emilio opened it. The sergeant, wordless, eyes small below forehead tightened into wrinkles, mouth set as if clamped, handed him another roll of names. He took it, found he could say nothing, gagged at the powerful odor of brandy. Closing the door as the sergeant walked away, he threw the roll of paper to the table. It knocked the candle over, rolled along the table top and fell to the floor. His wife looked at him. Grandmother continued her vigil.

Suddenly a morbid curiosity grew in him. Suddenly he had to know, to see for himself what was happening in the cemetery so long cared for, so long tended to, the cemetery that was no longer his. He put his hand on the door handle, fear fighting curiosity. The thump of his heart filled his head, his breathing became short and insufficient, he could hear the air scraping its way through his nostrils, feel it stopping halfway down his windpipe.

His wife called to him, his name in her mouth a low plea of fear and warning.

He said, "Quiet," slipped off his shoes, opened the door an inch, looked out. No one, only the long shadows of the tombs separated by channels of orange light from the sun sinking, unseen, into the horizon. He stepped out, pulling the door shut behind him. The heat of the day was beginning to lift and the bare skin of his forearms and neck detected intimations of the evening coolness.

Bent over double—instinct, this, for it served no purpose beyond the sense of making himself smaller, less noticeable—he hurried among the tombs towards the one he had been working on the morning before, this work of tidying and patching long forgotten. He took the ladder down, slung it on his shoulder, and walked quickly towards the open ground. The gravel, hard and stony, hurt his feet through the socks, and fine grains of sand worked their way through the wool to between his toes, coating the skin like a granular powder.

Approaching the last tomb, he began walking on the balls of his feet. The stones and pebbles became sharper, the ladder more difficult to balance on his shoulder. He was breathing through his mouth, his tongue felt thick and dry. He leaned the ladder against the wall of the tomb, tested it once by pulling on it; then, placing his feet with care on each rung, he climbed slowly to the top. He moved from the ladder to the roof of the tomb on his hands and knees. He was out of breath, he had taken no air throughout the climb. Gasping shallowly, he crawled over to the far edge of the roof.

I lie flat on the roof of the tomb for a few minutes, the rough concrete pressing into the flesh of my cheek and ear. My breathing is still labored; somehow, no matter how I try, I cannot get enough air into my lungs to satisfy them. I want very much to raise my head and look over the edge but simple fear keeps me down flat and tight against the still-warm concrete.

Minutes pass, and it is only after this time that the strange quiet strikes me. There are, not far below me, many men, many guns. But this silence is the silence of the cemetery asleep, the dead undisturbed. Encouraged, grasping onto the thought—absurd, I know, but the possibility offers the prospect of joy as an unearned gift—the thought that somehow, without my noticing and for reasons all their mysterious own, they have left, I raise my head and look down.

No, they are there, figures standing still in the gathering dark. In a quarter of an hour I will be unable to see them and they will be unable to see to do their work. But then from the right there is the low rumble of an engine and a flash of light. A car is being slowly manoeuvred between the tombs. They will have their light, they will do their work.

In a minute the headlamps of the car, the sergeant's, I imagine, the one in which he first came to the cemetery, flood the scene before me in a thick yellow light that is more like a mustard fog. Almost directly below me are the soldiers. Before them a large pit, dirt piled to one side, into which the light does not reach. On the other side of the pit, the cemetery wall, the concrete just above the lip of the pit nibbled and stained. The car engine is turned off, the lights focussed on the wall.

Without orders, knowing what is expected of them, five soldiers form themselves into a line, rifle bolts clicking in near unison. From out of the darkness other soldiers push five men before them, men similar in their raggedness and a numbed docility, hands bound behind them with what, glinting in the light, looks like wire. They are lined up in front of the wall at the edge of the pit, facing the soldiers. All but one keep their eyes open, looking around not with courage but with a kind of stunned wonder. It is almost as if they do not know where they are, what is about to happen, and they are searching for an explanation. The one with his eyes closed, the youngest, I think, maybe seventeen or eighteen, appears to be praying.

The sergeant comes into the light, stands casually beside the soldiers. He says, in a voice so low I am sure the prisoners do not hear, "Okay, boys." The soldiers raise their rifles and take aim. Quietly: "Fire." The rifles crack. My eyes seem to follow the bullets from the quick flames of the barrels to their targets; red stains appear as if by magic on the chests of the four who have been watching. Faces contorted, they tumble into the pit. The fifth, the boy, is hit in the right eye, blood explodes on his face, he does not fall forward, crumples instead as if sitting back against the wall, head lolling lifelessly onto his right shoulder, blood gushes down onto his shirt, spreading rapidly. A soldier runs up and kicks the body into the pit. As it disappears a groan comes from the darkness: one of the men has not died. The soldier stops, puzzled, unsure, bends over and peers into the pit. "Use your pistol, damn you!" screams the sergeant. The soldier removes his pistol from its holster, points it down into the pit but cannot find a target. Another groan. It is too dark, the soldier still cannot find the man. Suddenly he opens fire, six, eight, ten shots sent crashing into the darkness. Smoke from the pistol hovers before him in the yellow light, rising silver curls, as if exhaled from a cigarette. Pistol still pointed, he listens. There are no more groans.

A biting, sour juice rises to my mouth from my stomach. I gag. A warmth comes to my face and chest. Grandfather's blood washes onto me, that smell of freshly cut meat fills my nostrils.

The soldiers bring five more men to the wall and the entire pantomime is acted out once more, the "Okay, boys", the "Fire", the crack of the rifles, the sudden appearance of red splotches on exposed chests. But this time they all fall forward into the pit.

Silence. For a moment everything seems to have come to a stop. I realize they are listening for groans. And so too am I.

Suddenly, a scream. From the distance. High and pure. A woman's voice: my wife. It takes me by surprise, sends a shiver of terror through me and, involuntarily, I say her name out loud, as if calling to her. A face from the firing squad looks up. I pull back but I know it is too late, I have been seen. I scramble across the roof to the ladder, down the ladder, jump from halfway down: the gravel bites into the soles of my feet. Run. Run. The house.

The crunch of gravel behind me. Boots, running, growing louder. The door, just ahead of me. To my left a soldier, rifle held before him, charging at me: the young guard, Isidro. I smash the door open and almost fall into the house; he is right behind me. He screams, "You saw me! You saw me!" And then his gun crashes, and again and again and again. I feel nothing. He has missed me. But I see where his bullets hit. My wife. My baby. Magical splotches of red. My wife pinned to the wall, the baby still in her arms suddenly headless. Another shot. The young guard pitches forward, rifle clattering to the floor. Behind him, pistol outstretched, the sergeant fires a second shot into his back.

I think: Why? Why did I run to the house?

Over at the window Grandmother turns her head slowly towards me. "The wind, son," she says softly. "The wind."

Grandfather wakes me. He says nothing, beckons to me with his finger, leads me over to the window, to Grandmother. He points through the window, urging me to look and, suddenly, I see the wind. I am amazed I never saw it before; it is there, real, more real than anything I've ever seen.

And so now I sit at the window with Grandmother, holding my breath and looking out, counting the wind, counting the endless wind, the wind that blows all before it, the good, the bad, all the countless sad. And what visions we see flying by, Grandmother and I.